I Just Want To Be Happy, Olivia

By Danny Baker

CONTENTS

Part I

May, 2010

The last time I saw her was when she was running away from me cradling her broken arm, moments after I'd crashed the car into a suburban street pole in a mania-induced frenzy. I'd been hallucinating, chasing imaginary waves at 140k's an hour when the car fish-tailed and flew off the road. Her arm snapped in two and she ran hysterically away, before I nearly killed myself and got committed to a psych ward. The diagnosis: medicine-induced bipolar disorder. After treatment I felt much better, and that's when I decided to send her the letter.

Even after everything that's happened, I still love you as much as ever. I'm going to overcome this illness and live a normal life, and nothing would make me happier than to do it by your side.

I'm so glad to hear you're doing better, she'd replied. *Regarding "us" – we'll talk properly when you get out.*

Three weeks later I finally did, and we agreed to meet the very next day. I thought I'd be able to handle it, but as I walked from my house along Manly Wharf and up The Corso to Three Beans Café where I was due to meet her, I found myself shaking with every step. My stomach churned. Two blocks away, I leaned over a garbage bin, thinking I was going to puke before coughing up bile for the next five minutes. For fuck's sake, I was meeting my lover for the first time since I'd nearly killed her to see if we could start things up again. How could I not be an anxious wreck?

When I arrived at Three Beans I found her sitting by the window, brown and beautiful, her thin hair cascading down her olive-skinned shoulders, her eyes as soft, dreamy and hypnotically blue as ever. She waved when she saw me, and I smiled weakly and sat down in front of her.

'N-nice place,' I stammered, referring to the relaxed, laidback atmosphere and the view of all the couples, friends and families strolling through The Corso.

'Yeah,' she replied. 'Have you been here before?'

I shook my head.

'Have you?'

'No, I haven't either.'

Someone then said something about the weather. The other person agreed. Then awkward fidgeting. Silence. No eye-contact. Nothing.

Thankfully, the waitress then arrived at our table with menus, which we studied uncomfortably until she finally came back again.

'What would you both like?' she asked.

'Just a Diet Coke.'

'Two, thanks.'

She brought them straight away, and then we were alone. Just Olivia and me.

'So, ah ... how've you been?' she asked.

'Yeah ... much better,' I said, before briefly summarising what I'd been doing in hospital to get myself stable again – like working one-on-one with my psychiatrist Dr Delacor, participating in group therapy sessions, and reading self-help books.

'How about you?' I reciprocated. 'Have you been feeling OK?'

She nodded.

'Yeah, I'm doing alright.'

She elaborated a little before talk quickly petered out, as I knew it would with our future so up in the air. I was readying myself to broach the gigantic elephant in the room, but Olivia brought it up first.

'S-so, Jimmy,' she stuttered. 'Do you want to ... d-do you want to talk about your letter?'

My heart pounded in my chest as I cleared my throat, did my best to compose myself.

'OK,' I managed to croak.

She nodded nervously, and looked down at the table. My heart thumped harder and harder and a frenzied chill shot down my spine, turning my skin to gooseflesh as I stared at her anxiously, frantically, so much so that I forgot all about The Corso, forgot all about the café, forgot all about everything but her and our perilous predicament. Her face tightened, squinted uncomfortably as she wrestled for the right words, wrestled with our fate, before she finally, finally, lifted her head to look at me. And then, with a tremble in her voice, the love of my life said that even though she forgave me for everything that had happened, even though she still cared about me, and even though she wanted us to remain really close, that our relationship – as boyfriend and girlfriend – was over.

'B-but Olivia,' my voice shook. 'Things are better now. *I'm* better now.'

I reached across the table to hold her hand, and reiterated what I'd said in my letter.

'Liv, I ... I know we've been through a lot. I know I've put us through a lot. But that's over now – it's all in the past – and I'm back to being the same guy I always was. I'm back to being the same guy who was your first love. The same guy you gave your virginity to. The same guy you did everything with for four whole years. The same guy who you wanted to marry and spend the rest of your life with.'

I squeezed her hand, gazed intensely into her eyes.

'Just give me one more chance,' I begged. 'Please, Olivia. *Please.*'

But she looked right back at me and shook her head sadly.

'I'm sorry Jimmy, but when I think of you, I can't help but think that you're also the same guy who I had an abortion with; the same guy who I helped through alcoholism; the same guy who I broke up with a year ago because you had depression and you weren't getting help; the same guy who proposed to me four weeks after we got back together again because you were manic ... and you're the same guy who broke my arm and nearly killed me two months ago.'

She sighed.

'I'm so sorry, Jimmy – I really, really, really am. But we've been through too much together. Our relationship ... it's just too broken to be fixed. And as much as it hurts me to say it, it always will be ...'

And at that, she pulled her hand away from mine and started crying into her palms.

'It's over, Jimmy,' she sobbed. 'We're finished ...'

The rest of the morning is sort of a blur. I remember Olivia bawling her eyes out, and I remember me bawling my eyes out too. I remember pleading with her, with all the desperation I could possibly muster: *"don't give up on us, Liv. Just give us one more chance. Please, baby. Please."* I remember doing everything I could to try and convince her that despite all the drama we'd been through, that we could start fresh and make it work this time.

That we were made for each other and that it was crazy to abandon what for the most part had been so damn good. But it fell on deaf ears. Her mind was made up, and there was nothing I could do to change it. Months later, I'd find out exactly why. But in that moment, I didn't understand how deeply scarred she was. I couldn't see the raging tsunami that was swirling beneath the surface. I had no idea I'd triggered what would turn out to be the most confronting, debilitating, challenging experience of her life. All I heard was her gut-wrenching refrain:

"It's over, Jimmy. We're finished ..."

Coping sans Liv

Somebody once told me that recovering from bipolar disorder meant not getting high-as-a-kite manic when something good happens to you, and not sinking into a debilitating depression when something bad happens. I hoped and strived for a time when I'd be that stable, but at that point in my life, I wasn't yet equipped to handle something as devastating as the girl of my dreams telling me that our relationship was over.

And as a result, I was suicidal again.

In that heart-shattering moment, a life without Olivia did not seem a life worth living. The nine months I'd spent apart from her the previous year had been excruciating, and when we finally got back together a month before the accident, I was the happiest I'd ever been. I was sure that we'd made it through hell and that there were only good times and love and laughter ahead. I was convinced that we'd get married and live happily ever after, just like they do in the movies. But now, bereft again, I felt overwhelmingly crushed.

And, I felt so cheated.

It's not my fault my GP Dr King gave me the wrong medication! I thought furiously to myself. *It's not my fault it made me manic and crash the car! What the fuck have I done to deserve this? What the fuck have I done to deserve being alone and suicidal again?*

But as the saying goes, holding on to anger is like drinking poison and expecting someone else to die. I knew being bitter and acting like a victim wouldn't get me anywhere, and after all I'd been through, I knew that even though I felt the urge to kill myself, that I'd never actually do it. Instead, I knew that I needed to deal with my issues by confronting them, resolving them, and then moving on from them.

So with that thought in mind, I saw my psychologist Dr Kendall the following afternoon and told him what'd happened. After he said how sorry he was, I asked him what he thought I should do going forwards.

'It seems to me like you have three options, Jimmy,' he said. 'Firstly, if you're not content to be "just friends" with Olivia, then you could make a clean break for it and never talk to her again. Secondly, you could resign yourself to being "just friends" with her, do what you need to do to get over her, and then when you're ready, start trying to meet a brand new girl. And lastly, if you're still set on getting back together with her, then you could see her as a "friend" for the time being, but hold on to the hope that she'll eventually change her mind and want something more.'

I nodded thoughtfully as I carefully considered my options.

'Do you think there's a chance she might change her mind?' I asked.

Dr Kendall nodded softly.

'It's possible,' he said. 'After all, Olivia's just been through an extremely traumatic experience, and it's still very raw in her mind. There's a chance that – given time – she might be able to move past it, and be ready to start fresh with you again.'

He sighed.

'But of course, there's a chance that she may never get over everything that's happened – and, if you hold out hope that she'll change her mind about you and she never does, then you're going to prolong your suffering for a very long time.'

He was right. If I continued pining for Olivia and she never reciprocated, then my already broken heart would crumble into a million more pieces. In many ways, it would've been easiest just to give up on her now and start gluing myself back together again. But as you know, I've never been one to take the easy road. Deep down, I still believed that Olivia was my one true love, and when you think you've found that person, you have to do everything in your power to make it work with them.

'I can't give up on her,' I whispered. 'I love her ... I love her so damn much ...'

'I understand that Jimmy, but what if she never loves you back? What are you going to do then?'

I felt tears begin to well in my eyes.

'Then I-I'll ... I'll be devastated,' my voice shook. 'But at least I'll be able to live with myself. If I give up on her now ... then I just think there'd always be a part of me that would think "what if?" And there's nothing ... there's no feeling in the world more painful than regret.'

'OK,' Dr Kendall agreed. 'If she really means that much to you, then you should go for it.'

I wiped my eyes, nodded my head softly. Dr Kendall then started saying something, but he stopped mid-sentence when I broke down crying in the palms of my hands.

'It's OK,' he whispered gently, patting me on the shoulder. But the floodgates had been opened, and for the next five minutes, out spilled my pain as I just cried and cried and cried. It was only with great determination that I was able to pull myself together again so we could continue the session.

'Now Jimmy,' Dr Kendall resumed, 'while I agree that you shouldn't give up on Olivia yet, I also don't want her to dominate your thoughts. As we've talked about before, if you want to live a happy, stable life despite the fact that you have bipolar disorder, then in addition to taking your medication and living an active, healthy lifestyle, you need to learn – through therapy – how to manage your "triggers", so to speak – which are the events, thoughts and circumstances that can cause you to feel either manic or depressed. Now at the moment, it goes without saying that your primary "trigger" is your separation from Olivia – and, since getting back together with her is not an option right now, then the best thing you can do for yourself is to accept that you're not with her and focus on the other aspects of your life. After all, there's a lot going on for you at the moment: you're two days out of hospital and trying to adjust to life with a serious illness; you need to study for your mid-year exams that are coming up in three or four weeks; and you're still aiming to submit your novel to a number of literary agents before you go with your friends to Japan in a couple of months' time. You've got enough on your plate as it is, so try not to ruminate on not being with Olivia. Just focus on getting your life in order, because that really is the best thing you can do for yourself right now. I mean it, Jimmy.'

I nodded.

'Yeah. You're right.'

We talked for a while longer before we parted ways with a handshake and I drove back to Manly. It was still light outside, so in line with living healthily, I went for a swim amongst the calm, gentle waves at the beach. After that, my mum and dad – who'd made a special point of coming home early from their jobs as a lawyer and an investment banker, respectively – took me out to dinner in The Corso.

'We know you're going through a hard time right now,' they said, 'but you're going to get through it. After all, you've never faced anything that you haven't been able to overcome.'

I nodded.

'Just have a little faith, Jimmy,' they continued. 'Everything will turn out OK. It always has.'

'Yeah,' I said. 'I know.'

As we continued talking, I gradually felt more and more refortified, so when we arrived home, I retreated to my room, sat on my bed, and opened my wallet to the picture of Olivia. Brushed to one side, her thin brown hair blew slightly in the wind. Her warm blue eyes stared straight into mine. She was smiling at me, her face full of love and life and laughter as I gazed ardently right back at her.

'I know you, Olivia,' I whispered softly. 'And I know us. And in my heart, I know that this isn't the end. You may not be able to see it right now, but I know that one day, we're going to get back together again, and then we're going to get married, and have babies, and spend the rest of our lives together – just like we'd always planned. I know it, Olivia. I just know it.'

And at that, I leaned forwards, and gently pressed my lips against hers. I held them there, second after second, recalling the subtle scent of her perfume, the fresh taste of her breath, and the warmth of her tongue intertwined with my own before I gently pulled back, smiled at her one last time and then closed my wallet, said my prayers and slipped into bed – feeling strengthened and ready for the fight ahead.

The following day was much like most days owing to the next two months. I woke up at 7:30 after an eight hour sleep, washed my face, and then got laced up to go for a run. I'd jog up The Corso past all the cafés, bars, restaurants, ice-cream shops and surf stores, turn left at the end to run along Manly Beach, and then go for a 15 minute swim before jogging all the way back again. After having a shower and eating a healthy breakfast of five Weetbix with skim milk and a bowl of fresh fruit on the side, I'd then drive to uni. When I'd first checked in to hospital, I'd assumed I'd have to defer the third year of my commerce/law degree, but thankfully, most of my lectures were recorded and available online, plus my classmates had been really helpful by sending me their notes, so I'd been able to scrape by and not fall too far behind. That semester, I was taking Advanced Economics, Mathematical Economics, Regression Modelling and International Law. International Law, like most of my previous law subjects, didn't interest me at all, and while regression modelling and my economics subjects were tolerable, I could hardly say I was passionate about them – or for that matter, that I even enjoyed them. But I knew that acing my commerce/law degree would put me in a very good position to snag my dream job of being an investment banker or a management consultant and thus make me a fortune, so I was more than willing to study my ass off even though I didn't like the work itself very much.

After going to my classes, I'd then tutor a couple of students to make some money to pay for my Japan trip, before studying in the library for a while and then heading back home when the peak hour traffic had died down at around seven o'clock. After having dinner – typically a lean piece of meat with a serve of veggies – I'd then usually either email one or two literary agents a pitch for my book about the orphan in the Great Depression that I'd written over the previous three years, or wind down by reading a Penguin Classic. Other times, I'd read a self-help book about how to better manage bipolar disorder – which was hardly my first choice of things to do after a tiring day at uni, but anything that would help me manage my illness was well and truly worth it.

During those couple of months, I also made sure I saw Olivia. The first such occasion was about two weeks after we'd parted at Three Beans. I was listening to a lecture on a Saturday morning about statistical analysis and random sampling when her name all of a sudden lit up my phone. I immediately paused the recording, cleared my throat, and then nervously, excitedly, answered her call.

'Hey, Liv.'

'Hey, Jimmy. What's going on?'

'Nothing much, just studying. How about you?'

'Yeah, the same.'

'Cool.'

A few seconds passed.

'So …' she eventually said. 'You feel like taking a break in a couple of hours and meeting up for lunch?'

'Ah, yeah. OK. Where do you want to go?'

'Hhmmm ... I kind of feel like pizza. Want to go to Hugos?'

'Sounds good. Say 12:30?'

'Yep.'

'Great. I'll see you then.'

'OK. See you, Jimmy.'

We hung up. I tried to get back to my lecture, but I was too preoccupied to be able to focus.

I mean, it's all well and good to say *we'll be friends,* I thought anxiously, *but how do we know that's actually going to work in practice? What if she finds it too awkward? What if I find it too awkward? What's going to happen to us then?*

At 12:25, I nervously left home and walked to the restaurant. Olivia was already sitting down at a table overlooking the harbour when I arrived, wearing a floral dress with thongs and her hair tied back in a ponytail. She smiled softly when our eyes met, and stood up to hug me before I sat down across from her. After a few minutes, she ordered a seafood pizza and an orange juice, and I got a chicken salad and a Diet Coke. It was a little uncomfortable at first – being new territory and all that – but to my relief, we quickly broke the ice, and before long, we were talking and laughing just like old times.

'It's so funny to see you eat a salad after all these years!' Olivia giggled. 'I don't think you've ever ordered one with me before!'

'Hey,' I smiled, 'I'm trying to be healthy. You should be supporting me!'

'And a *Diet Coke!*' she teased. 'You're such a little princess!'

'I am *not* a princess.'

'You are so!'

'At least I can finish my meal.'

'And what is that supposed to mean?'

'It means you never finish your food.'

'What?'

'Seriously, every time you order something, you eat a bit of it, put some of it on my plate, eat a bit more of it, and then take the rest home in a doggy bag.'

'That is not true!'

'Of course it is.'

'I didn't do that today.'

'You wanted to. I just didn't want any pizza.'

'That's because you're a little princess.'

'Whatever Miss I-can-only-eat-half-a-pizza.'

At that point, a waiter came by.

'How were your meals?' he asked.

'Very good, thank-you. But would you mind putting the rest of her pizza in a doggy bag? She eats less food than a baby.'

'If you're going to do that, then could you please get him another Diet Coke? He's on a diet and really watching his figure.'

The waiter – looking slightly puzzled – took our plates and walked away. Olivia smiled playfully.

'That guy *definitely* thought you were a princess.'

'He definitely thought you were a baby.'

'I should've asked him to put a little pink umbrella in your drink. Maybe even a flower, too.'

'I think you've done quite enough as it is. I don't even want another Diet Coke.'

'I'll drink it then.'

'Liv don't be silly – you wouldn't be able to finish it.'

'Shut up!' she laughed.

We stayed at Hugos well into the afternoon, and afterwards, because the weather was nice and we were enjoying ourselves so much, we decided to walk down The Corso to the beach for a swim. By the time we were finally about to leave each other at the crossroads to our homes, it was dark.

'I had a really good time today,' Olivia said.

'Yeah, me too. We should do it again soon.'

'Of course,' she nodded. 'Maybe we can make it like a weekly Saturday thing we do – just spend the day together.'

'For sure. That'd be great.'

She smiled at me, and we said our goodbyes with a warm hug and a peck on the cheek.

It became kind of like a tradition. Every Saturday, we'd meet up for a long lunch somewhere in Manly, and then depending on the weather, either go for a swim, relax in a coffee shop or head to the movies. We always had such a great time together, and I was always so happy when I was with her. At times, I'd be so suffused with joy that I'd feel the overly tempting urge to take her hand in mine, look into her eyes, tell her that I loved her, and ask her if she wanted to rekindle our romance. But I had to admit that Olivia hadn't shown any clear indication that she wanted to start things up again, and regardless, Dr Kendall had advised me not to.

'I'd leave it for the time being,' he said. 'Just enjoy your Saturdays with Olivia for what they are, and focus on continuing to get your life back on track. You've been doing a really good job since you left hospital, Jimmy – make sure you keep it up, and in the meantime, keep giving Olivia space and the time she needs to recover.'

I took his advice all the way up until December of 2010 – six months later – when I eventually relented and opened up my heart to her. And when I did, she finally revealed her true feelings towards me – and in the process, wound-up divulging the devastating secret she'd been trying so hard to hide.

Japan

But a lot happened before December and me telling Olivia that I wanted to get back together with her, starting with my trip to Japan. I'd booked it with my mates Corey, Brent, Sean, Chris and Steve a couple of weeks before I'd gotten out of hospital, and I'd been looking forward to it ever since. After all, even though it was only July, it had already been one hell of a year – what with reuniting with Olivia in February, the car crash in March, being in hospital until the end of May, having things implode with Olivia the day after I got out, the struggle to adjust to a new life with a serious illness after that, and the race against the clock to try and catch up on all my uni work before the end of semester exams in June. After so much upheaval, what I felt like more than anything else was a holiday, and Japan, with its breathtaking landscapes, enchanting history, exotic culinary delights, pulsing party scene, mind-boggling technological progression and bizarre cultural idiosyncrasies figured to be the perfect destination to take a break from my life. From the day my exams ended on June 27 to our July 10 departure date, I literally counted down the days until we left, crossing them off the calendar that hung above the desk in my room. I was giddy for it, and when my parents dropped me at the airport with a hug and I went inside to meet the boys, I felt a tingle in my chest, a whirling excitement that only comes when you're about to embark on an unforgettable adventure.

But when I arrived at the airport, I was snapped out of my reverie by my best mate's petulance.

'Well look who decides to finally turn up,' Corey chided, shaking his head.

'What? We're not boarding for another two hours.'

'We agreed to meet at 5:15. It's now 5:23.'

'So?'

'Mate, at 5:30 Maccas starts serving *breakfast*. How am I supposed to get a Big Mac then?'

'Who wants a Big Mac at 5:30 in the morning?'

'Who doesn't? The breakfast menu's shit.'

'Are you guys listening to this?' I asked the fellas.

'Corey, you're a fuckwit,' Brent said. 'There's nothing better than a Bacon and Egg McMuffin.'

'Especially when you slip a cheeky hash brown inside,' added Steve.

'They should have the breakfast menu 24/7,' chimed Chris.

'Piss off,' said Sean. 'I'm with Corey – let's hurry up so we can get a hamburger.'

We lined up at the check-in counter, dumped our baggage, and arrived at Maccas at 5:41. Corey and Sean were forced to order Sausage and Egg McMuffins; Brent, Steve and Chris got two rounds of Bacon and Egg (hash browns inside, of course); and I got a large fruit salad and a bowl of oatmeal from a coffee shop.

'What time do we arrive?' Sean asked.

'About seven o'clock.'

'Sweet! Just in time for dinner and a really big night!'

'Hell yeah!'

We all slapped each other fives and then smashed down our breakfast and charged for the gate, eager and ready to get our trip under way.

After an uneventful ten hour flight, we arrived in Tokyo, sped through customs, and then caught the fastest, cleanest, most on-time train I've ever been on and flew to Shinjuku, which is where we'd arranged to stay for the first few days of our trip.

'Fuck me ...' Brent marvelled when we got off. 'Look how crowded it is!'

And he was right. With over three million people passing through it each day, Shinjuku Station is the busiest transport hub in the world, and that Friday night it was teeming with people – from businessmen in suits on their way home from work to Japanese youths gearing up for a night on the town. Pandemonium was the only word you could use to describe it, as thousands of people raced up and down the escalators between the 36 platforms, and thousands more appeared and disappeared through the 200-plus entrances and exits. Our hostel was only a few blocks away in Kabukichō, but given the chaos surrounding us and the extremely limited number of English signs, I had no idea how we were going to find the place.

'Anyone got a map?' I asked.

'Yeah,' Steve said. 'Follow me.'

But it turned out that all Steve did was take us to a different platform. Brent, Sean and Chris only managed to get us even more lost when they tried to navigate. I gave the map a miss and decided to just ask passers by for directions, only to realise that hardly anyone in Japan knew how to speak English. Corey ran into similar language barriers when he tried to talk to a booth teller. Finally after 20 minutes, an English teacher kindly led us out of the station and pointed the way towards Kabukichō.

'This place is going off!' Chris exclaimed as we walked down the street. And going off it was. Kabukichō, also known as the "Sleepless Town", was an Asian embodiment of big-city chaos. Fluoro-coloured Japanese signs and advertisements covering the tall buildings towering over us flashed everywhere we turned, and the sound of bustling footsteps and chattering voices filled our ears as throngs of people packed the streets. We were passed in every direction by groups and individuals going in and out of sushi-, ramen-, udon-, tempura- and *okonomiyaka* (cook what you want) restaurants; *izakayas* (pub eateries); and *shokudōs*, which are those cheap places with the plastic food displays outside the shop window. Others went to movie theatres, massage parlours, bars and nightclubs with promoters outside trying to entice people in, while a few youngsters and wealthy businessmen discreetly slipped into strip joints, brothels and love hotels. Hardly anything was written in English, nor were there any other Westerners in sight, but we didn't care. This was Japan's biggest red light district, and we couldn't wait to get amongst it.

After buying a dozen cans of Sapporo beer one by one from a vending machine outside our hostel, we checked in at reception and carried our bags up to our 24 person dorm. Typical of many Japanese hostels, instead of sleeping in beds, we were sleeping in capsules – literally wooden boxes enclosing a mattress with doors that are lockable with a key from the outside. Ours were about three feet high, three feet wide and six feet long, lined up in two rows of six capsules resting on the ground and another two rows of six stacked on top of them.

'Hope y'all aren't claustrophobic,' Corey laughed.

'Nah, it's all good,' Brent said, lying down inside one. 'This just makes it all the easier to take a wank.'

'Can't argue with that!' said Sean, cracking open a beer.

'Here's to a big night tonight and a sick time in Japan!' Chris exclaimed, raising a can.

'Yeah, boys!'

We started drinking as we talked excitedly about all the things we planned to do on the trip (even I was drinking, for the first time since my 21st birthday about four months previously. As a rule, I didn't drink – due to my bipolar disorder and my history of alcohol abuse – but it was night one of a much-anticipated holiday, and I figured that I should be OK just this once). We got through our first twelve beers pretty quickly, and after doing a second run to the vending machine and downing another couple of Sapporo's each, we started getting ready to hit the town.

'Any of you guys used the toilets yet?' Steve asked as he emerged from the bathroom.

'Nah. How come?'

He shook his head.

'They're fucking crazy, man.'

Feeling curious – and needing to go anyway – I decided to check them out.

After closing the door in the cubicle, the first thing I noticed was a control panel on the right-hand side of the toilet with an array of buttons in Japanese labels that I couldn't understand. Feeling game, I pulled down my pants, sat down, and pressed the first button.

'What the fuck!' I cried, jumping up from my seat as a warm jet of water squirted my balls. At the time I had no idea what it was, but after developing a fascination with the Japanese "super toilet" and Googling it later on, I learned that it was a spray used to wash one's vulva.

Sitting back down, I pressed the second button ready for anything, and this time received a similar squirt of water up my ass (the aptly named "anus cleaner"). Then I pressed the third button, and the next thing I knew the seat was heating up. When I pressed the fourth button, I started getting a massage.

During the next half hour, I had by far the most fun I've ever had on a toilet. I messed around finding the ideal temperature and pressure for the anus cleaner, experimented with different types of nozzle positioning, and tried out a variety of vibrating and pulsating jets of water (which, according to my later research, was claimed by manufacturers to alleviate constipation and soothe one's haemorrhoids). Towards the end of my pooing experience, I figured out how to mix the water jet with soap to improve the bum cleaning process, then I blow dried my ass – after tinkering with the blow drying temperature – before last but not least, I capped off the most luxurious crap of my life with a few sprays of peachy perfume (I would later discover that more advanced toilets have even more ludicrous features, including a built-in air conditioner below the seat for hot summer days, being able to glow in the dark, the ability to play music to relax the user's sphincter, and for those who like to stick to a pooing schedule, the ability to track at what times of day the toilet is most being used, and then automatically warm the seat at those times. Even more unbelievably, future developments to the Japanese super toilet include adding medical sensors which can measure the user's pulse, blood pressure, blood sugar levels and body fat content from their urine, and then via built-in, internet-capable cellular telephones, automatically send that data to the user's doctor. Talking toilets that greet the user are also under development, as are voice operated toilets that understand verbal commands. As I would come to learn, the Japanese are nothing if not technologically advanced).

By the time I'd finally finished in the bathroom, the boys were all ready to go so we headed to an *izakaya*, which like I mentioned before my toilet tangent, is a Japanese pub eatery.

'*Irasshaimase!*' a waiter exclaimed with a smile when we arrived.

Not knowing what *irasshaimase* meant, we just nodded politely before being led to a low table where we sat down on rice straw mats and were handed hot wet towels to wipe our hands with.

'Alright boys,' Steve began, 'according to the hostel manager, we pay a fixed price and get unlimited food and booze for the next three hours – so let's get stuck into it.'

And get stuck into it we did. Until 11pm, we shared plate after plate of *sashimi* (slices of raw fish), *kushiyaki* (grilled meat skewers), *yakitori* (grilled chicken skewers), *karage* (bite-sized pieces of fried chicken) and *edamame* (boiled and salted soy bean pods); and we also had so many rounds of *sake* that we quickly lost count. Suffice it to say, by the time our three hours were up, we were shitfaced. Before we'd even managed to make our way to a club, Brent had slipped the glasses off a sleeping homeless man, put them on his head and started running around in circles before slipping them back on the homeless man again; Chris and Sean had started talking to two young Japanese businessmen, who within five minutes were all taking it in turns whacking each other on the ass with the businessmen's umbrellas; and after seeing a half-eaten box of teriyaki chicken on the side of the street, Corey and I – still evidently feeling a little bit peckish – picked it up and started eating it.

'You guys are a fucking disgrace,' Steve slurred.

'Come on mate, have some chicken,' I laughed, pushing the box in his face. 'It tastes really good!'

'Fuck off!' he exclaimed, batting the box away. 'You guys are disgusting.'

When we stumbled into a club, we ordered another round of *sake*. Steve and Sean then found themselves speaking to two Japanese girls in the most broken English I've ever heard, before the four of them weaved through everyone on the dancefloor and started taking group pictures in one of those small photo booths on the other side of the room. Brent, Corey, Chris and I then joined the crowd on the dancefloor and started fist pumping to disco music we couldn't understand a word of.

'This place is pumping!' Chris yelled above the music.

'Damn right, brother!'

A few minutes later, Steve and Sean returned with the two Japanese girls and a few of their friends, and when the next song began, one of them started grinding on me. I didn't stop it, but I didn't exactly encourage it either.

'Dude!' Corey yelled in my ear. 'Fucking hook up with her!'

But I was thinking about Olivia. Where she was right now. What she might be doing. How wrong it was that we weren't together.

Corey could read my mind.

'You're not with Liv anymore, so it doesn't make sense to reject other chicks. Just go for it!'

I sighed, knowing he was right. *After all*, I conceded, *what good does it do to make myself miserable over Olivia when she's in Australia and there's a hot girl right here rubbing up against me?*

So with that in mind, I spun the Japanese girl around and we started hooking up. She tasted different from Olivia ... kissed faster ... used less tongue ... but I tried to forget about drawing comparisons and just do my best to enjoy the moment – a moment which turned out to last for a few more songs on the dancefloor, the ten minutes it took us to have another drink at the bar, and the two absolutely ridiculous hours we spent at a "love hotel".

Now, the reason love hotels – which are rooms rented by the hour purely for having sex – exist is because Japanese youths have no privacy, since they often live with their parents well into their 20s, and it's customary for grandparents to move in with their children after they've retired. As for the reason love hotels are so ridiculously strange ... I have no idea. But it makes for one hell of a story that I can't resist telling you.

Here's what happened: after walking for a few blocks, the girl – whose name I never managed to catch – led me into a windowless building lit up with neon lights. In the lobby, there was a panel on one of the walls with images of each room on the premises. Even in my wasted state, I remember being shocked at all the absurd set-ups they had available: for example, there was one room where the walls and bedspreads were covered with anime characters; another that was dungeon themed and had chains and bondage equipment hanging from the ceiling; one that was designed to look like a children's playground and included a built-in, horse-themed merry-go-round that circled the bed; one that looked exactly like a school classroom complete with desks, lockers, chalk boards and a cane; another that was S&M themed and decked out with a flogging frame, whips and handcuffs; one that was a mock hospital ward containing a nurse's uniform, stethoscope, thermometer and other surgical instruments; and there were numerous rooms equipped with rotating water beds, heart-shaped Jacuzzis, and mirrors that covered the ceiling and each and every wall. While I gawked at all the different lay-outs, the girl selected a Hello Kitty themed room by pressing a button below the picture of it. When a key emerged from a slot beneath the picture, she picked it up, grabbed my hand and led me to the room.

As soon as she'd opened the door, I instantly regretted not choosing a different one. All the walls were covered with Hello Kitty pictures. So was the quilt cover. Stuffed Hello Kitty toys were arranged deliberately around the bed and were dangling from the ceiling. It seemed like a place where paedophiles would lure unsuspecting little kids, and the idea of having sex in there freaked the shit out of me. But the girl didn't seem the slightest bit phased. While I stood by the door looking awkwardly around, she poured us drinks she'd gotten out of the fridge before slipping into a Hello Kitty G-string that she'd found on the bed.

Here's how the next two hours went: after finishing our glasses of *sake*, I pleasured her with a Hello Kitty vibrator she'd found in the fridge until she came. Then we tried to have sex, but due in part to being fucked out of my mind and in part to being completely wigged out by the idea of doing it in a child molester's lair, I was finding it really hard to maintain an erection. After a while, the girl got the jack of it, so she marched to the fridge, retrieved a "Hello Kitty Blow Light" and handed it to me. I shrugged at her, indicating that I wasn't sure what to do with it – at which point she unwrapped the blow light, grabbed my dick and tried to shove it inside the hole. After getting over the initial shock of it, I figured what the hell, and started thrusting myself back and forth inside the object while the girl checked her emails on the computer beside the bed before deciding to play *Dragon Quest IX: Sentinels of the Starry Skies* on the Nintendo. When I finally managed to come, the Hello Kitty Blow Light lit up brightly – courtesy of some sort of chemical reaction (didn't I tell you the Japanese were technologically advanced?). Then, as if things couldn't get any more bizarre, the girl convinced me to start singing karaoke with her, so after slotting a few notes into the karaoke machine by the Nintendo, we started chanting the lyrics to random Japanese pop songs that I didn't understand a word of.

> *"Chanjing, chanjing, koo doo won doh!*
> *Chee koo chee koo, sai won don!*
> *Chanjing, chanjing, soo me kai won!*
> *Kawaoh! Keecho! Danjing monono!*
> *Nanananananana ho!*
> *Nanananananana hey!*
> *Nanananananana ho!"*

After another round of *sake*, the girl passed out in bed cradling one of the stuffed Hello Kittys. Figuring that was my cue to get the hell out of there, I started inserted money into the machine at the door, which opened as soon as I'd put in the right amount. I quickly sneaked out without looking back, and then began the drunken walk of shame back to the hostel.

The next morning, when I told the boys what'd happened they all laughed their heads off.

'She shoved your dick into *what?*'

'That Hello Kitty room sounds *fucked.*'

'I would've taken her to the hospital room, no doubt. Dressed her up like a nurse and really gone to town.'

'I would've taken her to the classroom and pretended she was Miss Brownie from high school. I always did have a crush on her!'

I laughed along with them as we bantered about different fantasies and sexual scenarios before Brent had to get up and go to the bathroom.

'So how'd you like sleeping in the capsules?' I asked. 'How many wanks have each of you had?'

'One,' Corey replied.

'Ditto,' nodded Steve.

'I'm still yet to open the floodgates,' said Chris.

'Three,' admitted Sean.

'Three?'

'Yep.'

'But you would've barely spent four hours total in there!'

'Hey, when you need to do it you need to do it. It was all that Japanese chick – she seemed keen as fuck, and then – '

But he was interrupted by Brent's shriek from the toilet.

'The vulva spray?' I called out.

He laughed.

'Is that what the hell it is?'

After Brent had satisfied his bowels – and his curiosity with all of the toilet buttons – we all had showers and headed out for breakfast, before visiting the Imperial Palace, the Tokyo National Museum and Hama-Rikyū-Tienen, which is one of the most beautiful gardens I've ever walked through. The following morning we went to the world's largest seafood market before going to Disneyland, and the day after that, we were fortunate enough to catch one of the six sumo wrestling tournaments held that year, where after ceremonies that involved a lot of stomping, squatting, clapping and salt-throwing, we saw countless pairs of fat guys wrestle each other to the floor as the crowd yelled and screamed for their favourite wrestlers and even threw their seat cushions in anger when their guy lost. Next, we made our way to the Gion Matsuri in Kyoto, which is one of the most famous festivals in Japan where 32 amazingly decorated floats adorned with textiles, woven fabrics and sculptures parade through the streets, while musicians on the floats play Gion-Bayashi music with Japanese flutes, balls and drums. During the night the *onsen* kept us warm, where in naturally hot water from geothermally heated springs, we sat around chatting and gazing up at the stars. We went to a couple in Kyoto and then a couple more back in Tokyo, which is where we spent the final few days of our trip – visiting the toilet museum (of course), and eating as much sushi, ramen and tempura as we could fit in our stomachs.

Our second last day in Japan was a Saturday, and because it was traditionally my day to spend with Olivia, I decided to break away from the boys for a bit and head to an internet café to send her a Facebook message. But to my delight, I logged in to realise that she'd beaten me to it.

> *Hey Jimmy,*
>
> *As I'm sure you know, today's Saturday, and since you're not here to take me out, I have absolutely no idea what to do with myself. You're definitely in my bad books at the moment, but if you keep your promise and send me a message telling me all about your holiday, then it's possible I might just choose to forgive you.*
>
> *Haha hope you're having an incredible time!*
>
> *Love Liv xx*

I chuckled to myself and then started typing, telling her all about the amazing food, the capsule beds, the sumo wrestling tournament, the Gion Matsuri, the *onsen*, and of course, all about the crazy toilets and the love hotels (although I chose to omit the fact that I'd personally been to the latter). After I'd filled her in on everything, I also told her about a very important decision I'd made during the course of the trip.

> *While I've been here Liv, I've also decided that I want to be a management consultant after uni is finished. As you know, it's something I've always strongly*

considered – along with being an investment banker like my dad or possibly even a lawyer like my mum – but I've finally settled on management consulting. Like investment bankers and lawyers, they get paid a truckload of money, but what really sets consulting apart in my mind is the fact that consultants get to do a lot of travelling as part of their work, and this trip has reminded me just how much I love that. There's just something so magical about stepping foot somewhere you've never been, talking to people who you've never met and will probably never meet again, eating food that you've never tasted, and learning about a history and a culture that's so unlike your own that you realise just how small your hometown is and just how big the world is. Second to writing my novel, travelling is my favourite thing to do, and if management consulting will lead to me getting rich and doing a heap of it, then it sounds like the perfect job for me.

Anyway Liv, that's all my news. How's everything been with you?

Can't wait to see you next Saturday when I'm back!

Love Jimmy xx

I clicked send, and then tried to sign out of the computer so that the store manager could tell how long I'd been logged on for and thus know how much to charge me. But being unfamiliar with the system, I wasn't sure how to do it.

'Do you want help?' a voice behind me asked.

I turned around, and saw a young Japanese guy who was probably only a couple of years older than me.

'Yeah, I'm not sure how to log out of this thing.'

'Here,' he said, doing it for me.

'Cheers, mate. Thanks.'

'You welcome! My name's Fumio,' he grinned, extending his hand. I shook it.

'Jimmy.'

'You are from America?'

'Australia.'

'Ah!' he exclaimed. 'Harbour Bridge! Opera House! Kangaroo!'

'Yep,' I laughed. 'That's Australia!'

He nodded excitedly.

'What is your job back home?'

'I'm a university student. I study commerce/law.'

'Ah,' he murmured thoughtfully. 'I studied law as well.'

'Yeah? Do you practice it now?'

He shook his head.

'I did, but then I quit.'

'Really? Why?'

'Didn't like it,' he said simply.

'Why not?'

'Ah, many reasons. Work is not of interest to me ... hours very long ... bosses treat you like a slave.'

'But it pays so well!'

Fumio laughed.

'You sound like my parents.'

'What did they say when you told them you'd quit?'

He sighed.

'They did not understand. My parents ... they are very ... how do you say ... like from a long time ago, you know?'

'Traditional?' I offered.

'Yes! Traditional! They think life is about studying very much, getting good job, making a lot of money. That's what they forever told me – ever since I started school when I was a little boy. Study, study, study. Work, work, work. Nothing more important than getting good job.'

'Maybe they're right,' I suggested.

Fumio shook his head.

'For some people, maybe that is OK. But not me. I did not like being a lawyer. It did not make me happy. So I stopped being a lawyer.'

'But lawyers make so much money!' I insisted. 'They have great lives!'

He laughed.

'Make so much money, yes, but are they happy, Jimmy? Not me, my friend! Only my parents were happy with me being a lawyer.'

'So they were really angry when you told them you'd quit?'

'Yes, very, very angry. We have a big fight. They say I am a bad son. They call me *hanran*. How do you say in English? A rebel, I think. And they say they never want to see me again. Tell me to leave home and never come back.'

I was shocked.

'Wow ... I'm really sorry to hear that.'

'It is OK,' he said. 'When I was a lawyer, I was very, very sad. It feel like ... how do you say ... like I was in a prison, you know? But now, I am free! I can live my own life – the way I want to. It is much better this way.'

I smiled weakly.

'What are you going to do now?' I asked. 'Like for a job and stuff?'

'Ah!' he exclaimed excitedly. 'My whole life, I have always wanted to see the world. Can you believe I am 25, and I have never left Japan? But now, I am going to. I have come here today to book my flight!'

'Where are you going to go?'

'Everywhere!' he exclaimed with joy. 'I start in China, work there for a while. I will pour the drinks – I will be bartender! And I will keep learning English, and when I am – how do you say ... fluent? – I will go to England! And then I will take the train around Europe! And after that, I will go to New York! And one day, Australia too!'

'But you can't travel forever,' I said. 'Don't you want to settle down at some point and have a family?'

'Of course! But I am young, Jimmy. I have time.'

'Yeah, but ... what about when you *do* want a family? How are you going to support them? Bartenders don't exactly get paid very well ...'

'You can still support a family as a bartender!' he laughed. 'But who knows ... maybe I will have a better paying job by then.'

'Like what?'

'I do not know, my friend! But it is OK! I am smart,' he said, tapping his head. 'I work something out. I trust myself.'

I couldn't believe what I was hearing.

How ... ? I thought, flabbergasted. *How could this guy give up the Holy Grail of professional careers – an almost sure-fire way of getting rich – in exchange for such an uncertain, unpredictable, insecure life?* Hell, flabbergasted was an understatement. I agreed with his parents – this was fucking madness.

'Well, I wish you the best of luck,' I said, getting up to leave.

'You too, my friend! But before you go, give me your Facebook – I'll tell you when I come to Australia!'

So we added each other, and I wished him luck again before I went to meet the boys, convinced that I would never see Fumio ever again.

I love you, Olivia

When we arrived back in Sydney, it was late July of 2010, and time for the second semester of uni to begin. Straight away it was back to the daily grind: reading tort law case after contract law case after contract law case after tort law case; analysing economic data, graphs and statistics; and constructing economic models and deriving economic proofs – after which I'd spend a relatively boring hour submitting my novel to literary agents. On the bright side, though, returning to Sydney meant I could see Olivia on Saturdays, and on my first one back, we met up for lunch at Ribs and Rumps overlooking the beach. When we got there, I told her more about my trip and she filled me in on what she'd been doing, and then as she usually did, she asked me about my health.

'So how've you been Jimmy, bipolar-wise? Has everything been going OK?'

I nodded.

'Yeah, I've been pretty good. It's still hard coming to terms with it, you know? Like just getting used to the fact that I have a serious illness and becoming comfortable with that fact … it takes time. But I'm getting there, and overall, I've been feeling pretty good. It's hard work, of course – I have to take my medication, see Dr Kendall, read self-help books, and make sure I eat healthily, exercise a lot, and get at least seven or eight hours of sleep every night. But it's all worth it, because I do feel well again. In fact, this is probably the most stable I've been in the last two or three years.'

'That's fantastic, Jimmy!' she beamed. 'That's really, really terrific.'

'Yeah, it is. I'm so grateful. I thank God every night for letting me recover.'

'I do too, Jimmy,' Olivia said, reaching across the table to squeeze my hand.

I smiled at her, and then she asked me how my first week of uni had been.

'Uni's been OK, but I really hate my law subject – Torts and Contracts II.'

'How does a commerce/law degree work, again?' she asked. 'You finish the commerce part in the first three years while fitting in a year's equivalent of law subjects as your electives, right? And then you do straight law for the last two years of your degree?'

'Yeah,' I sighed, shaking my head. 'It sucks. I don't know how I'm going to cope with two straight years of full-time law.'

'You've never liked it, have you?'

'No. Not really.'

'So why do you keep studying it then? You've said yourself that you don't even want to be a lawyer – you want to be a management consultant.'

'Yeah, but I need something on top of a commerce degree to become a management consultant. Grad positions at all the best firms are really competitive, and with just one bachelor's degree, I wouldn't have a chance. I don't think I'd even get an interview anywhere.'

'So study something on top of commerce then, but does your extra qualification really have to be a law degree? Can't you do something else instead? Like, I don't know ... honours in economics? Or something else that you might actually enjoy?'

I raised my eyebrows thoughtfully.

'Um ... I don't know ... I'd never thought about that before. But I mean yeah ... maybe that would be OK.'

'Look into it,' she smiled.

'Yeah,' I nodded. 'Yeah I'll definitely do that. Thanks Liv, that's actually a really good idea.'

She kept on smiling at me. I thought about my options for a few more moments before pushing the issue to the side, and asking Olivia how she was currently enjoying her honours degree.

'Argh ...' she groaned. 'It's going OK, but it's *so* much work!'

I laughed.

'You'll be fine, Liv. I know you'll ace it.'

'I hope so. I'm studying like a maniac!'

'You'll ace it,' I repeated with a grin. 'This time next year, we'll be at your graduation ceremony, and when it comes to your turn, the presenter will say, "Olivia Cruz, First Class Honours in Psychology". And when you go up on stage to accept your degree, your mum and dad and I will all stand up and cheer our hearts out.'

'Aw, Jimmy!' she smiled, once again reaching across the table and squeezing my hand. 'Thank-you!'

There we were – smiling at each other, holding one another's hand. But she let go after a few seconds and started talking again.

'I can't wait for this semester to be over,' she said. 'This year's been such a grind, and it really doesn't help that I have to take the ferry to Circular Quay and then the train to Redfern every day just to get to uni.'

I frowned.

'You're still doing that? Isn't your car fixed yet?'

She looked away.

'I don't know … it keeps breaking down.'

It was a clue – a subtle one, yes, but still one that gave me a glimpse of the beast that was ravaging her. But like I've said, it would take me until the end of the year to finally understand everything.

'Are you *sure* you don't want a lift?' I asked. 'I said I could drive you, remember?'

'Oh no, don't worry. My classes are much earlier than yours are, and I don't want to trouble you.'

'It's no problem, really. I'd be glad to help.'

'It's OK, really. You just stay in Sydney and stop abandoning me for other countries,' she winked.

'Actually Liv, it turns out that I might be going away again soon. As you know, the travel bug has its teeth in me, and Corey and I are talking about spending the summer in South East Asia.'

'What! Jimmy you can't abandon me again!'

I laughed.

'Why don't you come with us? That way, I won't be abandoning you.'

'I can't come with you – I've got to do my placement at the psych ward this summer, remember?'

'So really, I could make the argument that *you* are abandoning *me* so that you can work.'

'You definitely *cannot* make that argument.'

I chuckled, and Olivia frowned playfully.

'OK fine. Go,' she said. 'I'm getting used to spending Saturdays by myself anyway.'

She turned her bottom lip inside out, pouting.

'Aw, don't do that, Liv,' I smiled. 'You know I can't resist you when you look sad – even when I know you're only joking!'

But she continued staring at me with her pouting, mock-sad face.

'I'm not looking,' I laughed, covering my eyes with my hands. 'I'm not looking!'

But then she leaned across the table and tickled my tummy.

'Hey!' I said, reaching down to stop her.

Olivia giggled.

'Don't worry Jimmy, I'm just messing with you.'

I smiled at her.

'Can I redeem myself by buying you Ben and Jerry's later on?'

'Maybe.'

'Come on …'

'OK fine. And since you're paying, I'm really going to go to town. I think I'll get three scoops of ice-cream, some nuts on top, a brownie underneath, some whipped cream, a handful of Hundreds and Thousands all over it, some chocolate topping, and maybe even some fruit if they've got it, too.'

'You're all talk, Liv,' I chuckled. 'There's no way you'll be able to finish even a fraction of that!'

'Shut up!' she laughed.

A few days after I caught up with Olivia, I got together with Corey to talk about South East Asia. We still hadn't technically decided if we were going to go yet (*maybe we should try and get work experience instead?* we'd thought. Or, *what if one of us decides to do honours next year and needs to start drafting their thesis?* And, *can we really afford it?*). But when two 21 year old best mates who've just come back from a wicked trip and are giddy for another one get together to talk about the possibility of going overseas again, it's more or less a forgone conclusion that they're going to go (*we'll just get work experience next summer; we'll catch up writing our theses when we get back; yeah, we should be able to afford it, and if we're a little bit short, we'll just borrow from our parents.).* Once that was decided, we then turned our attention to where specifically to go.

'I really want to go tubing in Laos,' Corey said.

'I really want to go to Vietnam and take a cruise through Ha Long Bay.'

'If we're going to Asia, then we've got to go to India and see the Taj Mahal.'

'The Philippines would be awesome, too – they've got some really cool islands down south and some sick rice terraces up north.'

'Got to go to Singapore as well.'

'And Thailand for a ping pong show!'

So we turned up to a travel agent with our hodgepodge of ideas, and after listening to a few suggestions and looking at some brochures, we booked an eight week holiday starting in Singapore, and then travelling to the Philippines, Vietnam, Laos, Thailand and India before coming back home again two days before uni was set to begin. And as an added bonus, when we told the rest of the boys what we were doing, they decided to hop on board for the Vietnam-Laos-Thailand leg of the trip.

It was bound to be epic, but until we left on December 26, there was still a whole lot of water that needed to go under the bridge. Uni was in full swing, and despite not particularly enjoying it at all, I had to study hard to stay on top of my subjects. Of course, I was tutoring a bunch of high school students too so that I could save up for the trip, going for my run four times a week to keep myself fit and healthy, and trying to find a literary agent at night – which was a task that was still yet to bear any fruits. The way it worked was that you had to send them a one page "query letter" describing your novel, and if they liked the sound of it, they'd then ask to see the first few chapters; if they liked those they'd then ask to see the rest of the manuscript, and if they liked the whole book they'd offer to sign you. Out of the 30 agents I'd pitched my novel to by the start of October, 28 of them had rejected me right off the bat, and after asking to read the first three chapters, the other two agents ended up passing on me too. On the bright side, however, those two had given me some valuable feedback, so I was experimenting with a few of their suggestions before I planned on querying a new batch of agents. I'd be lying if I said I hadn't had my doubts, but I hoped with everything in me that someone would sign me soon. Every night, I prayed to God that it would happen, as I did every Sunday at church as well. *Please God, please.*

And then of course, there was Olivia. We were still spending every Saturday together, and still getting along as well as ever. Like I always had, I just felt so comfortable around her, so naturally at ease, so carefreely happy. And I was sure she felt exactly the same way.

We are so right for each other! I'd often think. *How on earth are we not together?*

And when I found myself thinking that way, I'd start to wonder, *is it possible she's changed her mind? Is it possible she'd be open to being in a relationship again? And if so, wouldn't it be best for me to float the idea now?* But then I'd also be forced to acknowledge that maybe she wasn't ready, and that if that was the case, then making a play for her would completely ruin things. No matter how much time I'd spend analysing the situation, I'd never be able to reach a decision. I just had no idea what to do. I really, really didn't.

But then in December, I finally got my answer. It was a picturesque Saturday afternoon in the heart of summertime Manly, with the sun bright and beaming; the sky cloudless and blue; the water rippling and glittering as the ferries pulled into the wharf; and The Corso filled with shirtless blokes and girls in bikinis with joy in their faces and ice-creams in their hands, strolling towards the beach where couples, friends and families contentedly sun-baked and sun-tanned surfers danced along the waves. On such an idyllic day, it would've been lovely no matter which restaurant we went to, but for its amazing view overlooking the sea, we chose to have lunch at the Bavarian Bier Café.

'Just so you know Liv, I'm going to break my healthy eating habit for you today.'

'Oh really?' she smiled. 'And why is that?'

'Because it's a special occasion – after all, it's not every day you get first class honours in psychology! So today, no healthy eating. Schnitzels, apple strudels, champagne – whatever you want to eat, we'll eat.'

'Well in that case we'll get some champagne and a schnitzel to share – the servings are huge here, so I won't be able to finish one all by myself.'

'It's about time you finally admitted it!'

She giggled.

'Shut up, Jimmy. Today's my special day – you're not allowed to make fun of me!'

I winked at her, and she smiled before a waiter came over. As we agreed, we ordered champagne and a big schnitzel between us, and then Olivia asked me how my book was going.

'Still working on it,' I sighed. 'Like I told you a while back, I made a few changes based on what those two agents advised, and that ended up inspiring me to make a few more changes, and then a few more changes after that. Anyway, I'm hoping to have it all finished by the time I go to Asia with Corey after Christmas, so I'll start resubmitting it once I get back.'

Olivia nodded.

'What sort of changes have you been making?'

'I'm actually working in quite a bit of mental health related stuff,' I said. 'To try and give the novel a bit more present day relevance.'

'Yeah? Like what?'

'Just stuff to do with depression, really. I'm putting in a lot of the emotions I struggled with myself – you know, feeling worthless, feeling as if I'd never be happy again, wanting to kill myself – all of that. Those feelings are just so common these days, so I think a lot of people will be able to relate to them. And, if I show my main character able to overcome them – and able to overcome all of the other crazy stuff that happens in his life – then I think it will give people going through those problems hope, and inspire them to succeed as well.'

'That sounds really great. I really, really like that idea.'

'Yeah, I'm excited about it too.'

'You should be. After you make those changes, I'm sure your novel's going to be snapped up in no time.'

I sighed.

'I hope so, Liv. I really do hope so.'

'It will be. You just wait and see.'

She paused for a moment, smiling fondly.

'It's funny, Jimmy,' she continued. 'I really don't doubt your ability to do anything. I just have this unshakable confidence in you, and I believe that no matter what you set your mind to doing, you'll end up doing it. I always have – ever since the day we met, when everyone was calling you "Washed Up Wharton" and saying you'd amount to nothing because you'd injured your spine and couldn't be a professional surfer anymore, and you looked me in the eye and told me you were going to overcome everyone's doubt in you and finish Grade 12 at the top of the year. You just looked so determined that I knew you were going to do it. And you did. And I know you're going to do this too. I just know it.'

At that moment, I felt a hot flush of love for her – one that tingled with even more passion and desire than usual. She always had been, and still was, my biggest cheerleader, and as she sat there smiling at me, warmly and affectionately, I wanted more than anything in the world to be able to step around the table, cup her face in my hands, and just kiss her, and kiss her, and kiss her. But instead, all I did was return her smile.

'Thanks,' I said. 'That really means a lot.'

We finished our schnitzel, and ordered an apple strudel to share for dessert as well. And, feeling festive and nowhere near ready to go home yet, we also ordered a second glass of champagne each.

'So,' I said after taking a sip. 'How was the first week of your placement at the psych ward?'

'Great! It's been really interesting to finally do hands-on work with patients, instead of just reading textbooks all the time.'

'Yeah, for sure. What's been the most interesting part so far?'

'Honestly, just seeing how little mental illness discriminates. I mean I've always known it was common – I know that it affects one in four people on average – and I know that it can affect anyone with any type of background. But it's different actually seeing it in real life, you know? Like just this week alone, we've treated a war veteran, a lawyer, a school teacher, a retiree, a 15 year old high school student, a second year engineering student, an unemployed person, a stay-at-home mum, a nurse, a management consultant and ... and so many other people I can't even remember them all off the top of my head. It's just crazy – how unbelievably prevalent it is. And it makes you realise that anyone – no matter who you are or what you do – can go through something like that, you know?'

'Yeah, absolutely. It seems to be everywhere you turn these days. Even this week, I ran in to two people from school who told me they were suffering from depression.'

'Was one of them Kevin? I bumped into him at uni a few weeks ago, and he said the next time he saw you he was going to talk to you about it. See if he could get some advice.'

'Yeah, one of them was Kevin. We chatted about it for ages.'

'What did you tell him?'

'Just the usual stuff – get help, live a healthy lifestyle, and for crying out loud, to stop smoking so much weed all the time. Ever since he moved into that share house in Newtown he's been getting stoned nearly every night.'

'Yeah, I told him the same thing. He said he would.'

'I hope so.'

Olivia nodded.

'Anyway,' I continued, 'his house is having their Christmas party tonight. You're coming, right?'

She shook her head.

'Unfortunately not.'

'What? How come?'

'It's ... I don't know.'

She paused, looking away.

'It's so ... so *far,*' she eventually said. 'And I've had a really long week. I need to rest.'

'Come on, Liv,' I said, instead of picking up on what was really going on. 'That was your excuse all year during honours, but you've finished now, so come out.'

'No, I'm so tired, really. Newtown's too far for me tonight.'

'But you haven't come to a party in ages.'

'I go to all the ones in Manly.'

'Yeah, but lots of our friends have moved into share houses closer to the city, so that's where heaps of the parties are. And you never come. In fact now that I think about it, I haven't seen you at a single party outside of Manly since the start of the year!'

'I know,' she sighed. 'I know. But during the year I had to study for honours, and today I just feel exhausted. Maybe next time, OK?'

'Alright, next time there's a party – regardless of where it is – you have to come. No more excuses!'

'I'll think about it. Now, tell me all about your plans for next year,' she said, changing the subject. 'Did you end up deciding to do honours like I suggested?'

'You'll be happy to know that I did! As of yesterday, I'm no longer a law student, and I'll be studying honours in economics next year.'

'Really? That's great!'

'I just figured, what's the point in continuing to do law, you know? I mean I don't like it, and, not that I love economics or anything, but I prefer it over law any day, and since it turns out I can get a job at a top management consulting company with an economics honours degree, then it made sense to quit law and just do that.'

'That makes complete sense, and congratulations on getting into honours!'

'Thanks, Liv. And of course, thank-you so much for giving me the idea.'

I looked at her, smiling.

'You really do give good advice, you know that? Your patients at the psych ward are very lucky to have you.'

She giggled.

'Aw, thanks Jimmy!'

'It's true!'

We continued chatting as we drank our champagne, and then capped off our lunch with a swim at the beach. After that, since it was still warm and sunny, we decided to get an ice-cream from Royal Copenhagen.

'So,' Olivia began as we were strolling through The Corso back towards the wharf, 'where are you most looking forward to going on your trip?'

'To be honest, I don't know. I really love Asian food, so eating all the local cuisine wherever we are will be really awesome. Ha Long Bay should be incredible too – I've always been a sucker for those paradisiacal islands.'

'What about the Taj Mahal? That's what I'd be most excited for.'

'Oh yeah, that'll definitely be a highlight. Everyone says it's really amazing.'

By then, we were almost at the end of The Corso.

'Well, be sure to take lots of pictures for me, OK? I won't have time to go on holidays anywhere, so I'll have to live vicariously through you!'

'Of course! And I'll bring you back lots of souvenirs too.'

We reached the end of The Corso, and waited at the traffic lights so we could cross the road to the wharf. Olivia asked me something about the Philippines, and I'd just opened my mouth to answer her – but then a car turned into the wrong lane and smashed into another one in front of us.

'Ah!' Olivia screamed.

After barely taking a second to catch his breath, the driver of the car who'd been hit stormed up to the other driver's window and started pounding his fist on it.

'What the fuck was that?' he yelled. 'You turned right into my lane, you idiot!'

'Sorry,' muttered the other guy. 'I made a mistake.'

'You're damn right you made a mistake! Both my passenger side doors are smashed in!'

'Alright settle down, mate. I said I was sorry.'

'Don't fucking tell me to settle down! You just fucking smashed – '

But I stopped paying attention after that, because to my surprise, I realised that Olivia was running frantically away.

'Liv!' I called after her.

But she ignored me and kept on running.

'Liv!'

I sprinted and caught up to her, grabbing her wrist.

'Let go of me!' she cried, trying to pull away.

'Liv it's OK – '

'Let go of me!'

'But Liv – '

'I said let go!' she turned around and screamed.

Flabbergasted, I dropped her hand. She stood there on the spot, shaking violently. Gasping for air. Staring at me wide-eyed with a look of terror spread across her face as tears uncontrollably streamed down her cheeks. I stared right back at her, completely bewildered.

'Liv it's OK!' I stressed. 'No one was hurt – '

'No it's *not* OK!' she screamed.

'But Liv – '

'Just leave me alone!'

'But – '

'Just leave me alone! Just fucking leave me alone!'

And at that, she turned back around and started running home. I stood there frozen in complete and utter shock, watching her shrink smaller and smaller in the distance before she rounded a corner and disappeared out of sight. As everyone around me stared, all I could think was, *what the fuck just happened? What the fuck just happened?* before I eventually started trudging home myself with nothing but confusion walking beside me. In hindsight, I of all people – particularly by that point in time – should've been able to figure out what was wrong. But her reaction had come as such a shock that in the heat of the moment, I wasn't able to put two and two together.

By the time I got to my place it was 6:30pm. I should've been starting to get ready for Kevin's party in Newtown, but instead I just lay on my bed, stewing with perplexed worry over Olivia. At various points throughout the next hour I tried to call her, but she wasn't answering her phone. I gave up at half-past seven, at which point, I decided to text her.

Liv, I'm going to stop ringing you tonight to give you some space, but when you feel up to it, can you please, please call me? I really don't understand why you were so upset this afternoon (you know no one was hurt, right? It was just a minor accident). But whatever the reason is, I'm really worried about you. I hate seeing you this way, and I just want to do whatever I can to help, so please call me as soon as you can, OK? Xx

Just after I'd messaged her, Corey rang me. He'd been trying to get through for the last 20 minutes, but because of the fiasco with Olivia I hadn't answered until now.

'Dude, what've you been doing?' he said. 'Aren't you picking me up on the way to Kevin's?'

I really didn't feel like going anymore, but Corey was relying on me for a lift, and I knew it would do me good to get out of the house for a while instead of staying at home fretting pointlessly over Olivia (keys to good mental health 101: don't waste time worrying about problems that you can't solve). So I picked Corey up, and we arrived in Newtown about three-quarters-of-an-hour later. Most of the guests were already there, getting drunk and letting loose. I did my best to join in the fun, but it was a bit hard being one of the only sober people there, and as much as I tried not to, I couldn't help stressing out over Olivia – wondering if she was now OK, wondering what the hell had actually happened. As a beer bong was doing the rounds, I felt the urge to get on one knee and obliterate my anxieties – but I'd previously promised myself that I wouldn't get drunk until I was in Asia with Corey, and what's more, I knew from experience that drinking to forget about my problems was a slippery slope that I didn't want to start sliding down. Brent however chose to get amongst it, and after downing two funnels of party punch, started puking in the bathroom. I patted him on the back as he hugged the toilet bowl, and had just given him a glass of water when all of a sudden, my phone vibrated in my pocket.

I'm really sorry about this afternoon, Jimmy – for screaming at you and ruining our day together. Nothing was your fault – you didn't do anything wrong – but the truth is that I haven't been very well lately. I've tried to hide it from you for so long, because you really are the last person in the world who I wanted to know about this. But after how hysterical I was this afternoon, I know you'll drive yourself crazy worrying about me until I give you an explanation ... so whenever you're ready, we can meet up and I'll tell you what's been happening.

After texting back and forth a couple of times, we agreed that I'd leave the party and go to her place. I organised for somebody else to take care of Brent and another person to drive Corey home and then I was out of there.

Forty minutes later, I arrived at Olivia's. She answered the door wearing a white nightie, smiling weakly but looking nervous and afraid. We embraced each other, and then taking me by the hand, she led me to her room. Like we'd done so many times before, we sat down side-by-side on the edge of her bed. Second after second passed as Olivia stared apprehensively down at the carpet, still holding my hand, stroking it gently with the tip of her thumb. I watched as tears welled in her eyes and rolled silently down her cheeks before she eventually broke down in a quiet sob.

'Olivia what is it?' I uttered frantically. 'What's going on?'

I handed her a tissue and she wiped her eyes, dabbed at her cheeks. She tried to compose herself as I sat there trembling, genuinely frightened of the news I was about to receive.

'Jimmy ...' she finally began, wiping her eyes again. 'Jimmy like I said I ... I tried so hard to keep this from you ... because I didn't ... I didn't want you to feel ... *guilty.*'

She paused, looking at me sympathetically.

'But the truth ... the truth is that I have post-traumatic stress disorder ... because of the car accident we were in together when you were manic and we crashed.'

She paused again, squeezing my hand tightly.

'I haven't been able to drive ever since,' she continued. 'I've tried ... so many times ... but whenever I turn on the engine – or even if I'm just sitting in the passenger seat – my mind flashes back to the crash, and I get so scared that it brings on a panic attack. My heart starts pounding really quickly, and then I start shaking, and crying, and I start to feel dizzy, and I find it so hard to breathe that I just have to get the hell out of there. *That's* why ever since the accident, I've been taking the ferry and the train to and from uni every day. *That's* why I haven't gone to any parties that aren't in Manly. It's not because my car broke down or because I had to study or because I was tired ... it's because I just couldn't do it, Jimmy. It's because I was just too scared.'

She wiped away a fresh batch of tears that'd lacquered her eyes.

'I've been getting help for it,' she went on. 'I've been seeing a really good psychologist, and I am getting better. But it's something I still really struggle with. And today ... just seeing that crash ... it just made me get those flashbacks again, and ... and I couldn't handle it. I couldn't handle it, Jimmy ...' she trailed off, crying.

I was gobsmacked. Absolutely fucking gobsmacked. As I sat there with my arm around her, I found myself inundated by an avalanche of emotions. Of course, I felt a deep-seated concern. I felt shocked – that this had been happening for months and I hadn't suspected a thing. I felt angry – at my GP Dr King – for giving me the wrong medication which is what had caused me to become manic and crash the car in the first place. I felt a devastating sadness – at the fact that Olivia was suffering so severely. But above all else, I felt what she'd guessed I'd feel: guilt.

'Liv I'm so sorry … I'm so sorry about all of this. It's all my fault that everything – '

'No, Jimmy,' she said, squeezing my hand. 'Don't do this … don't blame yourself. It was *not* your fault.'

'But Liv – '

'*No*, Jimmy!' she stressed, clutching my hand even tighter. 'Please don't blame yourself. *Please*, Jimmy.'

But I couldn't help it.

'Look I know … I know what you're saying … and I'm grateful you don't blame me for everything that's happened. But I still feel so bad. I still feel so *guilty*. I hate seeing you suffering like this. I *hate* it.'

I paused, gritting my teeth to try and stop myself from crying.

'I wish it was me, Liv,' I murmured. 'I wish it was me who was going through all of this.'

She shook her head, bringing my hand to her lips and kissing it softly.

'I don't,' she said. 'You've suffered enough already.'

'It doesn't matter. I care about you *so* much, Olivia.'

I paused, looking into her eyes.

'Seriously … I care about you more than I care about myself.'

As soon as I'd said it, she broke into a smile – that warm, vivacious smile that I could gaze at forever – and she snuggled up closer to me, resting her head in the crook of my neck.

'Jimmy, you are the sweetest, most genuinely caring guy I have ever met,' she whispered. 'I know you didn't mean it. I know you'd take it all back if you could. And I know that if there was anything you could do to make me feel better, that you'd do it no matter what.'

'Of course,' I said, gently caressing her shoulder. 'I'd do absolutely anything for you.'

'I know you would. So can you promise me that you won't feel guilty?'

'But Liv – '

'No buts,' she said, lifting her head from my shoulder to look into my eyes. 'It wasn't your fault – plain and simple. I'm not just saying that to make you feel better – I'm saying that because it's the truth. You had absolutely no control over what you were doing that night, which is exactly why the police dismissed the charges against you, and exactly why I don't blame you in the slightest for everything that's happened. I honestly do believe that, Jimmy – with every fibre of my being. *I promise you.* So can you please promise me that you're not going to feel guilty and blame yourself for everything?'

I studied her carefully. From the look in her eyes, I knew that she really did believe what she was saying.

'OK,' I finally said. 'I promise.'

She smiled at me, and then laid her cheek back down on my shoulder again. I kissed the top of her head and cuddled her, doing my best to make her feel cared for.

'I want to support you though, Liv – in every way I can. But to be honest, I don't know very much about PTSD. So could you maybe … could you maybe try to explain it to me a little?'

I could feel her nodding into my neck.

'What do you want to know?'

I cleared my throat.

'Ah … I guess … I guess I'm curious to know … what it feels like … just so that I can understand what you're going through a bit better.'

'OK … I'll do my best to describe it, but like any mental illness I suppose, it's really hard to try and explain properly, you know? I think the closest I can come is saying that – for me at least – suffering from PTSD means that you're trapped in the moment when the event causing your PTSD occurred, and that you're plagued with overwhelming, crippling fear as a result. Depending on what caused it, that fear can manifest itself in different ways, but for me, it's the fear that I'll be in another car accident, and that that car accident is going to kill me. That probably sounds crazy to you – someone who doesn't have PTSD – because the probability of being in a life-threatening accident every time you go for a drive is incredibly small. But like I said, having PTSD for me means that I'm imprisoned in the moment of time that the car crash happened, so every time I even just sit down in a car, my mind is not really "sitting down" with my body – instead, it's flashing back to you and me speeding through the streets in the dark, and me begging you to slow down, and you just going faster and faster, and me feeling completely powerless, and then *bang!* The two of us crashing into the telegraph pole at a hundred miles an hour. And even though the flashback is only happening in my head, it feels so real, so lifelike, that I almost feel just as traumatised as I would if it was actually happening all over again. That's why I haven't been able to drive in a car since the accident, and that's why I completely freaked out when those two cars collided today – because it triggered a flashback, and in my head, I felt almost as panicked as if I was having the accident myself right then and there.'

Her mention of my involvement stirred a throbbing guilt inside me, but in line with keeping my promise, I did my best to squash it, and continue trying to better understand her condition so that I could support her as best I could.

'And you said ... you said you've been getting better ... but Liv, I ... do you mind if I ask you ... how bad it was at the start? And where your head's at now, exactly?'

Once again, I felt her gently nodding into my neck.

'For the first two weeks after the crash, that crippling fear I've been talking about was so overwhelming, so paralysing, that I didn't leave the house to even go for a walk – because I was terrified that if I did, a car would zoom off the road and hit me on the footpath. During that time I was able to do my uni work at home, but the mid-semester exams were coming up, so unless I wanted to fail or drop out of honours, I had to go to uni.'

She paused for a moment, sighing deeply.

'It was so hard. The first time I went outside – the weekend before my exams started – I challenged myself to walk down the street to The Corso, and it's not an exaggeration to say that I was literally frightened with every step I took. Again, it might seem insane to you – you're probably thinking, *what could possibly go wrong walking down the street?* But when you have PTSD, you're paranoid. When you're in a situation that reminds you of your trauma, you never feel safe ... and even though on an intellectual level you may know that you are, on an emotional level, you feel convinced that you're in imminent danger. So that first day, because I felt so vulnerable and under threat, I was scanning the road for cars non-stop, and every time I'd see or hear one approaching, my heart would pound even faster, and my whole body would shake even more, and I'd be so afraid that I'd freeze in my tracks, and not be able to do anything but stare at it wide-eyed and desperately will it to pass. Kind of like when someone who's really scared of spiders sees one close by, I wouldn't be able to take my eyes off it, because I was petrified that if I did, it would come and get me. In fact, I remember sneezing one time when an SUV was approaching, and even that split second of blindness was so traumatising that I screamed. That's how anxious, how on edge, how overly-alert I was. It's a state that people with PTSD call "hypervigilance", and it's so, so, *so* exhausting. By the time I'd made it to The Corso, I was so drained that I collapsed on a park bench and started crying, and I was so overwhelmed by the prospect of walking back home again that I called my mum so that she could walk with me, and we didn't start going until I'd made her promise that she'd hold my hand every step of the way.'

As she spoke, tears filled my eyes. It was just so devastating, so heart-wrenching to listen to.

'But you're better now, right Liv?' I murmured, gently rubbing her shoulder. 'Like you don't feel that bad anymore, do you?'

'No. Walking in the streets became easier and easier the more treatment I got, and the more I faced my fears and pushed myself to do it. I'm comfortable doing that now – like I have been for the last seven or eight months. But to this day, I'm still scared stiff of setting foot inside a car – let alone driving one anywhere. So that's my next obstacle to try and overcome.'

I wiped my eyes, and tried to take solace in the fact that she was slowly recovering.

'What sort of treatment have you been getting?' I asked.

'Like most mental illnesses, I guess, many people with PTSD take medication to help with their symptoms. There's no such thing as an "anti-PTSD" medication or anything like that, but I take an anti-anxiety medication to try and reduce my stress levels and that "hypervigilance" I told you about. I used to take a second medication too to help with all the nightmares I would get – but they stopped a few months ago, so I've gradually been able to ween off that one.'

'What about therapy?' I asked. 'I know that for depression, medication is used to treat the symptoms, but to actually recover – as in to get to the point where you can live a happy, healthy, depression-free life – therapy is needed so that the sufferer can learn how to deal with the triggers of their depression in such a way that, over time, those triggers are no longer able to trigger them. Is it kind of the same with PTSD as well?'

'Yes, pretty much exactly the same. Medication will help you cope, but therapy is needed for you to actually recover – which in my case, can be thought of as being able to think about the accident without becoming distressed, being able to walk around the streets and not feel constantly under threat, and of course, being able to set foot in a car without getting flashbacks, and to be able to go for a drive like everybody else can. To help me get to that point, I've been doing this thing called "trauma-focused cognitive behavioural therapy", where my therapist has carefully exposed me to some of the thoughts and situations that remind me of the accident. For example, she's given me exercises that involve thinking about it in detail, which over time, have helped me to come to terms with it and be able to recall it without freaking out. That type of therapy also involves my therapist identifying irrational thoughts that I have surrounding the accident, and then helping me to rethink those thoughts in a more logical sort of way. So to give you an example of how that works, remember how I told you that at the start, I'd get scared walking down the street because I'd be worried that I'd get hit by a car? Like that's obviously not a rational thought, right, so my therapist helped me challenge it, and replace it with another thought that *was* more rational – the thought that I *am* safe walking down that street; that the chances of being hit while doing so are extremely, extremely, extremely small; and that I've walked down the street thousands of times before, so I'm more than capable of doing it again. And it worked, because now, I'm able to do it.'

She sighed.

'But I still can't get in a car, Jimmy. Like I've said, I've tried … so many times. But it's still just too much for me. And what's worse, just the idea of it seems so confronting … so terrifying … that I don't know if I'm ever going to be able to do it. I honestly don't know if I'll ever be able to drive again …'

She trailed off, and I could feel her weeping quietly into my neck. Once again, I gently rubbed her shoulder, and softly kissed the top of her head.

'You *will* be able to do it, Liv,' I tried to encourage her. 'I mean look how far you've come already – you're miles ahead of where you were right after the accident. And the more therapy you get, the stronger you're going to feel, and then one day, you'll be able to get in a car and go for a drive, and it will be just as easy as it always was.'

'But how do you know that?' she asked. 'How can you be so sure?'

'I know it, Olivia, because I know you. You're a fighter, and like all fighters, you'll eventually get what you're going for – because you'll never give up until you get it.'

She raised her head from my shoulder, looking into my face with tear-coated eyes.

'Do you really believe that?'

I gazed right back at her.

'Yes, I do. And I'll be there to help you – whenever you need me to. I'll be there to talk to you every time you feel low, I'll be there to hug you every time you feel scared, and I'll be there to remind you everything's going to be OK every time you feel overwhelmed.'

I brushed a loose strand of hair out of her face.

'Whatever you need, Olivia, I'll be there for you. Every single step of the way.'

At that moment, she smiled at me – the purest, most genuine smile I have ever seen – and laid her head back down on my shoulder, snuggling up even closer to me.

'You're such a sweetheart,' she whispered, bringing my hand to her lips and kissing it softly. 'I really hadn't wanted to tell you about my PTSD because I thought you'd blame yourself, but now that you know … I'm actually really glad. I've missed having you to talk to. I've missed having you to comfort me. This really has been the most difficult thing I've ever had to go through, and not having you by my side throughout it has made it a hundred times harder.'

She sighed.

'I've missed you, Jimmy. I've really, really missed you.'

I held her close to me, and kissed the top of her head once more.

'Don't worry, Liv. I'm here now. And I'm not going anywhere.'

We talked and talked into the early hours of the morning. Olivia told me more about her PTSD, and I comforted her … and the more I comforted her, the more she told me, and the more she told me, the more I comforted her … and we were cuddled up so closely together … and it just felt so normal, so natural ... and then sooner or later, one thing just kind of led to another, and then ...

It began so slowly, so tenderly – just soft, gentle kissing with our arms around each other. But then an urgency crept in, almost a desperation, and we started kissing harder, hungrier, faster ... Olivia's hands moving to my cheeks, mine running through her hair and then sliding down her waist, rubbing her all over as I recalled the contours of her figure, the smoothness of her skin, the roundness of her small, perky breasts before I moved to her legs and then up towards her vagina, stroking it through her panties, backwards and forwards, backwards and forwards as Olivia panted heavily between kissing me, *ha* ... *ha* ... *ha* ... *ha* ... her juices seeping through the fabrics, dampening the tips of my fingers as I pulled her underwear to a side, started massaging her clit as my cock throbbed in my pants, as Olivia fumbled with my belt, unable to undo it quickly enough before she pulled me down on top of her and I slipped inside her, and there we both were, like we'd been so many times before, moaning, screaming, gasping for air as she dug her nails into my back and wrapped her legs around me, our eyes half closed and our mouths wide open as we rocked back and forth in a ball of passion, in a bundle of unbridled desire, and when you're that immersed in the moment – when your bodies, minds and spirits are that unwaveringly engaged – it always ends too soon. It always, always, *always* ends too soon ...

'Oh, Olivia ...' I panted afterwards, trying to catch my breath. 'Olivia ...'

I propped myself up on my elbows, stared fervently into her deep blue eyes. And as she stared right back at me, smiling through tears before she leaned in to kiss me, I remember thinking that I'd go through all of it again – all of the depression, the heartache and the countless lonely nights – just so that I could experience the ecstasy of this sublime reunion.

I promise, Olivia

How can I possibly put into words how magical it was, rekindling my love with the woman I adored? I don't think I can, which is why in the moments after Olivia and I agreed to dive back into a relationship and intertwine our lives together, all I could do was cry with joy into the crook of her neck. Tears streamed from her eyes just as freely, and when I lifted my head to gaze deeply into them, she kissed my lips, and told me she loved me.

'I love you too, Olivia,' I reciprocated, and when I said it, I remember feeling so vindicated – for believing in the strength of our love for the last nine months, and having faith that this day would finally come. As the sun rose to congratulate us, we just lay there in her bed, holding each other, smiling so giddily that we were almost laughing. We were both so suffused with such an intoxicating bliss; such a breathtaking, ethereal ebullience; such a perfect love for the world and everything in it. And in such a state, what is the need for words?

In those early December days before I went to Asia with Corey, I was reminded that one of the most enchanting things about being in love is that what would otherwise be ordinary mornings, evenings or afternoons can so easily turn into the best moments of your life. That Sunday, after eventually drifting off to sleep in each other's arms, we awoke at midday and went for a swim at Manly, before walking the scenic route to Shelly Beach, hiring a couple of snorkels and paddling hand-in-hand amongst the gorgeous corals. We ate fish and chips for dinner on our towels in the sand, and watched the sunset together before making love back at my place with a necessity spawn from spending too long apart. The following week, Olivia had to work at the psych ward during the day, but knowing we wouldn't see each other in January or February, we spent every night together. On Monday, we rode the ferry to Circular Quay, and talked and laughed all the way to Darlinghurst where we ordered *empanadas*, *churros* and cappuccinos at a cute little Spanish café called Hernandez. On Tuesday, we took the tour bus to Borgnis Street in Davidson, and joined the throngs of people eating Mr Whippy cones and marvelling at all the houses that were beautifully adorned with brightly-coloured Christmas lights. My mum had taken her holiday leave early that year, so on Wednesday, she helped me cook spaghetti marinara and make a peanut butter chocolate cheesecake, which I packed into a picnic basket along with some prawns, stuffed olives and a bottle of wine that I had with Olivia down by the beach. On Thursday, we went shopping for all our Christmas gifts together at Chatswood, and then shared a plate of *nasi lemak* and a chicken curry at Mamek by the train station. On Friday, we cuddled up on the couch at my place and watched *A Lot Like Love* starring Ashton Kutcher and Amanda Peet. They were evenings that were so simple, yet so wonderful, so lovely, that when I'm old and grey, I know they'll glitter in my memory as brightly as any others I've made on this earth.

Of course, while the ordinary days with your lover can turn out to be the best of your life, so can the extraordinary ones, which is why Olivia and I spontaneously decided to take a short trip up the coast together just before Christmas. Since Liv was busy with her final week of work for the year beforehand, it was left to me to plan, and I was determined to make it the most romantic five days of her entire life. There were a few limitations which made it challenging – the fact that we only had five days for starters, and of course, the fact that Olivia's PTSD meant that we weren't able to use a car – but after hours of research and over a dozen phone calls, I was confident I'd planned a trip that she'd never forget.

'So where are we going, exactly?' she asked the night she came over to my place to watch *A Lot Like Love*.

'I don't really want to tell you,' I grinned. 'Can I just book everything and you find out when we get there?'

'What?' she smiled back. 'Why don't you want to tell me?'

'I want to surprise you.'

'Oh come on, tell me as an early Christmas present!'

'You've always been this way, you know that?' I chuckled. 'For as long as I've known you, every time I've ever wanted to surprise you with anything, you've always badgered me to tell you what it is – but then every time you eventually found out, you were glad I hadn't.'

'That is so not true!' she exclaimed, slapping me playfully on the arm.

'Of course it is!'

'Give me an example.'

'OK, how about that time in our first year of uni when I said I had a surprise for you after your last exam, and then I came to pick you up with your little dog Snowy? Or when I took you to Waterworks that time and we went racing down the slides together? Or when I said I was going to take you out for a really special evening at a "secret location" on your 19th birthday, only to bring you back to your place where all your friends were waiting for your surprise party? Or when – '

'OK fine!' she laughed. 'Maybe you're right.'

'Of course I'm right! So does that mean I don't have to tell you what I have planned for us?'

'OK. But we won't be taking any cars though, will we?'

'No cars.'

'You promise?'

'Ahuh! All we need to get where we want to go is a train … and another form of transport that lovers used well before cars were ever invented.'

'Really! What is it?'

'I want to surprise you,' I grinned. 'But think along the lines of *Gone with the Wind.*'

'Gone with the Wind?'

'That's what I said.'

'What on earth have you got planned for me, Jimmy Wharton?' she smiled, snuggling up closer to me. 'The most romantic trip a girl could ever dream of?'

'Hopefully I do,' I smiled back, leaning in to kiss her. 'Hopefully I do.'

As the train left early in the morning, Olivia suggested that I spend the night at her place, and because I hadn't seen her parents since we'd gotten back together again, she invited me over to have dinner with them as well. I'd met them countless times over the years and had always had a good relationship with them, but in the hours leading up to dinner, a nervous anxiety welled up within me. You see, it wasn't just to be the first time I'd seen them since Olivia and I had reunited – it was also to be the first time I'd seen them since the night of our accident. The night when I'd broken their daughter's arm, nearly killed her, and made her develop a serious mental illness.

What if they don't think of the accident the same way Olivia does? I worried on the walk to their place. *What if they blame me for everything that's happened? What if they're only making an effort to be civil to me for Olivia's sake, but deep down, they really hate me?*

When I arrived, Olivia opened the door with a smile, and kissed me on the lips before leading me into the dining room where her dad was setting the table.

'Hey there, Jimmy,' he said, stepping towards me and holding out his hand. 'Long time no see.'

'Hi Mr Cruz,' I replied, shaking his hand. Of Spanish origin, he had olive skin just like Olivia did, wavy black hair that he parted to a side, and brown eyes that lay behind a thick pair of glasses. I looked into those eyes to try and detect any hidden emotion – any malice or dislike that may've laid behind them – but I couldn't sense any there. In fact, judging by his smile, he seemed genuinely happy to see me – or else he was just really good at hiding his contempt.

He asked how I was, and I replied that I'd been doing well before Olivia's mum came in from the kitchen. Even though she was Australian, her skin was relatively tanned too, and she shared Olivia's brown hair, blue eyes, high cheek bones and warm, vivacious smile – which to my relief, she flashed at me before kissing my cheek and giving me a hug.

'Hi Jimmy,' she said. 'It's good to see you again.'

'Hi Mrs Cruz. It's nice to see you again, too.'

We talked a bit about the heatwave and our plans for Christmas before sitting down at the table – me beside Olivia, and her parents directly in front of us. Her mum served us some of the roast lamb, vegetables and apricot stuffing she'd prepared, and her father poured everyone a glass of the red wine I'd brought over before we all said cheers and took a sip.

'So, Jimmy,' her mother began as she started cutting up her meat. 'Olivia says you've been doing really well lately.'

I nodded uncertainly. Not entirely sure whether she was referring to me acing my final year exams or the fact that I hadn't had a bipolar episode in the last several months, I decided to reply with something that covered all the bases.

'Yeah, that's right. I'm feeling much better than I was at the start of the year, and I was fortunate enough to do well in my exams and get into the economics honours program at uni.'

Her father fixed me with a serious look.

'So you really are feeling better?' he asked.

'Yes,' I nodded. 'Much better.'

'Would you say you were "back to normal", again?'

I couldn't tell whether he was inquiring out of concern or because he didn't trust me with his daughter. But either way, I tried to answer as politely and as honestly as I could.

'Well, um … I have to work really hard, you know? Like I see my psychologist once a week, and I read self-help books, and I exercise a lot, and I eat well, and I hardly ever drink, and of course I take my medication every day … but I find that if I do all of those things, I usually feel pretty good. In fact, I usually feel about as good as I felt before I developed bipolar disorder.'

His eyes softened.

'That's good, Jimmy. I'm really glad to hear that.'

'Me too,' Olivia's mum agreed. 'We were all really worried about you for a while there.'

'Thanks,' I smiled. 'But luckily, everything's turned out well.'

They then asked me about honours the following year and how I was fairing trying to find a publisher for my book. I asked them about their work too, and learned that Olivia's dad was considering early retirement from his job as a stockbroker, and that her mum had recently changed jobs and was now the head chef of a two hat restaurant in the city. After dinner we ate caramel *flan* for dessert and then drank tea as we chatted about Olivia's placement at the psych ward, and her parents – who'd been to Asia for their 20th wedding anniversary a few years beforehand – gave me tips on what to do in the countries I was visiting. They were warm and friendly towards me, and I realised that I'd probably been worrying over nothing. Nevertheless, I felt relieved when they said goodnight and I was alone in bed with Olivia. And, perceptive as she was, she sensed it.

'Hey Jimmy, is everything OK?' she asked. 'I might just be imagining things, but during dinner you seemed a little bit … a little bit nervous. A little bit on edge, perhaps.'

I admitted that I'd been anxious about seeing her parents for the first time since the accident, and scared about what they may've thought of me since.

'Jimmy don't be silly!' Olivia said. 'They know it wasn't your fault, and they still think you're as terrific as ever.'

She paused, smiling at me.

'They love you, baby. Just like I do.'

She kissed me, and I felt a weight being lifted off my shoulders as our tongue's slowly and sensually circled one another's. And then we just kind of melted into it, as you do when you're in love – our breathing deepening, our hands racing over each other's body, undoing buttons and flinging clothes across the room before we danced under the doona and eventually drifted off to sleep in each other's arms.

At six o'clock, our alarm started blaring, and after rubbing the sleep from my eyes I excitedly leapt out of bed, unable to believe that after being lonely and single not ten days beforehand, I was now about to go on a wonderful trip with the love of my life.

'Come on baby, rise and shine!' I chirped as I threw on a T-shirt and jumped into my board shorts.

Olivia kissed me and then hopped in the shower, and after I'd put a pot of coffee on and we'd both had a cuppa, we walked down to the wharf to take a ferry to Circular Quay, before boarding a short train to Central Station and then the long train for us to ride up the coast.

'I can't wait to see where you're taking me, sweetie!' Olivia smiled as we reclined in our seats and cuddled up together.

'You'll find out soon enough,' I grinned. 'We'll arrive at our first stop a little after lunchtime.'

'Our *first* stop?'

'Ahuh. It seems that when God made Australia, He chose to spread the most beautiful spots out, so to make sure you have the most romantic trip of your life, we have to go to two different places.'

'Wow, I'm getting swept off my feet just listening to you.'

I laughed.

'Glad to hear it, baby!'

We continued talking for the next few hours, stopping from time to time to read a little bit or to look out the window at the rolling green hills, the sandy coastlines or the magnificent vastness of the Pacific Ocean. For lunch, we had a couple of roast lamb and apricot stuffing sandwiches that Liv's mum had made us from the previous night's leftover dinner, and afterwards picked at a jar of black olives until a little after two o'clock when we arrived at our first stop – a relatively small coastal town home to several beautiful beaches and the only place where the Australian mountains meet the Pacific Ocean: Coffs Harbour.

'Here you have it, my dear,' I said, sweeping my arm through the air to showcase one of the town's golden-sanded, sun-drenched beaches that was sprinkled with sunbathers and caressed by smooth, curling, white-tipped waves.

'I love it,' she said, looping her arm through mine. 'Want to go for a swim?'

'Sure,' I said. 'But not here.'

Taking her by the hand, I then led her along the beach where all the people were and up on to one of the pointed, emerald-green headlands.

'I hope you're taking me somewhere nice, baby,' Olivia said as she moved with cautious, flat-footed steps over the uneven terrain. 'I'm finding it really hard to walk in my thongs!'

'Oh I am, don't worry.'

We continued treading carefully for a couple more minutes until we found ourselves at a small, deserted cove by the base of the headland, where calm, cool water washed up gently against the rocky embankment. There was no one there. It was just us and the Pacific Ocean against the backdrop of the rocks.

'I just wanted you all to myself,' I smiled. 'Do you like it?'

'It's perfect,' she said, giving me a hug. 'You're two out of two so far, honey!'

I leaned in to kiss her before we put our bag down on a rock outside the water's reach, kicked off our thongs and took off our t-shirts. I was about to take Olivia's hand and wade into the sea with her, but given that we were by ourselves, I was suddenly struck by inspiration.

'Let's go in naked,' I said.

'What?' she laughed.

'You heard me.'

'But we're in public!'

'Not really. There's no one in sight.'

'What if someone comes?'

'They won't be able to see anything – we'll be in the water.'

She was shaking her head, but I could see the sides of her mouth curling into a smile.

'OK,' she said. 'I will if you will.'

My pants were off in a second, and at the sight of my nakedness, Olivia pulled the string of her bikini top so that it slipped off, and hooked her thumbs in the sides of her bottoms before sliding them down her legs and leaving them at her feet. I stood there mesmerised by the roundness of her breasts, and the smoothness of her olive, sun-kissed skin before inevitably, I felt my dick harden with a stirring of horniness.

'Let's fuck,' I murmured.

She laughed.

'You can't be serious.'

'Come on, just here on the rocks.'

A seductive smile spread across her face.

'Please?' I said.

Taking a step towards me, she slid her hand up my spine to the back of my neck, and pulled me in to kiss her. Her warm tongue swam around my own, and then her free hand grabbed my prick, squeezing it up and down for a few seconds before she led me towards the water by its tip.

'Come on, tiger,' she winked. 'You need a cool swim.'

We spent most of the afternoon in the sea, holding each other as we bobbed up and down amidst the gentle waves; made out as the bright, friendly sun warmed our faces; and licked the saltwater off each other's nipples, just because we could. After putting our swimmers back on, we held hands and swam around the surrounding coves, and then looped back along the beach for a walk in the cool evening breeze.

'What do you want to do for dinner?' I asked.

'Does that question imply that you don't have anything really romantic planned for me?' she pouted playfully.

'Not at all,' I grinned. 'In fact, I have two suggestions that I think you might like.'

'And what are they?'

'Which do you want to hear first – the traditional one, or the less-traditional-but-more-romantic-and-also-slightly-controversial one?'

'Let's save the best for last and start with the traditional option.'

'OK, so the traditional option is to go to the fancy restaurant around the corner, have a candlelit meal and a bottle of wine, and then go back to a hotel and have sex all night long.'

'Nice, nice,' she mused. 'And what about the less-traditional-but-more-romantic-and-also-slightly-controversial option?'

'Well, instead of going around the corner to the fancy restaurant, we could go around the other corner to the takeaway fish and chip shop, and then eat it by ourselves on our headland at sunset before making love and falling asleep beneath the stars.'

'You're right … that is a little controversial.'

'But romantic too, right?'

'Very romantic. But wouldn't it be uncomfortable?'

'I brought a blow-up air-mattress.'

'Wouldn't we get cold?'

'Not if we snuggle in our sleeping bag.'

Just like she had been when I suggested we swim together naked, she was shaking her head. But once again, a smile was playing on her lips.

'Alright, you're on then, Jimmy Wharton. Under the stars it is!'

So we ordered a big seafood basket and got a bottle of white wine from a liquor store, and strolled back to our headland to share it looking out at the golden-orange horizon. When night blanketed the sky and the wind picked up, I pumped up the air mattress, and just like I'd imagined us doing before we left, we copulated softly in our sleeping bag with only the stars as our witnesses.

We woke at dawn to the golden rays of the almighty sun, and after eating a bowl of muesli and fresh fruit salad at a nearby café, we boarded the train again and continued along the scenic route up to Tweed Heads on the New South Wales-Queensland border. When we arrived, I think Olivia expected us to follow the signs down towards the beach and check into a hotel – but instead, I pulled a hand-sketched map out of my pocket and let it guide me in the opposite direction.

'Where on earth are we going?' she laughed.

'Just trust me, baby.'

I got us lost twice, but eventually we arrived where we were supposed to: at a farmhouse annexed to a cow paddock, chicken coup, and several fields of crops. As we approached the door, Olivia gaped at me in shock, but I just smiled back and repeated for her to trust me before knocking. A few seconds later, the door creaked open, and in front of us stood a middle-aged, heavy-bearded man in a blue-and white-checked shirt.

'You must be Jimmy from Sydney,' he beamed, extending his hand. 'And this must be your lovely girlfriend, Olivia.'

'That's right,' I grinned back, taking his hand. 'And you must be Andy.'

'That's what it says on my birth certificate.'

Andy and Olivia then shook hands too, and even though she smiled at him, I could tell by the look in her eye that she was thoroughly confused – as, apparently, could Andy.

'Now,' he said to her, 'you look like a girl who has absolutely no idea what's going on.'

'You got me!' she laughed.

'And I bet you're pretty curious to find out why your boyfriend has brought you all the way to a farm in the middle of nowhere, right?'

'Yeah, just a bit!'

Andy turned to me.

'Should we tell her?'

'Hhmmm ... could we show her instead?'

'OK, let's go.'

So he led us around the corner, past a sleeping Labrador and a clucking chicken to a wooden stable, which housed four bronze, well-groomed horses.

'I'm sorry,' Olivia said, 'but I still don't ... I still don't get it.'

'Because we want to avoid travelling by car to where we're booked in to stay,' I said, 'and because it's too far to walk, I arranged for us to arrive on horseback.'

'Are you serious?' she smiled.

'Yeah.'

'But ... but how did you possibly plan that?'

'It's quite a story,' Andy said, 'but to cut it short, after thinking up the idea, Jimmy managed to track down one of the local farmers here called Fred, who put him in touch with another local farmer called Steve, who put him in touch with his sister Peggy, who put him in touch with her cousin Cindy, who also happens to be my wife. And after explaining how much it would mean to him if Cindy or I could take the two of you to where you're staying on a couple of our mares, we were happy to oblige – being the friendly country folk we are!'

'Wow …' Olivia said. 'Thank-you, Andy … thank-you so much. And Jimmy,' she murmured, turning to me. 'You're … you're amazing, you know that?'

I beamed at her, and then Andy got the three of us set up with our horses Tom, Dick and Harry before we all trotted off into Tweed Valley, where I'd organised for Olivia and I to spend the next three nights at an adorable pavilion situated by the mountains amidst 100 acres of tranquil bushland – an area that was so luscious and green you couldn't help but marvel at its beauty; that was so quiet and peaceful you felt your worries evaporate; and that was so romantic you just wanted to take your lover in your arms and never let them go.

Our stay was nothing short of heavenly, and how could it not be, when our days were spent going for walks through the beautiful rainforest, dipping our feet in one of the nearby lakes, or lying together in the hammock on our veranda and listening to the birdsong; while our evenings involved toasting marshmallows and feeding them to each other, watching the passing wallabies at sunset, bathing together in our timber bath surrounded by fragrant candles, and making love underneath our 19th century crystal chandelier. In fact, it was so celestial that as much as I'd been looking forward to going to Asia with Corey, I no longer wanted to – I no longer wanted to do anything but stay with Olivia in our near-mythical oasis, and then when our money ran out, go back to Manly and spend the whole summer with her, and every future summer with her, and all the autumns, winters and springs in between until the day we died.

Fittingly, on our last night before we were due to return to Sydney, I dreamed of Olivia and I getting married. The day began at 8 o'clock in the morning when Corey, Brent, Sean, Chris and Steve came over to my place, at which point – in a ridiculous, nonsensical occurrence that's so typical of dreams – we had my bachelor party. After getting really, really drunk, I was hand-cuffed to my living room door before a blonde-haired, big-boobed stripper gave me a lap dance, poured hot wax all over my back and then started whipping me while the boys smoked cigars and laughed their heads off. After we'd miraculously sobered up and all had showers, we got changed into our tuxes and then took a limousine to St Patrick's Estate in Manly for the ceremony. The church was packed with all our friends and family, including my uncle and auntie and my little nieces and nephews who'd come up from Melbourne; the Spanish side of Olivia's family who'd flown all the way from Barcelona; and in another bizarre occurrence that could only happen in a dream, the congregation included Gavin – that wanker who Olivia had dated at the start of the year and who I'd gotten into a fistfight with at my 21st – and also Lydia – the girl I'd briefly been seeing around the same time, who'd broken up with me when she found out that I was suffering from depression.

The music started playing, and Olivia came walking down the aisle looking more beautiful than I'd ever seen her. She took my hands when she reached me, and smiled radiantly through her veil with ruby-coloured lipstick. The priest spoke for a bit, and then, we said our vows.

'I, Jimmy, take you, Olivia, to be my wife. For as long as I've known you, you've been my strength, my inspiration, my joy, and my biggest supporter. Thank-you for always loving me at my worst as well as at my best, and in return, I promise to always respect you, cherish you, care for you, and be devoted to you for the rest of my life.'

'I, Olivia, take you, Jimmy, to be my husband. Over the years, we've overcome every obstacle standing in our way, and you've led me out the other side feeling more alive, exuberant, and happy than I ever thought possible. I promise to forever love you, look after you and treasure you, and to spend the rest of my life trying to make you as happy as you've made me.'

Then the priest went on with the 'do you take this man, do you take this woman' part. Tears were rolling down Olivia's cheeks when she squeezed my hands and said 'I do', and when I said it back, my voice shook and came out croaky.

'Then by the power vested in me, I now pronounce you husband and wife. You may kiss the bride'.

I pulled back Olivia's veil, and we gazed at each other through watering eyes before melting into the most beautiful, ethereal kiss as all our loved ones began clapping and cheering, and continued doing so as we walked down the aisle, beaming at one another, beaming at everyone, happier than we'd ever been at any point in our lives.

We'd just had our first dance as a married couple at the reception when I woke to Olivia sitting up in bed and bawling her eyes out.

'Olivia, what? What is it?' I panicked, jumping up and putting my arm around her. But she just buried her head in my chest and cried and cried. I kept asking her what was wrong, but it quickly became obvious that in the state she was in she wasn't capable of speaking, so I stopped asking questions and just tried to comfort her, holding her gently and stroking her hair until she'd finally stopped crying. A few moments later, she lifted her head to look at me, appearing nervous and afraid with a tremble on her lips. I thought she was going to tell me about a bad dream she'd just had that'd triggered her PTSD, but it turned out that that wasn't it at all.

'Jimmy this ... this is the hardest thing I've ever had to do,' she murmured.

I was taken aback. It wasn't what I was expecting her to say.

'What is it?' I asked nervously.

She sighed deeply, wiping her eyes.

'Jimmy you have to ... you have to understand that I would never, *ever* do anything to intentionally hurt you ... and it absolutely breaks my heart that I know I'm going to ... and it breaks my heart even more to know that our relationship has come to this ... but we can't ... we can't be together anymore.'

'What?' I panicked. 'Why, Olivia?'

'Jimmy I'm so sorry for doing this to you ... for putting you on this rollercoaster and leading you astray ... but that Saturday two weeks ago when we first had sex ... I was scared. I was vulnerable. I was really confused. And you were being so sweet and caring and ... I don't know ... it just happened. I'm not saying you took advantage of me or anything like that, because I wanted it as much as you did. But it was a mistake. It shouldn't have happened. And I should've put a stop to it right there but ... I don't know. I guess ... I guess I did really enjoy spending time with you ... and I guess I really did want to try our relationship again to see if we could make it work. But the truth ... or what I've come to realise over the last few days, at least ... is that we can't be together, because I can't properly reciprocate your feelings towards me.'

'What do you mean you can't properly reciprocate my feelings?' I exclaimed. 'Olivia, that … that …' I trailed off, wiping my eyes before I frantically gathered myself and stared at her intensely, squeezing her hands, my face tightening as I tried to fight back tears of my own.

'Olivia, I … I *know* you love me,' I stressed. 'I *know* you do.'

She nodded.

'You're right, Jimmy – I *do* love you. I …'

She paused for a moment, gathering herself.

'I've … I've never told you this before … but ever since we broke up after the accident … there's always been a part of me that's wanted you back. Because Jimmy, when you said in your letter from the psych ward that we were made for each other … when you said we were soulmates … I *agreed* with you. I *still* agree with you. And I haven't been lying the last two weeks when I've said I love you, because I *do* love you – I really do. But … but …' she trailed off again, weeping.

'But what, Olivia?' I cried. 'What is it?'

'But … but Jimmy,' she finally resumed. 'What I've come to realise while we've been away together … what I've come to realise over the last few days is that sitting beside my love for you … is *fear*. I know this sounds bad, and I'm not saying this to hurt you … but the truth is that there's a part of me that's afraid of you. And I don't mean just getting in a car with you. I also mean being in a relationship with you.'

She sighed, wiping her eyes again.

'We've been through so much together, Jimmy … so much pain, so many struggles, so much heartache … and it's broken something in me. I don't feel safe with you. And while I love the Saturdays we spend together more than anything in the world, I'm afraid that moving forward, that's all I have to give you.'

'But Liv you'll get through this!' I panicked. 'Saying that something's broken inside you … saying that you don't feel safe with me … that's just the PTSD talking. But you're getting help, and you *are* going to beat this. And when you do, everything is going to be OK.'

She shook her head sadly.

'No, that's *me* talking.'

She sighed again, squeezed my hand with all her might.

'I know we love each other, Jimmy. I know we're soulmates. But we've had our chance to make it work, and we've blown it. I wish it hadn't turned out this way ... it breaks my heart that this is how it is ... but it *is* how it is.'

'That's not true, Olivia! We can still make it work!'

'No we can't – '

'Yes we can! Olivia, you *cannot* give up on us! Like you said … we love each other. And as long as we love each other, we can get through all of this. We can be happy and enjoy the rest of our lives together.'

She was crying now.

'I w-wish ... I w-wish I could b-believe you,' she sobbed. 'B-but ... b-but it's over.'

'No it's not, Olivia!'

'It's over, Jimmy.'

I couldn't believe it. After all the sweaty, steamy, passionate love-making; after all the wonderfully simple evenings we'd shared together in Sydney the previous week; and after the magical last four days which I knew in my heart that she'd truly enjoyed, I felt like all of this was coming so out of the blue. Not only that, but it didn't make any sense to me at all. And because I couldn't think of any other logical way to explain it, I figured that it must be a product of her PTSD – that her illness was doing something in her head to make her afraid of me, and to scare her into running away. I pleaded with her for the rest of the night trying to convince her not to do so, trying to convince her that because we loved each other, that we could get past whatever was troubling her and make a happy life for ourselves. But no matter what I said, I couldn't persuade her, and by the time it was dawn – only a few hours before we were supposed to return by horse to Andy's place and then take the train back to Sydney – I found myself sighing in defeat.

'OK, Olivia – you don't want to be together right now. I get it. But I know that one day you're going to change your mind, and until that day comes, I'll be waiting for you.'

'No, Jimmy!'

'Yes.'

'Jimmy, *no!*' she cried. 'I don't want you ruining your life over me!'

'I'm not ruining my life over you, I'm – '

'If you wait for me, you will, because you're going to end up all alone!'

It came out so bluntly, so harshly, that I was shocked into silence. Olivia took my face in her hands, gazed at me earnestly as she spoke in muffled sobs.

'J-Jimmy ... Jimmy I'm n-not saying this to hurt you ... I'm saying this because I care about you. Because I *love* you, OK? And because I don't want you to end up old and alone.'

She paused, trying to pull herself together.

'Jimmy, you ... you are the most wonderful person I have ever met, and you deserve to be happy. You deserve to get married to a lovely girl, to have babies with her, and to grow old with her.'

She paused again, squeezing my face intensely.

'And Jimmy, I am so, *so* sorry ... but that girl is *not* me. I'll still always be there for you ... and I'll still always be your friend ... but we are never, ever, ever, *ever* getting back together again. You need to accept that, OK? And you need to move on without me. *Please,* Jimmy.'

'But Olivia – '

'*Please,* Jimmy.'

'But Liv – '

'*Please,* Jimmy!'

'But –'

'Jimmy *please!*'

She fell to her knees, clutching my hands tightly.

'Jimmy *please! Please!*' she shrieked. 'I'm begging you! For your sake, Jimmy, I'm fucking *begging* you!'

It was the most impassioned, emotional outburst I'd ever seen from her, despite everything we'd been through together over the last six years. As she continued squeezing my hands with all her strength, tears streamed down her cheeks, and she stared at me wide-eyed with a crazed, hysterical desperation that screamed exactly what she was saying even louder than her voice did: *"please, Jimmy!"*. Hell, she was so sure about what she was saying and so desperate to convince me of it that she was on her hands and knees pleading with me to believe her. Literally on her hands and knees pleading with me to believe her. And as I too burst into tears, I finally found myself doing so, and for the first time – ever – admitting that Olivia and I were completely finished.

'OK,' I managed to croak.

'*Promise* me, Jimmy.'

To this day, they're the most painful words I've ever spoken.

'OK, Olivia. I promise.'

Asia

Over the years, I'd been asked what it felt like to suffer from depression, and what made it different from just being "sad". I'd reply by saying that for me personally, having depression feels like you're living in a body that fights to survive, with a mind that tries to die. I'd say that it was fear, despair, emptiness, numbness, shame, embarrassment and the inability to recognise the fun, happy person you used to be. That it's the incapacity to be able to construct or even envisage a future. That it's seeing no answers for any of the problems in your life, and feeling absolutely powerless, completely and utterly overwhelmed, and unbearably helpless as a result. I'd say that you always feel so miserable – more miserable than you've ever felt in your life – and so scared. So unbelievably, unimaginably, gut-wrenchingly scared. I'd say that every day, it feels like you have to fight to keep your head above water when it's up to your nose, and it keeps getting deeper, and you don't know how to swim, and there's no one around to save you, and no matter how much you kick and struggle and scream, you just keep sinking, and after a while you start thinking *what's the point? What's the point in continuing to fight when you have no chance of winning?* And I'd say that that was the worst thing about depression – that that's what makes it so much more than just being sad – the fact that it can convince you that there's no way out. The fact that it can convince you that you'll never get better, and that your misery will suffocate you for the rest of your life. And, I'd say that it's when you're in that horrifically black place, staring down the barrel of what you truly believe will only be a lifetime of wretched agony, that your thoughts turn to suicide – because depression has convinced you that it's the only way out.

For several months, I'd managed to keep the beast at bay. But when Olivia broke up with me – all over again – in such an unexpected, heart-wrenching, devastating way, depression grabbed me by the throat and squeezed as tightly as it ever had. In the few days before my flight to Asia, instead of having farewell dinners with my friends, devouring the Lonely Planet Guides to find out as much about my destinations as I could, and feeling full of excitement about the adventures ahead, all I did was lie miserably in bed as depression boxed me in, crushed me every which way. Just like there'd been no way to put into words how elated I'd felt at getting back together with her, there's no way to describe how shattered, how heartbroken I was by us splitting up again. All I know is that I was consumed with a misery that was more potent than any I'd ever experienced. A misery that was so potent that I found myself wishing I'd just died in that stupid fucking car accident that I viewed as the source of all my and Olivia's problems. And, it was a misery so potent that there were many times I'd thought, *why don't I just kill myself now? Why don't I just get a steak knife from the kitchen and slit my wrists in the bathtub? I can do it while my parents are asleep. By the time they wake up, it will be too late.* But, I knew as well as anyone that you can't sleep away your depression, because it will always be there when you wake up. I knew as well as anyone that suicide wasn't a viable option, because all it does is pass your pain on to the people who love you. And of course, I knew as well as anyone that if I ever wanted to feel well again, then I had to face the music, and do what Olivia had said: move on from her. Somehow, some way, I had to move on from her – despite how overwhelmingly, impossibly difficult such a prospect seemed.

On the morning Corey and I were due to go to Asia, I dragged myself out of bed, and forced myself to get in the car when he and his parents came by my place to pick me up on the way to the airport. He didn't know what'd happened yet – I hadn't spoken to anyone about it except for my mum and dad – and as his folks chatted in the front seats, I told him everything in the back.

'I'm sorry, dude,' he replied. 'I'm really, really sorry.'

'It's just so hard, man. I mean ever since we started dating – six whole years ago – I always thought we'd spend the rest of our lives together, you know? But now, knowing that we won't ... I mean it just hurts so much ...'

'I know, mate,' he said, clapping me on the leg. 'I know.'

We were silent for a while.

'Hey Jimmy, at least we're going away though, right?' he eventually said. 'Think about how good eight weeks in Asia will be to get your mind off it.'

On some level, I knew he was right. But in the despair of the moment, I was so distraught, so broken, that I couldn't imagine myself being happy ever again.

When we arrived in Singapore, we were engulfed by its hot, sticky, humid air as soon as we walked outside and took a cab to our hostel in Clarke Quay, which is situated upstream from the mouth of the Singapore River. Being the hub of the city's nightlife, it was filled with smiling couples and exuberant groups of friends walking along the boardwalk on either side of the river, and going in and out of the plethora of bars and restaurants – many of which were either restored warehouses or moored 19th century Chinese wooden boats that had been recently refurbished and were floating by the walkway. As night had set in, each building was also lit up with rainbow-coloured strobe lights – a stunning array of blues, purples, oranges, reds, yellows, golds, greens, and pinks – that beamed with life and reflected magnificently in the shimmering water. Under other circumstances, I would've gaped at its beauty just like Corey did and been dying to get amongst it – but in my state, all I wanted to do was be left alone to sleep in the darkness.

'I'm starving,' Corey said as soon as we'd dumped out bags in our room. 'All the restaurants here will be really expensive, so how about we go and find a hawker's market?'

The bed beside my bag looked so inviting. So, so, so inviting. But I tried to make an effort for Corey.

'What's a hawker's market?' I forced myself to ask.

'They're like a Singaporean version of food courts back home. Let's go.'

So we went to a typical, open-air one a few blocks away. About half the size of a football field, it was bordered with a variety of different food stalls selling popular Singaporean seafood dishes like chilli mud crab and oyster omelettes; Singaporean-Chinese dishes like *bak kut teh* (pork rib soup), Hainanese chicken rice and *bak chang* (savory rice dumplings); Singaporean-Malay dishes like *mee goreng* (fried noodles), *epok-epok* (curry puffs) and *otak-otak* (spicy fish cakes grilled in banana leaf wrapping); and Singaporean-Indian dishes like *naan bread*, tandoori chicken and *soup kambling* (spiced mutton soup). Most of the stalls boasted a queue of people, which, after placing a packet of cartoon, cat-themed tissues at a space on a table to reserve their seat, more and more people would continuously join. Unlike Japan, there were a noticeable number of other Western tourists and expats there, and Corey even got talking to one beside a food stall who recommended we try the chilli mud crab. So when we reached the front of the line, we ordered two.

'Anything else?' the proprietor asked.

'I don't know,' Corey said. 'We just arrived in Singapore. What would you recommend?'

'Stingray to share. Very good.'

'Stingray?'

'Yes.'

'But aren't they ... aren't they poisonous?'

'Of course not! Taste very good!'

Corey and I looked at each other. Too depressed to care, I shrugged my shoulders, and eventually, Corey did too.

'Good, good!' the proprietor smiled, pushing a square object towards us over the counter. 'This your buzzer – it beep when food ready. If you thirsty, you can get drinks a few stores down. I recommend barley tea. Very good!'

So we got ourselves a barley tea each, and started drinking it as we waited for our dinner. When our buzzer went off ten minutes later, we picked up our food and sat down at a free table.

'This chilli mud crab is amazing!' Corey said.

He was right, but depression has the power to stifle the hunger of its victims, and I was only able to manage a couple of mouthfuls.

'Yeah,' I mumbled. 'How's the stingray?'

'It's really good too. Here, have your half,' he said, putting it on my plate.

I tried a forkful. It tasted even better than the chilli mud crab did, but I was too depressed to have any more of it. Corey ended up finishing my share, after which, we walked back to Clarke Quay. Being later in the night, it was buzzing even more so than it had been beforehand, with even more people talking and laughing up and down the boardwalk, young locals and tourists drinking beer and mixed bottles of spirits on the bridge, and cacophonies of loud music emanating from all the bars and clubs. In such a vibrant atmosphere, I should've been hyping up for a spectacular night, but my heart just wasn't in it. No matter how much I tried to forget about Olivia, not five minutes could pass without me thinking of her, and so I remained imprisoned in my cell of anguish. Corey could tell, and understood – which is why instead of joining the rest of the city partying, we just walked back to our hostel and went to sleep.

It was the same story the next three days too as we explored the city. Whether we were lying in the sun on the man-made beach in Sentosa, watching lions roar at Singapore's night safari, tasting beer at the Tiger Brewery, learning about Singapore's colonial history at the National Museum, eating crocodile paw soup for lunch at a local restaurant, racing up and down the roller coasters at Universal Studios or dancing at the Ministry of Sound nightclub, I just couldn't break free from my depression. The beast had me by the throat, and kept whispering in my ear:

Everything with Olivia is over, remember? So how can you possibly enjoy yourself right now? How can you possibly be happy knowing that you'll never be with her again? That you'll never make love to her again? That you'll never buy a big house with her in Manly? That you'll never marry her? That you'll never have kids with her? That you'll never grow old with her? That when you're lying on your deathbed taking your last breaths in the world, that she'll be somewhere else, holding another guy's hand? Knowing that, how can you possibly be happy right now? How can you be happy ever again? Your life, as you've known it for the last six years, is over, and because you will never be with Olivia again, this horrid misery that you feel, this paralysing sadness, will stalk you everywhere you go until you manage to get over her and find someone else – if in fact you ever do.

And my depression had such a strong grip around my throat that I believed it – I believed every single thing it was telling me. And I think Corey sensed that – which was why he did what he did the following afternoon.

It was our fifth day in Singapore, and we decided to visit Marina Bay. After going for a ride on the Singapore Flier – at that point in time, the largest Ferris wheel in the world – and wandering around the colourful Gardens by the Bay, we took a lift to the top of the Marina Bay Sands. One of Singapore's newest and flashiest hotels, the Marina Bay Sands is comprised of three 55 storey towers, with a boat-shaped SkyPark resting on top of them that boasts 360 degree views of Singapore's skyline – including the glittering bay on one side that's surrounded by the city's tallest skyscrapers. Being a drawcard for almost every tourist, dozens of people gazed out at the view from the SkyPark alongside us – either from the bar and restaurant, the crowded railings where we stood, or the magnificent infinity pool where you could swim up to the edge and overlook the entire city.

'I'd do anything for a dip in that pool,' Corey said, wiping the sweat from his brow in the 35 degrees Celsius heat.

'Yeah, me too.'

But there wasn't a hope in hell of that happening. The entire pool area was fenced off, and was only accessible via a small door that was manned by a full-time guard checking hotel passes. Knowing we'd never get past him, we remained in our cramped spot of the SkyPark until we were so hot and sweaty that we decided to cool off in the lobby before walking to the famous bar at Raffles Hotel a couple of kilometres away.

Like the majority of people, we ordered the traditional Singapore Sling, and like most other tourists who were there for the experience and for whom in usual circumstances a swanky bar like that would've been well and truly out of their price range, we almost had a heart attack when we were charged $63.60 for our two slings that were filled mostly with ice.

'I always thought Sydney was expensive,' Corey said, 'but this is ridiculous.'

'Yeah, I've only had three sips and my glass is already half empty.'

We talked for a few more minutes as we finished our slings. That's kind of how it had been since we'd arrived in Singapore – a bit of talk here and there as we did this and that, but mostly just silence. I'd tried my best, but I just didn't have it in me to smile and shoot the breeze. Corey had let me be up until that point, but after finishing his sling, he finally said something.

'So, mate ... are you feeling any better about everything?'

I shrugged my shoulders.

'I don't know.'

'You're not finding Singapore to be a distraction at all?'

I shrugged again.

'Maybe a little bit. But everything's still so raw, you know? I'm trying not to think about Olivia but I just can't help it.'

Corey nodded.

'Just give it time, man,' he said.

And at that, we fell into silence again. Corey nibbled on some peanuts, and I just stared blankly into space, wondering what Olivia was doing at that moment.

'I really wish we'd been able to go for a swim in that infinity pool,' he eventually said.

I nodded.

'Yeah. Me too.'

'There's got to be a way of getting in without being a guest at the hotel.'

'I don't think so. That security guard wasn't budging.'

Corey laughed.

'We could always pick up one of the rich single businesswomen staying there and just use her pass.'

Even I broke into a smile at that one.

'Yeah, because they're really looking for broke uni students, aren't they?'

A few moments elapsed where his mind was ticking.

'I'm going to go for it,' he said.

'What?'

'I'm going to do it! I'm going to score two passes and get us in!'

'Don't be ridiculous.'

'I'm not being ridiculous. I'm going to do it! Meet me there in an hour!'

'You can't be serious.'

'Just trust me! Meet me there in an hour!'

'This is crazy. What am I supposed to do in the meantime?'

'Just get a pen and some paper from the bar and do some writing. That's what Raffles is famous for, bro! Heaps of big-name authors have written here – even Earnest Hemmingway! So it's only right that you work on your book for a bit.'

We debated the matter for a couple of minutes longer. I was convinced that Corey had no chance of getting us into the infinity pool, and for that reason, saw absolutely no point in walking all the way back to the Marina

Bay Sands in the suffocating heat. But Corey insisted, and the next thing I knew, I was by myself. Since I didn't have anything else to do, then like he suggested, I borrowed a pen and pad from the bar and tried to write for a while before leaving to meet Corey at the SkyPark.

When I arrived, he was grinning from ear to ear. I couldn't believe it.

'Don't tell me …'

'Yep! I got someone's day pass!'

'How? You didn't pick up a chick, did you?'

'Come on, mate. You know how much of a smooth talker I am.'

'Seriously, what happened?'

'I just told people the truth.'

'What truth?'

He looked away shyly.

'I approached people in the lobby and told them that my best mate had just broken up with his girlfriend … and that I'd like to try and cheer him up by getting him into the infinity pool.'

I was shocked.

'Really? You went to all that trouble … just to cheer me up?'

He shrugged.

'Yeah, man.'

I couldn't help but smile.

'Corey I'm … I can't say how touched I am, bro.'

'All good, buddy.'

I punched him affectionately on the shoulder.

'Thanks, mate.'

He was still looking away awkwardly, so to break the discomfort that arises from one guy doing a sweet and thoughtful act for another, I suggested that we head in for a dip.

'Yeah, here you go,' he said, pushing the day pass into my hand. 'I could only get one.'

'Wait, I can't – '

'Just go,' he insisted. 'You need it more than I do.'

I tried to give Corey back the pass but he wouldn't hear of it, so I set him up with a beer at the adjacent bar before passing the security guard and diving into the water. It was so cool against my skin as I floated dreamily on my back, before moving to the end of the pool, resting my arms on the edge and gazing out at the bay. It sparkled beneath me against the backdrop of the skyscrapers, and the sky burned a breathtaking orange-yellow as the sun began to whisper "goodnight" to the city. The view was even more beautiful than it was earlier in the day, and as I sat there looking dreamily out at it with the gentle breeze in my hair, the taste of saltwater on my lips, and a heart full of gratitude for the magnificent sight that was caressing my eyes, I came to a profoundly moving realisation.

Yes, there are some things in my life like my relationship with Olivia that aren't going well right now, but on the other hand, there are so many things that are going well. I'm much healthier than I was at the start of the year, I've quit law and am about to do honours in something that I'll hopefully like, I get to spend the next two months travelling all over Asia, and I'm surrounded by great friends like Corey who go to all sorts of trouble to try and cheer me up when I'm feeling down.

I kept on thinking.

Over the last week or two, I've been dwelling so much on the negative aspects of my life that I've completely forgotten about all of the positive aspects. As a result, I've been feeling depressed, and if I continue to think this way, I will always be depressed. But, if I can instead make a conscious effort to focus on all that's good in my life – if I can instead make a conscious point of being mindful of- and grateful for all the blessings that I have – then I'll be able to find light even on the darkest of days, and be able to prevent myself from tumbling into depression every time adversity strikes.

So for the rest of the trip that's exactly what I did, and as a result, I felt infinitely better. It's not that I all of a sudden stopped caring about Olivia and magically put all the pieces of my broken heart back together again; rather, I just stopped letting my heartbreak over losing her cause an aftershock through my soul and destroy the rest of my life, by constantly reminding myself that my relationship with Olivia was just one part of my life – not my *whole* life – and that aside from that one part, all the other parts were going pretty well. Hell, that was an understatement – I was 21 years old and travelling around the world with my best mate. I was living the dream! And from then on, I embraced the experience to the max, and ended up having some of the best times of my life.

After spending New Year's Eve watching the fireworks at a rooftop bar, we spent New Year's Day at the man-made beach in Sentosa once again before taking a flight to Manila in the Philippines. As soon as we got there, Dapidran our hostel manager tricked us into eating duck foetus. I say "tricked" because he didn't tell us what it was beforehand – he just gave us an egg-shaped treat with a deep-fried coating as a "welcome to the Philippines snack", and then laughed uncontrollably at our astonished faces once we'd realised we'd just chomped in half a tiny baby bird. But if we thought eating duck foetus was cruel, a couple of days later we learned just how little the Filipinos cared for birds when we went to a live cockfighting tournament.

It was held at a cockpit in one of the poorest areas I'd ever been to. The streets were dark and grimy and lined with derelict shacks that were falling apart, some of which that had nothing more than a ripped dirty sheet for a door. In the dimly lit carpark of the decaying cockfighting arena, about 100 Filipino men – no women, no children – stood around talking in groups, and when our taxi dropped us off, all of them eyed us ominously. I thought I'd feel more at ease once we were inside, but we found ourselves stretched even further out of our comfort zones. In the cockpit, about a thousand men surrounded a blood-stained boxing ring, all yelling and screaming at one another and tossing around rolls of money, while a dozen employees raced around the ring doing a whole lot of yelling and screaming and money-throwing of their own. Like in the carpark, there was not a single woman or child in the entire arena, and we were, without exaggeration, the only two Westerners there.

'Come! Come!' an employee exclaimed, grabbing Corey and I by the arms and frantically leading us to seats right in front of the ring.

Then the next thing we knew, two cocks were going at it, stabbing each other with razor blades attached to their feet as the crowd roared their rooster on. Feathers flew all over the place and blood spattered on the floor, and before we knew it, one of the chickens was dead. The winning one was then held up to the crowd, which incited even more yelling and screaming and money-throwing than before.

'This place is crazy,' I said, half excited, half afraid.

Corey nodded uncertainly.

'You got that right.'

A few seconds later, the guy who'd led us to our seats came charging up to us.

'My friends, if you want beer, food, you ask me. If you want to bet on a chicken, you ask me too.'

Corey and I nodded.

'OK.'

'You need anything now? A beer?'

'Sure,' Corey shrugged.

'Diet Coke for me, thanks,'

'OK, I get your drinks. You watch fight. When you want to bet, you tell me.'

He hurried off, and then the next fight got ready to start as two owners entered the ring with their roosters. To get them ready for battle, one owner held down his rooster while his opponent violently pecked at it, working the victim into an agitated frenzy. Then they swapped roles. With both cocks fired up, they were then separated and held back from one another, at which point the fans all started yelling and screaming at each other once again and the employees began racing around the ring negotiating all the bets – and somehow remembering them all without writing a single thing down. Once everyone had placed their wager, a buzzer sounded, and the roosters were released. They charged at each other and met in a feather-flying crash as they began stabbing one another with the blades attached to their feet. More blood sprayed all over the ground, and after 15 seconds, one of the cocks could hardly walk, and the other one lay twitching on his side. The referee picked them both up by the feathers at the back of their necks; the one that had been limping started squirming straight away, and after a few seconds, so did the one who'd been twitching. Convinced there was still some fight left in them, the umpire threw them back together again to the roar of the crowd. With a second wind, the one who'd been twitching managed to strike the one who'd been limping with a kick to the throat, and he went down instantly. The referee once again stepped in and held up both of the chickens, but this time, the one who'd gone down just hung there motionless, and so the fight was declared over. I later learned that while the crowd cheered, groaned, threw- or caught rolls of pesos, the winning chicken was carried away to get stitched up by a bloody-handed man with a needle and string, while the dead one was taken away to be de-feathered, gutted, and wrapped up in a plastic bag to be given to the owner of the winning cock for food.

Corey and I stayed there for the next two-and-a-half hours, sipping cans of San Miguel beer and Diet Coke, watching the fights, and finally placing a few bets of our own. Our method of picking which chicken to back wasn't exactly sophisticated – the two factors we based our wager on were firstly, which chook was the biggest, and secondly, which one seemed to get the most pissed off when it was being pecked by the other one before the fight. But we managed to win five out of seven matches, and net a tidy profit that covered our 1000 peso entrance fee, the half-dozen drinks and two packets of chips we'd had between us, and the bus tickets we bought to the famous rice terraces in Banaue the next day.

To my naked eye, they looked like a huge cluster of breathtaking, rich green mountains that were all layered with steps that one could seemingly climb all the way to the top. We'd arranged to do a trek the following day, and we were excited to try and get as far up one of the mountains as we could. But instead of reaching the apex and being king of the world for a moment, I ended up spending the entire day glued to the toilet.

As is the case with so many mishaps, mine was the sum of one part stupidity and one part bad luck. It's bad luck getting food poisoning no matter how it happens, but when it's by eating a plate of chicken *adobo* in a tiny mountainous town that's already warned you they've "lost power for the day", then you've also got to shoulder some of the blame yourself. I mean seriously, without any power, how did I think they were going to cook it? But what was done was done, and after eating my *adobo,* I started to feel queasy on the walk back to the bed and breakfast we were staying at. I was better after some quality time on the toilet, but within half an hour my nausea had returned with a vengeance, and I was right back on the can, cursing in discomfort with my head in my hands.

Such was the tale of the rest of the day. Hoping I could sleep it off, I had an early night, but I felt just as ill when I woke the next morning. I wanted so badly to be able to hike the rice terraces with Corey, but in the state I was in, doing heavy exercise all day in the middle of nowhere without access to a bathroom was my idea of torture, so with great regret, I had to stay behind. Corey returned at sunset, physically spent but emotionally high on life.

'That was fucking awesome!' he exclaimed. 'I'm sorry you missed it, bro.'

'That's alright. No way in hell I could've gone feeling like this.'

'So you're not doing any better?'

'Nah.'

'Shit, man. How are you going to take the bus back to Manila tomorrow night?'

'I don't know,' I said, shaking my head. 'Hopefully I'm OK by then.'

But 24 hours later, I still felt like shit (no pun intended). If it had been possible to, I would've delayed the trip until I'd recovered, but we had to catch a flight to Vietnam to meet the rest of the boys a few hours after we arrived in Manila, so the most I could do was pray, and pop some Imodium an hour beforehand to slow my digestion and control my diarrhoea. I'd hoped it would allow me to get through the nine hour bus ride without needing to crap, and I'd hoped the medication I was taking for my bipolar disorder – one of which doubled as a heavy sedative – would put me to sleep for most of the journey. But unfortunately, neither of those two wishes came true – and as a result, it was the most ghastly, physically uncomfortable, horribly unpleasant nine hours of my entire life.

The trip began with me taking my medication, which made me feel overwhelmingly lethargic and sleepy. I tried to doze off, but I was sitting in the middle of the back row of the bus, and because the seats were so small and we were driving over bumpy, uneven roads and there was no belt to hold me in place nor any seat in front of me to lean my legs into, I found myself slipping off my own seat every 30 seconds. And, since I couldn't sleep as a result, I was unwaveringly conscious of the queasy cyclone stirring in my gut. As I tried my best to balance on my seat, I sipped water in an attempt to calm the storm in my stomach, and kept clenching my ass to try and hold back a shit. I managed to make it through the first three or four hours in exhausted, groggy, nauseous discomfort, but then, I felt my crack begin to give way. In a rush of panic, I charged towards the front of the bus and started banging furiously on the door, yelling at the non-English speaking driver to pull the fuck over. After a few seconds he did – I think more out of shock than anything else – and before I'd even made it ten steps I had to rip down my pants, squat in someone's yard and start shitting my bowels out in front of the entire bus of tourists. Most of them were asleep, but I was so desperate to go that I didn't give a fuck whether they were watching or not. Hell, I was so desperate to go that they could've been taking pictures for all I cared.

As I was wiping my ass with a little packet of tissues I had with me for that very purpose, I noticed that the bus driver had started the engine again and was frantically waving at me to get back on. Worried that he might take off without me, I left the pooey tissues in the yard and ran back on board – or at least moved as quickly as I could in my drug-fucked, stomach-churning state. As I stumbled back to my seat, Corey – who'd popped a Valium to try and sleep through the night – stirred beside me.

'Oi, you alright?' he muttered with his eyes half closed.

'Nah, just shat in someone's yard.'

'Shit, dude,' he mumbled, before dozing back off to sleep.

The second half of the trip was just as awful as the first. By then, I'd accepted that I wasn't going to get a wink of sleep, so I turned my focus to achieving one very simple goal: arriving in Manila without crapping my pants. Time seemed to stretch on eternally as I passed dreadful minute after dreadful minute in a comatose haze, groggily sipping water, clenching my ass and cursing every time I slipped out of my seat. Five horrific hours and another diarrhoea-fuelled-pit-stop-in-the-middle-of-someone's-yard later, we finally arrived in Manila, where we immediately hailed a cab to the airport.

Once we got there, we checked in before I headed straight for the bathroom. It was so nice to have the use of a seat again – and a flush! – but as I was about to wipe myself, I realised that the toilet water was bright red with blood. I resolved to see a doctor as soon as I got to Vietnam before I finished wiping, found Corey and boarded the plane – where I was finally able to drift off to sleep and escape my horror for a couple of hours.

This food poisoning story ends at baggage claim in Hanoi, when after attempting to only fart, I accidently shat my pants a moment after I'd collected my luggage. For a few seconds, all Corey and I could do was gape down at the runny poo on the floor, completely and utterly paralysed with shock. The rancid smell permeated through the air and the people near us started squinting around for its source, before my eyes met Corey's and I mouthed "run!" and we quickly bolted away. I dumped my soiled clothes in a bin in the bathroom and we hailed a cab straight to a hospital. The doctor gave me some medicine that bound me up something fierce, and then we finally made our way to our hostel to get some proper sleep.

When I woke later that afternoon, I felt a hundred times better – although of course, I was forced to endure a razzing from the boys for the rest of the day.

'Hey Jimmy, it sounds like you had the *shittiest* bus trip ever!' Brent laughed.

'Oi do you need to borrow some underwear since you crapped in yours?' Sean cracked.

'What about some sheets?' Chris added. 'Did you accidently take a dump in your bed while you were sleeping?'

'Fuck off, dickheads,' I smirked.

'Better not piss him off, boys,' Steve said, 'otherwise he'll shit on you!'

We all had a laugh, and then caught up on everything else that'd happened over the last few weeks before deciding to leave the hostel and wander around the city. For the next three hours, we walked past countless scooters parked on the side of every street we saw; weaved in between an abundance of riders and all the horn-beeping cars, buses, locals and tourists that crowded the loud, hectic, chaotic roads; marvelled at the beautiful French colonial architecture; and stirred our metaphorical spoons so to speak in the raging Vietnamese coffee scene by trying coconut sorbet with espresso poured over it, yoghurt coffee, and believe it or not, egg coffee. After a while, we started feeling peckish, so we snacked on a variety of cheap, delicious Vietnamese street food sold by local proprietors from portable carts and stalls including *bun cha* (slices of pork belly served with fish sauce, tangy vinegar, sugar and lime), springs rolls (some deep fried, some fresh), *pho* (rice noodle soup), barbeque chicken, and sticky rice. Then, upon seeing a roadside barber – or in other words, a man with clippers standing by a chair that was facing a mirror hanging from a wall – Brent decided that he could do with a trim, so amidst the chaos of the crowds and the cars and the scooters and all the incessant horn-beeping, there he was getting a haircut while the rest of us talked and laughed at the ridiculous scene.

'Feeling fresh?' Chris asked him when he was finished.

'Tops, mate. And it only cost me $2!'

'Two bucks? Shit, maybe I should get one too.'

'Not now,' Sean said. 'I'm still hungry.'

'What do you want to eat? More street food?'

'Nah, let's go to the snake village.'

'The *what?*'

'I heard someone at the hostel talking about how snake is a delicacy in Vietnam, and how you can go to this special village and eat a whole meal of it.'

'Are you serious?'

'Yeah, let's go!'

I wasn't really sure what to expect when we got there, but it certainly wasn't to be greeted by cage after cage of snakes when we opened the front gate of the restaurant – which was a dimly-lit house that appeared to double as the owner's home.

'Welcome! Welcome!' a short, elderly Vietnamese man said as we approached the front door. 'Where are you from, my friends?'

'Australia.'

'Ah, yes! Very nice country! I have not been there, but hear it's very nice! You want to hold snake?'

'Huh?'

'Here!' he exclaimed, taking a one metre long python out of a cage and thrusting it into Sean's hands. He held it nervously around the midsection as it slowly manoeuvred its tail and head in the air, taking us all in. Sean then palmed the snake off to Brent, and we squeamishly passed it around between us. I was the last person to hold it, and I gave it straight back to the restaurant owner as soon as the snake swivelled its body to face me eye-to-eye, which freaked the absolute shit out of me. The owner laughed at my fear as he took back the snake.

'All you tourists, so scared of the snakes! But they should be the ones who are afraid of you, because you are about to eat them! Now, each of you pick the one that you'd like for dinner!'

We uncertainly did as we were told, and after sitting down, the owner brought our snakes around – alive, mind you – with a waiter who was holding a pocket knife.

'Now get ready to drink!' he said jovially.

And then right there in front of us, he held one of the snakes while the waiter cut open its belly, aiming its blood – and its heart – into a shot glass on the floor. As we watched on in shock, the process was repeated six times with the six different snakes we'd picked, after which the waiter handed us the shot glasses.

'OK, bottoms up!' the owner exclaimed.

It was with great hesitation that we all chinked our glasses and wolfed down the shot as quickly as we could. The blood tasted thick and metallic, and although the heart was so small that it didn't really taste like anything, it felt strange having solid food – and a *beating* solid food at that – running down our throat with the liquid. All in all, it was hideous, and the owner laughed at our cringing faces.

'OK!' he said, holding up the snakes. 'Now I cook your dinner!'

And while the blood tasted disgusting, the seven course feast was absolutely fantastic, as for the next hour-and-a-half we had plate after plate of all things snake, including snake soup, snake spring rolls, and snake meat cooked in a variety of different ways.

'You like? You like?' the owner asked enthusiastically.

'Yes, very much so!'

'Good, good! Snake is very special – a real treat in Vietnam. Only the rich Vietnamese eat it, and only on special occasions!'

When we were finished, we washed down our meal with glasses of rice wine, and then took a taxi back to our hostel to meet some other backpackers and then hit the town. And it's on this very special night, of all nights, that I met Jessica.

Aside from both living in Sydney, Jessica differed from Olivia as much as any girl could, but early on at least, I think that's what drew me to her. Where Olivia's hair was brown and straight, Jessica's was blonde and curly. Where Olivia's skin was olive-coloured, Jessica's was marble-white. Her eyes were brown instead of blue. She had a big tattoo of a pirate that covered her upper thigh as well as a piercing on her clit, whereas Olivia never would've dreamed of doing anything of the sort. Jessica was wild as opposed to playful, a drama major as opposed to a psychology student, a pill-popper as opposed to a wine-sipper, a Bondi surfer as opposed to a Manly-sunbaker, a freak in bed as opposed to tender and romantic, and where Olivia was sweet and conservative, Jessica was adventurous, a risk-taker, and a thrill seeker up for practically anything.

To be honest, I don't even remember how we met. Like I said, the boys and I had had a few glasses of rice wine at the snake village, and after a few beers at the hostel and a few more on the pub crawl, we were all pretty sloshed. At some point, I found myself talking to her, and after ten minutes, we were hooking up on the dancefloor.

'You're hot,' she said.

'You're hot, too.'

'You're a good kisser.'

'You're a good kisser, too.'

'Want to fuck?'

'Sure.'

'My hostel's just down the road.'

'Let's go.'

The next four hours were wild. We did it in her bed. We did it in the stairwell. We did it in the kitchen downstairs after sharing a tub of ice-cream we'd raided from the freezer. Then we did anal on her bedroom floor. When I was completely spent, I fingered her until she came another two times, and after each time, she'd pull my hand out of her pussy and shove my fingers in her mouth, moaning loudly as she'd suck all her juices off them. At four in the morning once we'd finally appeared to be finished, I remembered that I hadn't taken my medication, and told Jessica that I had to go to my hostel to get it. She joined me on the walk back, and snuck into my dorm with me to get the pills. The rest of the boys were passed out in their beds – Sean and Chris with chicks of their own – and at the sight of everyone, Jessica straddled me and started kissing my lips.

'What, here?' I said, pulling away.

'Hell yeah. Let's do it on the top bunk. We'll rock it so hard we'll wake your mate up.'

I looked at Corey sleeping peacefully on the bottom and then looked back at Jessica. She was grinning mischievously, and after a few seconds, so was I.

'Let's do it!' I said.

Jessica was on top, and rode me so hard that the bunk creaked and shook and kept banging into the wall, but Corey was so drunk that he didn't wake up. After I came, Jessica almost looked disappointed.

'Hey,' she sighed, 'I tried,' before we finally fell asleep.

I'd assumed it would just be a one night thing, but Jessica gradually carved a place for herself in my heart, and from that night on we were almost inseparable. Corey and the rest of the fellas loved having her around, because she was cool and funny and the best wingman any of them had ever known. As for me, I didn't think I was capable of feeling anything for a girl besides Olivia – particularly so unbelievably soon – but Jessica was made of something intoxicating, and against all conventional wisdom, I found myself drawn to her. Part of the reason was because the sex was spectacular, but even more captivating than that was the fact that she was so daring, so fearless, so full of life. Every day with her was an adventure, and the more I got to know her, the more I wanted to join her for the ride.

And that ride's first destination with me on board was Ha Long Bay, where Jessica, the boys and I arranged to take a cruise with a crowd of other young backpackers just like ourselves. The head tour guide was a bloke nicknamed "Limp Dick" – a 30 year old surfer with long blonde hair from Australia's Gold Coast, whose only concern was to make sure that everybody had a raging time.

'Now everyone,' he began once we'd boarded the boat. 'If you came on this cruise to learn about Ha Long Bay – about how it was formed or about the early settlers who lived here or anything like that – then you are on the wrong cruise, because I don't know a fucking thing about it. But, if you came to party in one of the most beautiful areas of the world, then you're definitely on the right boat, because for the next three days, we're going to have a blast!'

'Yeah!' everyone cheered.

'Now while Bazza the other tour guide passes around beers, let me explain some very important rules. Firstly, holding a drink in your right hand is strictly forbidden. Anyone who notices someone holding a drink in their right hand should point and scream "buffalo!" to draw their crime to everyone's attention, at which point, the person who's been buffaloed must immediately scull the rest of their drink. Once buffaloed, if anyone is actually stupid enough to scull their drink with their right hand, then they must jump in the water naked – girls, losing the bikini top will suffice. Rule number two is that anyone who says the word "sex" must also scull the rest of their drink – but all slang terms are allowed. And now that we've hashed out all of the laws of the cruise, let's get this party started!'

So even though it was only midday, everyone started hitting the cans (except for me, since I'd already had the one big drinking night I allowed myself each month). It was a relaxing, carefree afternoon as we sipped drinks on the roof of the boat and chatted happily amongst ourselves, the wind cool in our hair and the sun warm against our skin as we glided over the calm, turquoise water in between all the limestone islands. The only thing that disrupted our peaceful tranquillity was the occasional cry of "buffalo!" and then the inevitable screaming, laughing, chanting and cheering that followed while the poor fool sculled their drink. Most people got done by either that or the sex rule on a few occasions, so by the time we'd arrived at the island we were due to stay at for the next two nights, everybody was pretty tipsy – excluding me who was sober, and also Chris and a couple of Brits who were fucked off their face.

'I keep getting buffaloed, man,' Chris slurred.

'Hey dude, can you hold my drink while I go to the bathroom?' Jessica asked.

'Alright,' he said, taking it with his free hand.

'Buffalo!' she yelled.

We all burst out laughing as Chris groaned and sculled another beer.

'That's the third time she's got you, man!'

But the fun was only just beginning. At the island, we had a fresh seafood dinner at our lodge on the beach, all watched the sunset together, and then wheeled out tables to play rounds of beer pong before blasting music from the speakers and all getting jiggy with it. Jessica felt a bit guilty for getting Chris so wasted, so she hooked him up with a smoking Parisian girl, and introduced Sean and Brent to a pair of Swedish twins who they probably could've got with if their friend hadn't kept cock-blocking them. Then while we were dancing together, she whispered in my ear that we should do something crazy, so after sweet-talking one of the bartenders into heating up a bottle of milk for her, she took me by the hand and led me down to the beach.

'Dare I ask what the milk's for?' I said.

'Do you want to know why I like doing ridiculous things?' she asked.

'Why?'

'Because I don't take life for granted. I may only be 22 now, but there's going to be a time when I'm old and grey and glued to a hospital bed, and when it comes, I want to be able to look back on my life and think that I made the most of it. That I did as much as any person could possibly do. That I squeezed every last drop out of the orange. Because my dream is to die with no regrets.'

'So you like pushing the boundaries?'

'More like making memories. Take tonight for instance – we could drink and dance and fuck the night away like everyone else will, or we could do something wild. Something that we'll never forget. Something that will bind us to each other forever.'

There was a twinkle, a vivacity in her eyes that I'd never seen before. I had no idea what she was thinking, but whatever it was, I was game for it.

'What did you have in mind?' I asked.

She winked at me, and pulled me into the calm, cool sea.

'Swim out to the boat with me, babe.'

Intrigued, I followed suit. When we reached the deck dripping with water, Jessica grabbed a glass and a handful of straws from the bar and we made our way up to the roof of the boat where we'd spent the day with the rest of the backpackers. I found a couple of towels to dry us off with, and as I wiped myself down, Jessica poured the hot milk into the glass.

'Ever done a ballcuzzi?' she asked.

'What the hell is that?'

'I've never done one either,' she said. 'And it's so bizarre that I bet neither of us will ever do it again with anybody else.'

'You still haven't told me what it is yet.'

She smiled.

'Take your pants off and I'll show you.'

I shrugged and did what I was told, at which point, Jessica took hold of my dick and gently pulled me down towards the glass of milk that rested on the ground. I thought she was going to stick my cock in there, but instead, she held it vertically in the air and dipped my balls in instead. The milk was so hot that it scalded me slightly, and then the next thing I knew, Jessica had put two straws in the glass and begun blowing bubbles.

'What the fuck?' I squawked.

She stopped blowing.

'I told you – it's called a ballcuzzi. Like a Jacuzzi for your balls, you know?'

'Yeah, I get it. But what's the point of it? I can't come doing this.'

'The point isn't to come. The point is to create memories.'

She sighed.

'Don't you get it? For the rest of your life, people will ask you, "have you ever been to this place?" or "have you ever been to that place?" Well, sometime someone's going to ask you if you've been to Ha Long Bay, and when they do, you'll be able to say to them, "hell yeah I've been to Ha Long Bay! And when I was there, this crazy blonde chick dragged me onto a boat in the middle of the night and dipped my balls in a cup of hot milk and started blowing bubbles in it! And then we left the empty cup and the bottle of milk there, so that when everybody got on the boat the next day, they all said, 'what the fuck's that bottle of milk doing there? Who the fuck was drinking a bottle of milk in the middle of Ha Long Bay?' And then me and the crazy blonde chick laughed and laughed, and no one knew why." That's what you'll tell them, Jimmy, and whenever you do, you'll laugh about it all over again, and so will the person you're telling the story to. And they'll never forget it – just like you never will.'

She paused for a moment.

'Like I told you, Jimmy Wharton, that's what I believe life's all about – making memories. Trying everything once. Squeezing every last drop out of the orange. Being able to die one day with no regrets. Because if I can do that, then I know I'll die happy – and I can't ask for anything more than that.'

She spoke with such passion, such conviction, that I couldn't help but listen to her. And, as she continued blowing bubbles in the glass, I found myself believing her.

'Yes!' I screamed with joy. 'That's what I'll say when someone asks me if I've ever been to Ha Long Bay! I'll tell them that I got a ballcuzzi on a boat deck in the middle of the night, and when they ask me what that is, I'll tell them it's when a girl dips your balls in a glass of hot milk and starts blowing bubbles in it like a fucking spa jet!' And as soon as I said it, I tipped my head back and laughed uncontrollably up at the stars. And as I did so, and as Jessica continued blowing, she squeezed my dick, and I knew right then and there that we were sharing a moment that would live as long as we did.

*

The next day was a paradisiacal 27 degrees Celsius, and we enjoyed it playing water sports. After spending the morning swimming, kayaking and racing around in a banana boat, it was time to go wakeboarding, and that was when the fun really got started.

'I bet I can wakeboard faster than you can,' Jessica teased.

'No way.'

'I bet I can!'

I laughed cockily.

'Did I ever tell you I was the Under 15 World Surfing Champ back in the day? No one can balance on a board better than I can.'

'Yes, you told me a couple of nights ago – I gave you an extra nice blowjob because I felt bad that you got injured, remember? But you haven't surfed in years, and I surf every day back in Sydney. So I'd beat you.'

'I don't think so.'

'Want a bet?'

'How much?'

'Money's boring. Let's do something fun.'

'Like what?'

She thought about it for a minute.

'Has anyone had to jump in the water naked yet? For sculling with their right hand after getting buffaloed?'

'I don't think so. But come to think of it, you buffaloed last night when I dared you to take a sip of the milk after the ballcuzzi. Would you like me to go soak my balls in another cup of hot milk now for you to scull?'

'Fuck off. So no one's had to jump naked in the water yet?'

'Nah.'

'Alright, well how about the loser does that? But, instead of jumping in the water, let's make it a nudie run in between all the tables at dinner. That'd be more embarrassing.'

'I'd feel bad making you do that.'

'I'm not going to lose. In fact, I'm so confident I'll kick your ass that if you somehow beat me, I won't wear undies either.'

'Are you *sure* you want to do this?'

'I told you – I'm not going to lose.'

'Alright. You're on then, babe.'

We kissed on it, and then laid out the rules of the race. The way we'd set it up, we both had to start from the same rocky formation, and then race to see who could reach a second rocky formation first, which was about 200 metres away from the starting point. By the time the race was about to begin, the other backpackers had found out about the stakes and were ready to cheer their contestant on. All the guys were clearly going for me because they wanted to see Jessica run around naked, and all the girls were behind Jessica, because in that moment, she embodied girl power to the max.

'Alright!' Limp Dick the tour guide yelled. 'Ready, set, go!'

We both took off as the crowd started screaming. I was sure that Jessica had been all talk before the race, and was just using the bet as an excuse to get her kit off. But to my disbelief, she was actually winning.

'Faster!' I yelled at the boat that was pulling me. 'Faster! Faster!'

I picked up speed but Jessica was still out in front, flying towards the finish line.

'Faster!' I kept yelling. 'Hurry the fuck up! Come on!'

The driver accelerated, but he did so so quickly that I slipped off my board and belly-flopped into the water. When I came back up for air, all of the girls were cheering like mad.

'Told you, babe,' Jessica winked as she circled back towards me.

'Any of you other boys want a go?' she asked the disappointed group of guys.

Thinking he was unbeatable, Brent stepped up to the plate, and while he didn't fall off his board and make an ass of himself like I did, he didn't win either. Sean then had a crack and got smoked as well, and after that, all the other blokes were too scared to face her.

'Getting three guys to run around the dining hall naked,' Jessica mused with a laugh back on the shore. 'Not bad for a day's work!'

We all grumbled and shook our heads. Jessica laughed again before heading off to the bathrooms to shower and freshen up for dinner, leaving Brent, Sean and I on the beach looking nervously at one another.

'Alright, let's smash down some drinks,' Sean said. 'I don't want to have to run naked around 100 backpackers stone sober.'

He had a bottle of tequila left over from the previous night, and Brent grabbed a handful of beers from the bar which they both started downing on the beach. Since I didn't want to break my once-a-month drinking rule and had already resigned myself to the fact that I was going to feel embarrassed as hell, I decided to take a leaf out of Jessica's book, and create a memory that none of us would ever forget.

'I kind of want to shock everyone when we go in there,' I said.

'What do you mean?'

'Well, have a think about it – everybody's expecting us just to bolt through the door, run around the tables for 15 seconds and then bold straight out again, right? But instead, we should slow it down. Work the crowd. Really strut our stuff, you know?'

They were both eyeing me uncertainly.

'Are you for real?'

'Yeah! It'll be fucking hilarious!'

A smile formed on Brent's lips, and he started nodding.

'Yeah, let's do it!'

I slapped him a high five and then turned to Sean.

'How about you, brother?'

He was shaking his head, but a grin was slowing creeping on to his face as well.

'Alright,' he finally laughed. 'A few more shots and then I'm in.'

So they polished off their bottle of tequila and finished the beers, and then once everyone had sat down and started eating their meal, we slowly entered with our arms raised triumphantly above our heads to the roar of the crowd. And then, all hell broke loose. As the three of us sauntered right through the centre of the room – Sean with his chest puffed out and pointing to random girls sitting down, me flapping my arms around to pump up the crowd, and Brent flexing like he was Arnold-fucking-

Schwarzenegger – two American girls took their tops off and started waving them in the air and screaming. This prompted Craig the South African to start pegging calamari rings at them from across the room, Jessica to pick up a jug of iced water and try to pour it all over our dongers so that they'd shrink to embarrassingly small proportions, and Limp Dick to live up to his nickname by standing up on a table, pulling down his pants, and flapping his flaccid cock up and down as he yelled "anarchy! Anarchy! An-ar-chy!" at the top of his voice. Someone then got the music going and we all started raving, dancing around as we ate and drank and sang as if it was our last night on earth.

The next stop on our adventure was Laos, which was a full day and night bus ride from Hanoi, and except for Jessica giving me a handjob under the blanket in the middle of the night while everyone around us appeared to be asleep, it was a relatively uneventful trip since I thankfully didn't have food-poisoning this time. After 24 hours we finally arrived in the capital city called Vientiane, and like most tourists, we got pretty bored there, so after one night we took another bus to Vang Vieng – Laos's mid-country paradise on the Nam Song River that was home of the daytime tubing phenomenon, and the centre of everything that's young and wild and free. For the next three days, myself, the boys, Jessica and a group of British girls she'd hooked the fellas up with floated down the river with hundreds of other backpackers in donut-shaped inflatables, stopping every half an hour to jump off rope swings or flying foxes and bomb into the water, toke on spliffs of marijuana or opium in the bushes, or let bar promoters on the riverbank throw us a rope and pull us into their establishments, where we'd drink bootleg whiskey, take shots off each other's bodies, hook up with random people we'd never speak to again, and break it down to loud, blaring music in our bikinis and board shorts. Despite me taking it relatively easy on the booze and laying completely off the drugs because of my bipolar disorder, it was still one of the craziest three day periods of my life. In the span of those 72 hours, a random girl jumped into Corey's lap and they started making out while drifting down the river. Brent got caught smoking weed on the riverbank by an undercover cop, who was all too happy to keep him out of jail for a $640 bribe. A bartender at one of the pit stops thought Jessica was the hottest girl he'd ever seen, so he let her get behind the bar and serve shots for an hour – where at one point she poured vodka straight from the bottle into Chris's mouth, getting him so wasted once again that he was puking in the bushes before it was even three o'clock in the afternoon. Meanwhile, Sean rooted one of the British girls in the toilets. Steve fingered one of them on the dancefloor. Corey claimed he took his river bird somewhere semi-secluded and did her doggy-style in his float. The same cop who busted Brent tried to sell me opium, but I palmed him off to some cocksucker who wouldn't leave Jessica alone and then he got in strife. On Australia day, the whole clan of us and all the other Aussies there paid a dollar to let a bunch of guys spray our bodies green and yellow and cover us with clichéd sayings from the homeland like "G-day mate!", " 'Straya mate!' and "Aussie! Aussie! Aussie!" before we jumped up and down to Triple J's Top 100 at one of the bars along the river. At the end of each day, we'd all go to cafés and order fresh baguettes, omelettes or fruit platters and lie down watching re-runs of *Friends* or *Family Guy* on the big screen TV at the front of the café, before moseying back to our hostel at midnight to crash so we could wake up the next day and do it all again. On our last evening there, we took another overnight bus to Luang Prabang, but when we arrived at our hostel in the morning they told us it was full. We were so tired we slept in hammocks outside until a group of people left, at which point, we snuck into their beds and passed out until midday.

After the insanity of Vang Vieng, Luang Prabang – a small, slow, laid back town encircled by the mountains at the confluence of the Nam Khan and Mekong Rivers – was a nice change of pace. Instead of starting to drink on the river at ten, we'd wake up at ten, and after ordering a round of ham, egg, cheese and avocado baguettes and a freshly squeezed juice each from our favourite street seller, we'd casually stroll through the village, admiring the beauty of the richly-decorated Buddhist temples before hopping on our rented mopeds and going for a ride. One day we visited the Kuang Si waterfalls, and spent the afternoon jumping off rope swings into the turquoise swimming holes surrounded by tropical trees and limestone rocks. Another day, we took a boat ride up the Mekong where we watched local fisherman hauling their nets, visited the Pak Ou caves, and stopped by some villages where we played catch with the children and gave them candy. On two separate occasions we drank freshly squeezed lemonades on piles of pillows at Utopia Bar overlooking the Nam Khan River, and at the staff's encouragement, dozed off for a nap. Once we'd returned from whatever we were doing during the day, we'd usually wander around the evening markets beginning at Wat Mai and running along Sisavangvong Road, checking out the embroidered bags and purses, screened "Beer Lao" t-shirts, fluro-coloured cotton pants collaged with elephants, woven scarves, opium pipes and paper lanterns – usually buying a cheap souvenir here or there before having street food for dinner. Our favourite dish was the salted barbeque fish, but we also loved *som tam* (spicy papaya salad), *kanom krok* (coconut rice pancakes) and of course the spring rolls and dumplings.

Then, at about eight o'clock, it was party time. In Luang Prabang, like in most other cities, the young tourists start off their nights drinking at a bar. However, at about twelve or one, all the bars would close, and instead of kicking on to a nightclub, everyone would go ten pin bowling, and play game after game with strangers and friends as they got even drunker on buckets of mojito or Long Island Iced Tea. Then at three or four in the morning, the backpackers would return to their hostels to smoke opium and chill, crash out in bed, or in my and Jessica's case, have sex in our 18 person dorm. Everyone appeared to be asleep, so we thought we'd tear one off on the top bunk in the corner of the room. Being sober, I finished before she did, and after throwing out the condom, I started rubbing her clit.

'Why are you biting your finger?' I asked after a couple of minutes.

'I'm trying not to scream and wake everyone up …' she panted.

'The Jessica I know and love would find it hilarious to wake everyone up.'

'Only people we know … not a room full of 20 strangers!'

I can't give you a good reason why, but at that moment, I became obsessed with the idea of making Jessica do just that. So I started fingering her harder, really thrusting up against the back of her pussy as she huffed and puffed and clenched and bit her bottom lip and pulled at her hair, doing everything in her power to stay as quiet as she could. As I kept going and going, it became a contest of wills, both of us giving our all to win. I felt sure I would come out on top – Jessica seemed like she was going to explode at any moment – but to her credit, she managed not to scream. Sensing I had to up my game, I played the card of last resort, and shoved my pinky finger up her bum. It nearly sent her over the edge as she buried her face in her hands and started convulsing even more wildly on the bed, but even when she came a minute or two later, the loudest noise I could get out of her was a soft cry as she smothered her face with her pillow before falling back in a gasping heap.

'Well played, babe,' she whispered once she'd caught her breath. 'The shocker was a clever move ... that nearly broke me!'

'I can't believe you held on,' I said, shaking my head with a smile.

'Can you two just shut the fuck up?' someone yelled from across the room. 'I'm trying to get some sleep!'

We muttered 'sorry' as we collapsed in a fit of giggles, before finally dozing off ourselves.

We'd all originally planned to head straight from Luang Prabang to Bangkok, but then Steve got talking to a guy who'd just done the "Jungle Jive", and when he told us about it, we were all keen as hell to do it too. The way he'd described it, we'd spend our days going for luscious bush walks in the Laotian jungle, swimming in clear blue lagoons, and zip-lining from tree to tree like Tarzan on a flying fox before curling up in a cosy treehouse 100 feet high and falling asleep to the soothing sound of the surrounding wildlife. And, because that's what we believed we were getting ourselves in for, we took a bus to the embarkation village right away, and signed up for a three day adventure filled with excitement. We were giddy for a once in a lifetime experience – and by anyone's standards, that's exactly what we got. But unfortunately, it was uniquely unforgettable in the worst kind of way.

The first sign that we'd made a terrible mistake occurred 10 minutes into day one's hike, when we crossed paths with a group returning from the trip that we were beginning.

'How was it?' we all asked enthusiastically.

Three of them wore solemn expressions and didn't say a thing. The fourth one, a 20-something-year-old girl, shook her head gravely.

'I'm going to have nightmares for the rest of my life,' she murmured.

'What? Why?'

She shook her head again.

'Spiders,' she muttered. 'So many spiders …'

'Huh?' we panicked. 'Where? How many were there?'

But she was too disturbed to answer as the group hurried away, eager to get the hell out of the jungle and put the ordeal behind them as quickly as possible.

We all looked at each other uneasily.

'I fucking *hate* spiders,' Brent said.

'Me too,' Steve and I nervously agreed.

I think at that point, the three of us were tempted to turn around and go back. But the tour guide – who hardly spoke a word of English – was charging ahead and never going to stop for us to ponder our options, so to avoid being stranded in the jungle, we marched on against our better judgment.

Half-an-hour later, Jessica felt something tickling her leg.

'What the fuck!' she cried as she rolled up her jeans. 'What the fuck, what the fuck, what the fuck!'

Not one, not two, not three but four leeches were latched on to her calf and sucking her blood. In a screaming panic she kicked them off, only to realise after pulling up her other trouser leg that there were another two on that calf as well. Then all of a sudden the rest of us started feeling itching sensations around our feet and legs too, and upon taking our shoe and sock off one foot while balancing on the other, we found that they'd crept into our socks as well. While we spent ten minutes trying to get rid of them in a panicked frenzy, it appeared that our tour guide had pushed on without us, because when we were ready to go again, we couldn't find him anywhere until 15 minutes later, when he reappeared scowling and cursing that we weren't moving quickly enough. From that point onwards, we stared obsessively down at our shoes so we could flick away the leeches before they crept into our socks, which sucked all the fun out of the hike. For this reason, Corey and Sean decided they weren't going to worry about the leeches and just hack whatever damage they did to them, so by the time we arrived at a waterfall a couple of hours later and they took off their clothes to go for a swim, their feet were literally covered with blood. But the cool water was blissfully refreshing in the 35 degree heat, and sublimely soothing for our sore and tired legs.

An hour or two later, we started hiking again, and after another uphill, exhausting, plagued-by-leeches walk through the jungle, we reached our first zip-line. Despite, thanks to the leeches, being riddled with anxiety for the entire bushwalk, if that was the worst of our tribulations, I would've enjoyed the Jungle Jive on the whole, because the zip-lining itself was absolutely amazing. At least 50 metres above the ground, we took turns flying through the sky, howling with joy as the wind whooshed through our hair and we soared over the treetops. But then our tour guide left us at the treehouse where we were to spend our first night, and that's when everything went horribly wrong.

You see, the treehouse was infested with bees. I do not mean that there were a handful of bees, but that there were literally hundreds of them swarming around everywhere.

And Jessica was allergic to bees.

I have never been more terrified for another human being in my life. Poor Jessica was hysterical – crying and screaming and flapping around, having nowhere to run, nowhere to hide, knowing that if she was stung she'd need to go to hospital – which in the middle of the jungle would've been impossible – and knowing that if she was stung on the neck, she would undoubtedly die. Everyone else was freaking out as well, all yelling out different suggestions of what to do to protect her. Eventually, we decided to all cuddle up to her and cover her with our arms to shield her from the bees, as she pulled on every piece of clothing she had so that except for her eyes, not a speck of her skin was left exposed – at which point, the six of us guys surrounding her all moved as a group over to our "tents", which were literally just mats beneath a sheet hanging from a piece of rope. We got Jessica in there as quickly as possible – me joining her for moral support – before the boys tucked the sheet under the mattress to try and make sure no bees would buzz in. Jessica was horrifically traumatised, bawling her eyes out into my chest, and shaking violently as I held her tightly. Only after she'd popped two Valium – which like many backpackers, she'd bought to help her sleep on the overnight bus rides – was she able to stop crying and shaking.

It was also around this point in time that Chris started to feel very ... *"iffy"* ... probably due to the water we'd been drinking all afternoon, which, as per the guide's example, we acquired by putting a strainer over a random tap in the middle of nowhere. Like everyone else, Chris had been hiding in his tent to avoid the bees, but as he'd later describe it, he grew more and more queasy, more and more desperate to take a shit. Not wanting to venture out of his cocoon, he tried to hold it in for as long as he could. But of course, just like I had on the bus in the Philippines, he eventually cracked, and was forced to charge right through the clusters of bees to the "toilet" – which turned out to be just a hole in the floor boards. He stayed in there for about five or ten minutes, crying out in pain at random intervals before charging back across the room and sealing himself up in his tent again.

'Dude, what the fuck happened? Are you alright?' someone asked, before Chris explained that right above the toilet was the beehive, and that every time he screamed, it was because he was getting stung. He managed to remain in his tent for another 45 minutes before a rush of diarrhoea forced him out again, and this time decided to sit on the railing and shit off the side of the balcony before hurrying back to his tent. I then remembered that I had some Imodium left, and also a spare packet of antibiotics that the doctor had given me in case I was still feeling ill after the first batch. I gave Chris the lot of it, and he took some Imodium to try and keep the runs at bay.

By sunset, the bees had finally retreated, so all of us except for Jessica – who was still too scared to leave the tent – emerged from ours to eat dinner, which the tour guide zip-lined over to us before immediately disappearing again. We enjoyed the spectacular views of the treetops that stretched as far as our eyes could see before the sun abandoned us below the branches, leaving us alone to eat in the darkness. Because there was no electricity in the treehouse, we had to use the torches on our phones for light, shining them in each other's chests as we talked about the day's chaos, believing the worst of it to be over. But after five minutes, Brent felt something splatter on his hand. Shining his phone on it, it looked like white bird shit, so we all then shone our phones up above us.

'What the fuck!' he screamed. 'What the *fuck!*'

On the ceiling rested 20 of the biggest spiders I've ever seen. *Twenty of them.*

And one of them had just shat on Brent's hand.

We started freaking the fuck out and scrambling in a wild panic to get back inside our tents. Our hearts pounded furiously in our chests and we drove ourselves crazy imagining a spider – or two, or three, or four of them – scurrying into our tents and crawling all over us. We slapped ourselves silly every time we felt even the slightest itch, and everyone besides me took a Valium to try and placate their fear (I took my legitimately prescribed medication, which served a similar effect). But even the drugs couldn't keep our anxiety at bay, and after another half an hour of this awful existence, our worst fears were confirmed when Sean started screaming and thrashing about in his tent.

'Is it a spider? Is it a spider?' we cried.

He was too hysterical to reply, although after about five or ten seconds, he stopped flapping about. But he *did* continue screaming.

'What is it? What the fuck is it?' we yelled.

'Oh my fucking God!' he shrieked. 'Oh my fucking God!'

'What? What?'

I nearly had a fucking stroke when he said it.

'Eggs!' he cried. 'There are fucking eggs in my bed!'

And then all hell broke loose. In a mad frenzy, we all then desperately searched our beds for eggs. Jessica broke down in tears again, and being even more arachnophobic than me, so did Steve. Refusing to sleep in his tent, Sean then crammed into Corey's, meaning that both of them were sharing a single mattress. Chris still had food poisoning and needed to take a dump, and while squatting on the rail of the balcony trembling with trepidation as liquid shit gushed out of his ass, he felt something crawl over his foot, and upon running to a different position along the railing, left a rancid trail of crap on the floor. Feeling as if he couldn't possibly endure another experience like that, he took one of my leftover antibiotics. After Brent swore he felt a spider race over his arm (although unable to ever find it), everyone but me popped another Valium.

While the drugs helped us get some much-desired sleep, we all had nightmares where big hairy spiders were crawling all over us, and at varying points in the night each of us woke up shrieking. But at around two in the morning, the spiders became the least of our worries when a vicious storm started raging outside. We were drenched by the rain as thunder roared in our ears and lightning attacked the sky, and the wind was so strong that our treehouse was shaking – it was literally shaking from side-to-side – and as we all yelled and screamed and Jessica and I clutched each other tightly and shook uncontrollably, I legitimately thought the treehouse might shake loose from its branches, and that we'd all plummet 100 feet to our deaths. In the following two years, there'd be times when I'd think miserably back to those hours and wish that the storm had in fact killed me – but when I was in Asia I was enjoying my life, so I breathed a huge sigh of relief at four am when the storm finally subsided, and we were able to catch a couple of broken hours of sleep until morning.

Suffice it to say, when we woke up, all we wanted to do was get the fuck out of the jungle as quickly as possible. But, it was extremely difficult communicating this to our non-English speaking guide. When we told him that Jessica was allergic to bees, he just stared at us blankly. When we pointed at the spiders up on the roof he just shrugged his shoulders. When we told him we wanted to leave, he kept saying 'we keep going now'. After some time, Corey remembered he had a map of the village we'd begun at, and frantically pointed at it to try and indicate that that was where we wanted to go. At first, the tour guide didn't seem to understand that either. But after a few seconds, he started shaking his head.

'Tomorrow,' he said.

'No! No!' we all insisted. 'Today! Now!'

We kept trying to persuade him for another five minutes before he finally consented to taking us back – thanks in whole to a US$66 bribe, which was most of the money we collectively had on hand.

Although we were extremely relieved to be returning to civilisation, the eight hour trek back was absolutely awful. Apart from having to be constantly on our guard for leeches, everyone was exhausted from the shocking night's sleep, and unbearably lethargic from all the psychiatric drugs – not to mention that because no one had planned for us to go back, we didn't have any food to eat for the entire day and were overwhelmingly starving.

But when we arrived at the village we'd started at, man oh man was it good! We checked into a hotel, showered ourselves clean, changed into some fresh clothes and then had a humongous feast of different types of curries, noodles, meats and freshly-squeezed juices, before we promised ourselves to stick to the cities from that point on and began making preparations to head to Bangkok.

Given that we only had two nights there after our disastrous jungle detour, we wanted to pack in as much excitement as possible, and because it was Brent's, Sean's, Chris's and Steve's last stop before they flew back to Sydney, we wanted to end their trip with a bang. So, as soon as we'd checked into our youth hostel, we went straight to the Hajime Restaurant, where we were seated at a table with a touch screen we used to order a range of dumplings, sushi, sashimi and barbequed meats, which were then served to us by human-sized robots. Since it was all-you-can-eat (for only $20 each!), we absolutely gutsed ourselves, before waddling into a couple of cabs that took us to a sporting arena where we spent the night getting really drunk while watching round after round of *muy thai* boxing (I, as was usually the case throughout the trip, stayed sober). We were pumped for some psycho, ruthless fighting and put-you-to-sleep knockouts, since that's what we'd been promised by the promoters outside the arena. But the fighting was very disciplined, and the contestants – at least in all the fights we saw – were too young and scrawny to pack a punch powerful enough to lay someone out. It was a disappointment, but the following night we went to one of Bangkok's famous ping pong shows, and that was anything but.

We started off the night at Khao San Road. In Alex Garland's novel *The Beach* (you're probably more familiar with the movie starring Leonardo DiCaprio), it was described as "backpacker land", which we agreed was an accurate description given the confluence of young travellers swapping stories; offering each other suggestions for where to go next; booking a flight, bus, train or guided tour from one of the countless travel shops; going in and out of youth hostels with their giant packs on their backs trying to shop around for the cheapest bed; buying T-shirts, sunglasses, shorts, bikinis, second-hand travel guides, novels, souvenirs or counterfeit DVDs from market stalls; chowing down on deep-friend insects, $1 plates of pad-Thai, chocolate and banana pancakes, mango sticky rice, green papaya salad or sweet coconut juice with jelly from the abundance of stores lining the street; or later on in the night, getting drunk on buckets of cocktails sold by mobile road stalls or Chang beers bought from the local 7/11, and going in and out of all the bars and clubs that lined the frantic, crowded, bustling street. There was so much to do that we didn't even know where to begin, but as soon as I saw someone selling a tray of deep-fried scorpions, worms, cockroaches and fully-grown tarantulas, I started going gaga.

'That's fucking awesome!' I exclaimed. 'Let's eat!'

'That's disgusting,' Chris said. 'I'm not touching that shit.'

'Forget it, man,' Corey agreed.

'No, let's all do it,' Jessica said. 'You only live once!'

At my and Jessica's insistence, everyone eventually got on board, so we all shared a big plate of bugs. And I swear on my life that everything tasted great.

After that, we headed to a club and got shitfaced on Chang beers and buckets of Long Island Iced Tea (me too this time, since it was our last night altogether). When we started to feel tired at about one in the morning, we went to a convenience store and downed an M150 energy drink each for a pick-me-up, before being accosted by some promoters to go to a ping pong show. They shoved us in a couple of *tuk-tuks* and then drove us half an hour to a dark and depressing bar where half-naked Thai girls performed on a small stage, and ten or so drunken tourists with glazy eyes sat slumped watching the show. We all took a seat in the front row, and within five minutes, found ourselves a part of the performance.

After taking off all her clothes, one of the girls lay down on her side so that she was facing us, and lifted one leg high into the air before inserting a large straw into her vagina. She then put a dart into the straw, held on tight, and shot the dart out, popping one of the balloons lying around in front of us. Then another dart – *pop!* Then another two – *pop! Pop!* Then one of the other girls handed a balloon to Brent in the front row.

'What the fuck,' he murmured, before *pop!*

As we all applauded, Brent was pressured into buying the girl an extremely overpriced shot of tequila. Moments later, the girl who'd handed Brent the balloon took the stage in a crop top and G-string.

'What's your name?' she asked, pointing to me.

'My name?'

'Yes. What's your name?'

'Ah, Jimmy,' I replied uncertainly.

She nodded with a smile, and then rummaged around in a nearby schoolbag, where she retrieved an A4 piece of paper and a permanent marker. Next, she pulled her thong to one side, inserted the marker inside herself, and then, leaning forwards on her knees and using her hands to balance, she began using her pelvic muscles to write on the paper. When she handed it to me, my jaw dropped, because in big blue letters that took up the entire page, it read:

'NICE TO SEE YOU, JIMMY.'

I was so impressed that I happily bought her a 200 baht ($6) tequila shot. Then, it was ping pong time.

Jessica was handed a paddle. Standing ten feet away from her, a naked woman then began dipping ping pong balls in water, inserting them into her vagina and then shooting them at Jessica, who tried to hit them back with the paddle. She nailed the first three or four, but then missed a fast one that hit her in the shoulder.

'Ah!' she cried, before shoving the bat in my hands. I then sent a top-spin forehand flying towards the bar before handing the paddle to Corey, who thought it would be hilarious to start smashing the balls at each of us, so after Sean received a wet one in the face, we all ran for cover as Corey laughed his head off and kept trying to hit us. When the girl was out of ping pong balls, we all had a shot with her at the bar and then left at the end of the show – the finale being another girl sucking up half a bottle of Coke Zero into her vagina using a straw, before squirting it back into an empty bottle as Celine Dion's *My Heart Will Go On* played loudly from the speakers (it goes without saying, of course, that *The Titanic* has since been completely ruined for me).

Unfortunately, the following morning it was time for Corey, Jessica and me to say goodbye to Brent, Sean, Chris and Steve before heading to India for the last leg of our trip, where the highlight of our stay was not seeing the Taj Mahal, but rather, having a local we met take us right into the heart of one of Delhi's biggest slums. To say it was unlike anything I'd ever seen before would be an understatement, and to say I was shocked by what I'd witnessed during the three hours we were there would be an even bigger one. But what took my breath away wasn't the fact that the half-a-square-kilometre-in-size slum was home to 25,000 people and crowded beyond belief. It wasn't that everyone wore dirty, ripped and tattered clothes. It wasn't that they all lived in huts made from scraps of metal, plastic, bamboo, cardboard or hand-woven reed-matting and were erected over bare earth. It wasn't that the huts were the size of a prison cell, and each housed as many as seven family members. It wasn't that everyone had to store their food in metal boxes so that rats wouldn't get to it. It wasn't that there was no electricity, toilets or running water. It wasn't that they had to bathe using nothing more than a bucket of water and their own hand. Hell, it wasn't even the fact that to relieve themselves, everyone had to squat in the football-field-sized latrine zone on the outskirts of the slum that at any one time was being used by dozens of people. Rather, what shocked me to my very core was that within the slum, amidst this overwhelming, inescapable, previously-unimaginable poverty, everyone appeared to be ... *happy*. Everywhere we turned, generations of women sewing garments, listening to Hindi love songs on the radio, preparing the evening's meal or bathing their infants in copper dishes laughed and chatted amongst themselves, and shared their glowing smiles with us as we passed. Groups of men carrying water in buckets, tending to goats and chickens, and playing cards in their doorways or on stools in their huts looked up at us with joy in their faces, and invited us to sit with them and sip chai. Children from all different ages joked and laughed amongst themselves, chased each other in circles, danced all around us, waved at us from afar, slapped us high fives, posed in our photos, climbed on us so we could give them a piggyback, sang to us, asked us if we were American and if we knew Justin Bieber, and smiled and smiled and smiled. All together, these people had filled the slum's filthy corridors with their love and their laughter, their spices and their incense, their ballads and their *ghazals*, and created not only a home, but a very cheerful one at that.

After we'd re-joined the throngs of people, cars, taxis, buses, bicycles, ox-carts, rickshaws and scooters on the street and begun the long walk back to our hostel, I mentioned how amazing I found it that everyone in the slum appeared to be happy.

'Why is it so amazing?' Jessica asked.

'What do you mean "why?" Because they're all so poor.'

'Why can't poor people be happy?'

'I guess they can. It just seems like it would be really difficult, that's all.'

'Why would it be difficult?' she pressed.

'It would just be easier to be happy with more money,' I said.

'Why?'

'Because ... you can live in a bigger house. And buy more things. And actually have access to a toilet and electricity and stuff.'

'And you think the bigger the house you live in and the more things you have access to, the happier you'll be, is that it?'

'I guess so.'

'Why?'

'What do you mean "why?" '

'Why do you think living in a big house and having lots of stuff will make you happy?'

I frowned at her.

'What's with the interrogation?'

'I'm not interrogating you. I'd just like to know why you're so obsessed with money, that's all.'

'I'm not obsessed with money.'

'Of course you are.'

'No I'm not.'

'Why do you want to be a management consultant?' she asked.

'Huh?'

'You heard me. Why do you want to be a management consultant? Is it because you think you'll find the work fascinating, or because it pays really well?'

'It's a combination of the two,' I lied, not only to her, but to myself as well.

'Bullshit,' Jessica said. 'You're doing it for the money, because like most people, you've let society brainwash you into believing that the people with the best jobs are the ones who get paid the most, and that the more money you make, the better.'

'And you don't think that's true?' I asked.

'I think it has a grain of truth to it, but only a grain. Provided that your job can pay the bills, I think the most important thing is that you do something you enjoy, and that the best jobs are the ones that make the person who's doing them happy. So if a lawyer is making a million dollars a year and is happy, then he has a great job. But if he's miserable because he hates his work, then he has a shit job.'

She sighed.

'Most people think having money is an expressway to happiness, or at the very least, that the more money you have, the better. But generally speaking, I don't think that's true. After all, if it was, law and medicine wouldn't have the highest rates of depression out of any profession in the world, no one rich and famous would ever commit suicide, and you, Jimmy babe, would never have suffered from depression either.'

She sighed again.

'In my humble opinion, you only need four things to be happy: shelter, food, freedom, and to be surrounded by the people you love. If you have those four things, then you can be happy – regardless of how much money you have in your bank account. And if you don't believe me, go and visit the slum again.'

It would be a year-and-a-half before I'd come to agree with her, at which point, my life would get turned upside down again for what would feel like the millionth time. But it was Jessica's brazen honesty, her courage to think outside the box that was part of the reason I was so drawn to her. Combined with her adventurousness, unbridled wildness and how unbelievably hot she was, she was a hell of a catch, and any guy in my shoes would've jumped at the chance to go out with her. But when she was seeing me off at the airport before I flew back to Sydney and broached the subject of us becoming a couple, I sadly shook my head, and said I couldn't do it. When I told Corey on the plane, he couldn't believe it, and I muttered an excuse about needing to focus on honours that year so that I could blitz it and get the university medal. But the real reason I said no to Jessica was because I knew that saying yes to her would've meant giving up on Olivia. I know she'd told me over and over again that we were never getting back together; I know she'd literally gotten down on her hands and knees and begged me to let her go; and I know I'd looked her in the eyes and promised her I would. But the more I'd thought about it throughout my travels, the more I'd realised that as long as I loved her, I couldn't possibly give up on her, because at the end of the day, I am a fighter, and a fighter never, ever, *ever* gives up. Throughout my life, being a fighter had always been my biggest strength: it's what had propelled me to become the best 15 year old surfer in the world; it's what had led me to get 99.60 in my Year 12 exams after I'd injured my spine and everyone said I'd amount to nothing more than a dumb washed up jock; and it's what had gotten me through depression and stopped me from killing myself when I was standing on the edge of the bridge in Rozelle near the writers' centre thinking of jumping, on the night of the car accident when I was running that piece of glass over my throat, and all the other times I'd felt suicidal. On the plane back to Sydney, however, I realised that – like the majority of human traits, in fact – my unwavering determination, my fighting spirit and my never-say-die attitude was actually a double-edged sword. After all, I thought, maybe it *was* ludicrous not to give up on a girl who'd gotten down on her hands and knees and pleaded with me to do just that, and perhaps clinging to the fantasy of us getting back together, marrying at a lovely ceremony, raising a family in a big house on Manly Beach and growing old in each other's arms would ultimately lead me to end up alone and depressed. I was fully aware that that may well happen – not only when I told Jessica that we couldn't be together, but also in all the time that followed where I continued pining for Olivia. And while ending up alone and depressed was my biggest fear in the world, I knew I had to face it in the name of love, and hope with all my heart that one day, she would change her mind.

Consequently, when Corey fell asleep in the seat beside me, I opened up my wallet, and took out the picture of her. Like I'd done so many times before, I marvelled at how beautiful she was, with her brown hair blowing slightly in the wind, and her warm, vivacious, beguiling smile. I lost myself in her brilliant blue eyes that were gazing right back at me, and, unable to resist, I gently pressed my lips against her own, before slowly pulling back and meeting her eyes again.

'I'm a fighter, Olivia,' I whispered softly. 'So for better or for worse, I cannot give up on you. I can never, ever, ever give up on you …'

Part II

~~~

The time I started honours was also about the time that I resumed keeping a diary. I say "resumed", because I'd sometimes logged my thoughts during the depths of my depression to try and make sense of my despair. But, during honours was the time I really got into it, thanks in large part to meeting Jessica.

'Writing diary entries is like taking photographs of your mind,' she once said, 'and our memories will be our most prized possessions when we're old and grey.'

The other benefit, I later came to realise, is that when our life implodes, it can help to have a record of our thoughts, feelings and emotions in the lead up to our demise so that we can understand what caused it, which is the first step involved in putting our life back together again. But before we get to all of that, let me share with you some of my diary entries about honours, Jessica, and of course Olivia.

2nd March, 2011

I had the first lecture of my economics honours course today, which was Advanced Applications of Microeconomic Theory. The lecturer gave the spiel they usually give at the start of those courses, the 'only the best students make it this far' and the 'if you work really hard you'll have a great future' type of stuff before he plunged into the content.

'It is imperative to note the critical distinction between actions and strategies. Suppose player "I" in an extensive form game has "L" information sets: "I.1", "I.2" ... "I.L" etcetera, and that she has a choice of M_K actions at her "K-th" information set. Then, player "I" has "M_1" x "M_2" x ... x "M_K" strategies. If an agent has only one information set, strategies and actions are synonymous for that player. In particular, for a simultaneous-move game, the notions of strategies and actions coincide for each player.'

I tried to pay attention and take notes, but all I could think while the lecturer was speaking was, *I wish I was still overseas! I wish I was still meeting new people every day, experiencing new cultures, eating insects and beating snake hearts for dinner, going ten pin bowling at two in the morning, getting ballcuzzis on boats in the middle of the night, watching girls shoot ping pong balls out of their vaginas, and exploring some of India's poorest slums in the middle of Delhi.* I was thinking the exact same thing throughout my Monetary Economics lecture as well, which I found just as dull as the morning's one.

'In 1963, it was postulated by Friedman and Schwartz that money growth is positively correlated with output, in the sense that faster money growth tends to be followed by increases in output, and slower money growth tends to be followed by decreases in output. However, this gives rise to a causality problem, since ...'

Who gives a fuck? I groaned in my head. *Take me back to Asia, please!*

After spending the afternoon in the library trying to catch up on what I'd been too bored to focus on in class, I met up with Corey and drove him home.

'We've only been back a few days, and I already miss Asia like crazy,' I said. 'Don't you wish we were still there? Don't you wish we were still there right now?'

Corey shrugged.

'Not really, to be honest.'

'What?' I exclaimed. 'Are you serious?'

'Yeah, man. Look don't get me wrong – I had a great time in Asia. But it's like ... even though I was having heaps of fun on the trip, there was always a part of me that wished I was home finishing my degree and doing my internship. I just love graphic design, man. I really love drawing, and making cartoons, and seeing my work come to life on a screen. It's my favourite thing to do in the world, and while we were travelling, I really missed it.'

As the lights changed from orange to red, I turned to look at my best friend. And right there, in that moment, I couldn't relate to him at all.

12th March, 2011

Today is a Saturday, and in keeping with last year's tradition, I spent the afternoon with Olivia. Since she'd thought it would be best if we had some time apart, it was the first occasion we'd spoken since the day of our break-up, and as I listened to her voice, heard her laugh, saw her smile and looked into her eyes, I knew that I'd made the right decision in saying no to Jessica, and holding out hope that there'd come a time when her heart would once again beat to the rhythm of my own.

As we each ate a club sandwich at Sugar Lounge by the beach, Olivia asked me questions about my trip – like what I'd done in each city, where my favourite place was, and what my most memorable experiences were. And then, she asked me a question that I hadn't anticipated.

'So who's that girl you were hanging out with?'

'Huh?'

'You know who I mean. The one with blonde curly hair who was in like half your Facebook pictures.'

'Oh. *Her.*'

'Yes. Jessica, I think her name was.'

'Yeah.'

'Tell me about her.'

I looked at her uncertainly.

'Why?'

'I don't know,' she said, looking away shyly. 'I was just wondering.'

'What were you wondering about?'

'I don't know. Was she ... was she nice?'

I shrugged.

'Sure.'

'Did you enjoy spending time with her?'

'Yeah, we had fun.'

'Did she treat you well?'

'Ahuh.'

'Did she realise how lucky she was to be with you?'

'Um, I don't know. I guess?'

'And are you going out with her now?'

I shook my head.

'No. We're not going out now.'

At that moment, I thought I saw a look of relief cross her face. Then again, it could've just been my mind playing tricks on me.

'Oh,' she said after a few seconds. 'Do you, um ... do you mind if I ask why?'

'It wouldn't have worked,' I said, glossing over the truth. 'How about you? Have you been seeing anyone?'

She shook her head.

'I haven't been on a single date since our accident, Jimmy. And I can't see myself dating anyone anytime soon, either.'

She sighed.

'I'm just not in the right frame of mind at the moment. This PTSD ... I want to move past it before I date anybody again.'

And hopefully when that time comes, that guy will be me.

2nd April, 2011

Every day, I wake up, have breakfast and then I study. Then I have morning tea and I study. Then I have lunch and I study. Then I have afternoon tea and I study. Then I have dinner and I study. Then I study some more before going to bed. I try to fit in some exercise and some time to pitch my novel to literary agents when I can, but it's mostly just study, study, study. And if truth be told, I don't really like it. I hoped I would, at the start of the year – and for me at least, anything's better than law. But there's still nothing about economics that excites me. There's nothing about it that makes me get out of bed and think, *I'm looking forward to studying "this" today,* or *I'm looking forward to learning "that" today.* For me, it is a chore – something that I *have* to do, not something that I *want* to do.

And when I acknowledge that, I also can't help but acknowledge that maybe Jessica was right – maybe I *am* only in it for the money. But it is a hell of a lot of money, and being rich will definitely be worth studying this boring degree.

14th April, 2011

Because honours has been so full on, I haven't had a chance to submit my novel to many literary agents lately, and just like last year, I haven't had any success with the ones I have found time to pitch to. It's something I've been really worried about, but over the last couple of days, I've started thinking that the lack of traction my novel's gotten may actually have been a blessing in disguise. I first started musing along these lines when I was talking to Andy – my new friend from honours – who told me that he'd been suffering from depression since halfway through 2009, but that because he didn't know much about the illness, it had taken him until last May to realise that he even had a problem.

'Me and my girlfriend had just broken up,' he'd said. 'I was really torn up about it, and because she was the one who'd ended it, I felt really worthless and I lost all my confidence. Looking back now, I can see I was depressed – but at the time, I didn't realise it. I thought I was just "sad", in the same way that everyone gets sad sometimes, you know? And I wanted to escape it, I wanted to feel good again, so I started going to raves every weekend and popping a lot of pills, and I got pretty messed up on all of that. Then one night last May I had a bad trip on some of the ecstasy I'd taken, and I tried to jump off a bridge. I obviously survived, but I broke both my legs and had a week-long concussion. That's when I realised something was wrong – that I was more than just feeling "sad". And by then, I had a drug problem and I'd almost killed myself.'

It was eerily similar to my own story, in the sense that it was a long time before I figured out that I was suffering from depression too – by which point, my illness was far more severe than it would've been if I'd gotten help sooner, and I was getting drunk five nights a week to deal with it. I kept mulling our experiences over, and I concluded that one of the biggest problems concerning depression right now is that many people who are afflicted don't even know it, and therefore don't seek the help that they really need. As a result, their depression almost always worsens, they often turn to drugs or alcohol to cope and get themselves hooked, they sometimes drive their loved ones away and end up alone, or in the worst cases, they resort to killing themselves. And that's when I got the idea to write a fictional story exploring the lives and relationship of two college-aged lovers who suffer from depression.

People might choose to read it because they enjoy love stories or coming-of-age novels or something like that, I figured, *but in the course of being entertained, they'll also come to really understand depression – including knowing what the symptoms are; how the illness can make a person think, act and feel; how it can affect a sufferer's relationship with their partner; and what to do (and not to do) in order to recover. And while depression may not be relevant to them now, since it affects one in seven people on average, chances are that it will unfortunately strike either them or someone they love at some point in their life – and if and when that happens, then at least they'll recognise it and know how to deal with it.*

I'm so excited by the thought of writing such an impactful novel, but if I did in fact choose to do it, I know I'd have to abandon the one I've already written, because in line with what those two agents who'd read the first part of my book last year had advised, I've inserted quite a lot of mental health-related content to give it more present-day relevance, and it would overlap with this new idea too much for me to be able to publish both of them. I've been thinking about what to do, and while on the one hand it seems a waste to give up on the original, on the other hand, I truly believe that my new idea could turn into a really great novel that's far better than the original currently is, and if I can only publish one of them, then don't I owe it to myself to release the best book I can possibly write? I don't know. I guess I'll just mull it over some more, and hold off on submitting the original novel to agents until I've decided.

26th April, 2011

I'm still not really enjoying honours, and because I slog away at it for 60 hours a week to get into a good management consulting firm next year, by the time the weekend arrives, I feel completely and utterly exhausted, and in desperate need of an escape. As a result, I've been drinking a lot more than usual lately, and last Saturday night, I got completely wrecked. I started at seven-thirty by having beers with the boys at the Steyne in Manly, and continued until eleven when they all decided to head home. Unable to face the prospect of going to sleep knowing I'd have to start studying again as soon as I woke up, I called up Jessica, who I hadn't spoken to since I'd gotten back to Sydney.

'Where are you?' I asked. 'I really want to see you.'

'I'm at a bar in Bondi. If you want to come, then come.'

So I took a ferry and a cab and met her there. We did three shots of tequila each as soon as I arrived, and then started smashing vodka Red Bulls as we danced the night away. By the time the bar closed at 4am, I was so blind that I couldn't get a boner when I was trying to fuck her back at her place. When we eventually gave up, she asked me why I'd called her.

'I don't know,' I replied. 'I wanted to see you.'

'Why? Was it just so you could fuck me?'

'No. Of course not.'

'Then why'd you call?'

'I told you – because I wanted to see you. I've had a really shit week, and I just wanted to blow off some steam and have a big night with someone who knows how to have a good time. And who knows how to have a better time than you?'

'Why'd you have a really shit week?' she asked.

I sighed.

'Just uni. You know how it is.'

'Not really. I love studying drama.'

'You're lucky. Economics is pretty boring.'

'I'm not exactly "lucky" – I just choose to study a degree I enjoy. You can do the same, you know? After all, no one's forcing you to study economics.'

'Yeah, but I need to study it – and absolutely blitz it – so that I can get a job at a top tier management consulting firm.'

'And why do you want to be a management consultant? Is it because you think you'd find the work itself interesting, or because you want to be rich?'

'You've asked me that question already – after we went on the tour of the slum.'

'I know. I want to see if your answer's changed at all.'

I sighed, thinking over her question carefully.

'I guess ... I guess if I'm being really honest,' I eventually said, 'then I must admit that I don't even know exactly what management consultants do – at least not beyond the vague definition that's something like "advising businesses on a different range of issues to make them more efficient". So based on that, I guess I'd have to say that I'm drawn to the job for the money.'

'Why don't you try and find a job that you actually *know* you'll enjoy, even if it doesn't pay as well as management consulting does? Remember what the slum proved to us – you don't need to have a lot of money to be really happy.'

I shook my head.

'I want to be a management consultant. It'll make me rich, and hopefully I'll enjoy the work as well.'

Jessica sighed.

'I hope for your sake that you do enjoy it,' she said. 'Because if you don't like your job, then all being rich will mean is that you'll be able to buy a really expensive handkerchief to cry into every night.'

1st May, 2011

Yesterday was a Saturday, and as usual, I spent it with Olivia. We caught one another up on each other's news, and in the course of doing so, we talked about my novel.

'So Jimmy, how's the book submission process going? Any update on the last time we spoke?'

'Nah, I'm still holding off until I decide whether or not I want to write this new one instead.'

She smiled at me.

'You want to know what I think?'

'Always.'

'I think you should forget about the old book and start writing the new one.'

'Yeah?'

'Yeah. Call me crazy, but I have this strange belief that you were almost destined to write a book about depression. Maybe I'm wrong, but I believe that God has a plan for all of us, and I believe that He led you into writing and made you go through depression so that you could write a great story that raises awareness about it. And it *would* raise a lot of awareness, because great novels have mainstream appeal, and by writing a great novel centred around depression, you can help make it a mainstream issue, and help people who wouldn't otherwise take the time to learn about the illness to really understand it.'

When Olivia stopped talking, I realised that my heart was pounding in my chest. When I think about working on my honours thesis or about studying economics all day in the library, I feel uninspired, and uninterested, and I have to force myself to do it. But the idea of writing a novel again – and particularly one that has the potential to be so powerful – sent a tingle down my spine, and for the first time in weeks, I felt energised, and excited, and completely alive.

'I would love to do it, Liv,' I said. 'I really, really would.'

'I'd love to see you do it too.'

I gazed into her sea-blue eyes.

'Do you really think I can, though?' I asked. 'Do you really think I'm capable of writing a novel that's so entertaining that it has mainstream appeal, and so insightful that it helps people understand depression?'

She reached across the table and took my hand.

'Of course I do, Jimmy. Ever since the day I met you, I've always believed that you can do anything you set your mind to, and ever since that day, you always have. So if you decide to write a novel that raises awareness about depression, then I'm sure you'll be able to do it, and I'm sure it will be a success as well. And the more I think about it, the more I believe that you were meant to do this. That we'll both look back one day after you've done it and see that it was part of God's plan for you. That it was part of your destiny.'

She squeezed my hand as she smiled at me, and I was so flushed with love for her that tears lacquered my eyes.

24th June, 2011

Uni is over for the semester, thank fuck. I'm so fed up with honours, so completely and utterly sick of it that when the bell to end our last exam finally sounded, my whole face lit up and I clenched my fists with joy. I punched the air in celebration as soon as I'd left the room, and then met Corey at the university bar to start slamming tequila shots. I was annihilated before it was even seven o'clock, and on the way to meet the rest of the boys in Manly, I started vomiting off the side of the ferry.

'Alright mate,' Corey said, patting me on the back. 'No more drinking for you tonight.'

But half an hour later, I was downing beers at the New Brighton Hotel.

'Why are you still drinking?' Corey frowned. 'You're drunk enough already.'

'Why are you being such a downer?' I slurred. 'Uni's finished for the semester, man! It's time to have some fun!'

At about half-past eight the rest of the fellas arrived, but I was so sloppy I was kicked out ten minutes later. I was refused entry when we tried to get into The Steyne, so we finally ended up at the Bavarian Bier Café. More alcohol was the last thing I needed, but as soon as we got there, I ordered myself a litre of Lowenbrau and a shot of Schnapps.

'Stop drinking, stop drinking,' everyone was telling me.

But I was so relieved to be done with uni, so at the end of my tether, so desperate to blow off some steam after feeling suffocated for so long that I couldn't stop. I couldn't stop. I just couldn't stop.

I woke up this morning feeling disgusted with myself. After all, I've treaded down the substance abuse path too many times before, and I know as well as anyone that it will only lead to disaster. So I made a promise to myself to stop drinking indefinitely, messaged the boys to tell them I was sorry for being such a nuisance, and then to sooth my soul, I wandered down to the beach with a deckchair and then settled in to write my new novel, *Lovesick*. Because honours was so intense leading up to the exams, today is the earliest I've been able to start, and it's hard to put into words how pleasurable it was. The best I can do is say that when I'm writing, and when I really lose myself in it, I feel as if I'm transported to a different place. All my pain just melts away, and I feel at peace with the world. I feel blessed to be alive. I feel blessed to be me. I feel a pulsing rush ... of excitement, of joy, of inspiration ... all at the same time. I feel invigorated. I feel alive. I feel free. And above all else, I feel happy. Purely and utterly happy.

31st July, 2011

It's a Sunday afternoon, and I just got back from Olivia's place. I'd love to be able to write that yesterday's Saturday lunch had turned into dinner and then turned into breakfast and then turned into lunch again, but the truth is that I went to see her today so that we could go driving together.

'I've been doing better lately,' Olivia said yesterday. 'With my PTSD, I mean. And I think ... I think I might be ready to face my ultimate fear. I think I might be ready to go for a drive.'

She asked me to come and pick her up today, because the way she put it, if she can stay relaxed and calm while the two of us went driving together, then it would be a huge, huge step forwards in her recovery. I agreed of course, and as I was cruising over to her place, I was filled with a tingling excitement, believing as I do that if Olivia could in fact do it, that not only would she be one giant step closer towards recovering from her PTSD, but that we'd also be one giant step closer towards getting back together.

So I arrived at her house this morning with a bounce in my step, but when she opened the front door, her eyes were damp and she looked stricken with fear.

'Woah, Liv, are you OK?' I asked concernedly, reaching for her hands.

'I'm ... I'm scared, Jimmy.'

'Look, we don't have to do this, you know. If you want, we can wait – until another time when you feel more comfortable.'

She was looking at me nervously, but then she shook her head.

'No, I want to do this.'

'Are you sure?'

She nodded softly.

'Yes.'

So with my arm around her, I led her to the car. I could feel her trembling as we walked together silently, and in hindsight, that combined with her watery eyes when she greeted me should've been a big enough clue that this was never going to turn out well. But I guess hope can blind our judgment, and be so strong that it convinces us that what we want still has a chance of happening – even when all the signs suggest the opposite.

When we reached the car, I opened the passenger-side door for her. She hesitated for a few seconds, breathing deeply, in and out, in and out, in and out, before slowly creeping inside. I gently closed the door and then got in the driver's seat. Before I started the engine, I looked at her. She was shaking even more now, and gritting her teeth to try and keep them from chattering.

'Are you *sure* you want to do this?' I asked her again.

She nodded softly.

'Y-yes.'

'OK, Liv. You just tell me when you're ready to go, and then we'll go. But take all the time you need, OK? There's absolutely no rush at all.'

She nodded again, and began taking deep breaths to try and calm herself down … one … two … three … four … five … all the way up to 22. And then, in a whisper I could barely hear, she said it: 'go'.

With my eyes on her, I turned on the engine. Her body tensed up even tighter, but once again, she whispered 'go', so I eased away from the curb as gently as I could, and started moving slowly down the street.

'Are you OK so far?' I asked her.

'Y-yes,' she croaked.

I was looking at her out of the corner of my eye. She was still trembling, and ever since we'd started moving, she was also clutching the cross around her neck. I glanced at her eyes, and noticed they were tightly bolted shut. I'm not sure what Olivia was thinking about at that moment, but she was probably trying to imagine that she was someplace else, someplace safe – anywhere but in a car with *me,* of all people. Knowing how traumatised she was, I was driving slowly – no more than 25 or 30 K's an hour in a 50km/hr zone. We'd only been driving for about 200 metres, but already there were two cars behind us – right behind us – clearly frustrated that we were going at a snail's pace. They put up with it for another 50 metres or so, but then one of them loudly beeped their horn.

'Aahhh!' Olivia shrieked, jumping up in her seat.

I quickly veered to the curb to let both of them pass, before taking hold of Olivia's hand.

'I'm so sorry, Liv. Are you OK?'

She was trying to fight back tears.

'I'm sc-scared, Jimmy. I'm really, really scared …'

'I know you are,' I whispered, stroking her thumb. 'I know you are. But you're doing well. You're doing a really good job.'

'I don't know if I can do it …'

'You can, Liv,' I said. 'I know you can.'

She looked at me nervously.

'Do you really think so?'

'Yes, I do. I believe in you.'

She sighed, and then took a few more deep breaths to try and gather herself.

'OK,' she eventually murmured. 'OK. Let's keep going, then.'

'Are you sure? If you're not ready, then that's OK. I'm not trying to pressure you.'

'No I want to try and do it. Let's keep going.'

But as much as we both wanted her to be, she just wasn't ready yet. About 30 seconds after we'd started driving again, we had to turn right near the hospital and go down Darley Road. The speed limit is 60 kilometres an hour, but since no one was behind us, I crept along at 30. Despite still shaking, and having one hand clutching the cross around her neck and the other clutching the arm rest on the door for support, she was holding up OK, and after we'd turned down Darley Road, she even opened her eyes a little as she squinted ahead of us.

'You're doing great, Liv,' I encouraged. 'You're doing really, really well.'

But at that moment, another car started coming down the hill behind us. Trying to avoid another horn-beeping incident, I sped up a little.

'Jimmy please slow down.'

'I can't sorry, Liv – there's someone behind me.'

'Then pull over – I can't go this fast!'

I scanned for a car space alongside the road, but they were all taken. Not knowing what else to do, I came to a halt and flicked the indicator on so that I could turn into a side street.

It was the wrong move to make. Because I hadn't given much warning, the woman in the SUV behind me slammed her horn. Just like before, Olivia screamed.

'I'm sorry!' I said. 'I'm so, so sorry!'

'Get off the road!' she shrieked, covering her eyes again. 'Just please get off the road right now!'

'I'm trying, Liv! I just can't turn quite yet – there are too many cars coming the other way and – '

But I stopped talking as soon as I heard the sound of an ambulance behind me, coming from the hospital.

'Oh my God, oh my God, oh my God!' Olivia cried, looking around in a panicked frenzy.

'Liv it's OK, I'll just – '

But then the woman in the SUV behind me started blasting her horn again because I was holding up the ambulance. Since there were still cars coming in the other direction that prevented me from turning, I instinctively floored the accelerator. Olivia screamed hysterically as we zoomed down the street.

'Stop the fucking car! Stop the fucking car! Stop the *fucking* car!'

There was so much commotion that I was freaking out as well until I managed to hang a left in a side street and stop by the curb. As soon as I'd turned off the engine, she threw open the door and started running away.

'Olivia!'

When I caught up to her, she stopped running and bawled her eyes out into my chest. I just held her, stroking her hair, doing my best to comfort her. And as I did so, my eyes began to moisten, and then before I knew it, tears were streaming down my cheeks too as I cried for Olivia, as I cried for us, and as I cried at the realisation that if we were ever going to get back together again, that it wouldn't be for a long, long time.

1st September, 2011

As usual, honours is batshit boring, and writing my new novel is the most enjoyable thing in the world – but because I study 60 hours a week and write for less than five, I constantly feel drained, uninspired, irritable and on edge. On the bright side, though, interviews for graduate positions at all the top management consulting firms are about to begin, and I can't wait for them. A job at one of the "Big Four" companies is the so-called carrot on the stick. The prize that I'll hopefully receive for putting myself through so much shit.

I've just started looking through all the recruitment brochures, and I'm already really excited. Each glossy page is sprinkled with quotes from employees about how "unique", "nurturing" and "dynamic" their firm is, as well as how "challenging", "stimulating", "diverse" and "cutting edge" the work is. Interspersed with these quotes are countless pictures of smiling team members enjoying the company of their fellow workers. In the brochure I just read, for example, there's a snapshot of two team members laughing while sipping a takeaway coffee in the hall between their offices. On the next double-page, there's one of three young team members with their arms around each other on the ski slopes, a second with another group of team members playing rounds of golf on a beautiful summer's day, and a third with people sailing on an even more beautiful summer's day – all weekend trips away organised by the firm. On the following double-page there are pictures of team members shooting hoops in preparation for the inter-firm basketball competition, another of them playing indoor soccer against each other, and yet another of a group running through Sydney's lush Botanic Gardens at lunch time as they trained for the City2Surf together. Next there are pictures of team members sipping champagne at a charity ball for breast cancer, and others of everyone dressed up as rock stars and playing air guitar at the company Christmas party. On the double-page that talked all about the pro bono consulting the firm does, there are shots of people sitting in plush boardrooms with harbour views listening eagerly and intently to one another speaking – the captions of each picture stating that they're working on projects that support animal rights, battered women, asylum seekers and other worthy causes. No matter what they're doing, however, the common theme in all of the photos and the accompanying text is that everyone loves their life and absolutely loves being a member of the firm. It's as if everyone in the company is all part of a family – a really big, warm, happy, caring family – and it's a family I'm willing to do anything to be a part of.

8th September, 2011

This week, I went to the information seminar for each of the "Big Four" consulting firms, and I really loved what I saw and heard. All of the companies handed out branded lollies, pens, mouses, umbrellas and chocolates; and treated us to glasses of champagne, hors d'oeuvres, sandwiches, pizza bread and mini-muffins. After a couple of the partners gave talks about how "unique", "nurturing", and "dynamic" their firm is and how "challenging", "stimulating", "diverse" and "cutting edge" the work is, everyone started mingling. At one of the presentations, I found myself chatting to a young team member wearing an Armani suit and a gold Rolex, who was probably only a few years older than me. He spoke of how compassionate and supportive his firm was; how enjoyable of a place it was to be a part of; how he got to travel overseas every three months to places like New York, Singapore, Brussels and even Kazakhstan to work on new and exciting projects, and how on more than one occasion while he'd been away, they'd flown his girlfriend out to see him. He regaled me with tales of afternoon golf trips and sailing regattas just like I'd read about in the brochures, and got me salivating for a lifestyle of fancy restaurants, fast cars, designer clothes, international travel, ritzy hotels and high-rolling parties. The way he described it, he lived in a world full of opulence and glamour, and I knew that all the hard yards I'd put in this year – all the weeks I'd spent studying subjects that I couldn't give a shit about and working my ass off on my thesis about 21st century fiscal policy that was duller than the phone book – would all be worth it if it could punch me a ticket to this corporate Utopia.

24th September, 2011

'How many balls are hit on a golf pitch in any given calendar year?'
'Are we assuming the pitch in question has 18 holes?' I asked.
'Yes.'
'And where is the pitch located? Australia?'
'Yes.'
'In Sydney?'

'Yes.'

I was stalling, since I wasn't really sure how to deduce a sensible answer. An excellent CV will get you an interview, but what management consultants really want to know is how well you can problem solve, so they'll test your reasoning with questions like 'how many ping pong balls could fit into a Boeing 747?', 'how many five peso coins are in circulation in Uruguay at any one time?', and 'how many balls are hit on a golf pitch during one calendar year?'

'OK,' I finally said after several minutes of thinking. 'To arrive at my answer, I'm going to divide golfers into six different segments: 'weekday beginner golfers', 'weekday intermediate golfers', 'weekday advanced golfers', 'weekend beginner golfers', 'weekend intermediate golfers' and 'weekend advanced golfers' – and what I'm going to do is see how many balls each segment hits each year, and then add the total of each segment together to see how many balls are hit each year overall. Is that OK?'

'Yes, that seems reasonable enough.'

'OK, let's then start with weekday beginner golfers. Assuming that throughout the year, a typical Sydney golf pitch is open from 9am to 6pm each day, and that every three hours, one group of three beginners will start, it follows that on any given weekday, nine beginner golfers will play on the pitch. Now, if the average par per hole is four, and we assume that it takes beginner level golfers double the par to get the ball in the hole, then that means that in any given day ...' I paused to calculate the answer to 9 x 4 x 2 x 18 by hand using a pen and pad.

'Yes,' I eventually resumed, 'that means that in any given weekday, 1,296 balls are hit by beginner golfers.'

I then multiplied 1,296 by five to get the number of balls hit by beginner golfers in five weekdays (6,480), and then multiplied that number by 52 to calculate the number of golf balls hit by beginner golfers on weekdays in one year (336,960). I repeated the same analysis for weekday intermediate golfers (assuming they averaged one-and-a-half times as many puts as the par), as well as for weekday advanced golfers, (who I assumed on average putted each hole on par). I then did the same calculations for weekend golfers of each segment, assuming that on weekends, there were double as many golfers each day as there were during the week. Then finally, after three A4 pieces of paper full of calculations and what felt like an incredibly stressful lifetime, I arrived at my eventual answer: 1,364,688.

Combined with asking me a bunch of questions about my resume as well as my future goals, extracurricular interests, and strengths and weaknesses, such was the typical management consulting interview I attended. They were rigorous and gruelling, and out of the three "Big Four" firms that'd invited me to their first round of interviews, only one asked me to return for their second and final round. But, before it began, everyone was invited out to dinner by the firm.

It was held at the Sydney Opera House, and was one of the most lavish experiences of my life. As we enjoyed an eight course degustation which included mud crab, oysters, smoked eel and a glass of vintage wine with every plate, we marvelled at the breathtaking view of the Harbour Bridge, and listened to the partners and team members talk more about how "unique", "nurturing" and "dynamic" the company is, and how "challenging", "stimulating", "diverse" and "cutting edge" the work is. They peppered their speeches with tantalising stories of corporate life – weekends away to Fiji, rounds of putt-putt in the office, and Christmas parties on private islands – making my body tingle from head to toe as I sat there listening intently and lapping it all up.

I just have to get one of those graduate positions. I just *have* to.

5th October, 2011

Fuck yes! Fuck yes! Fuck yes! Fuck yes! Fuck yes! Yesterday, a courier came to my house with a bottle of Moet and a letter saying that I'd been offered a job! I still can't believe it! I'm actually going to be a consultant at one of the Big Four Firms! And I get a $15,000 signing bonus! *$15,000!!!* And then at night, the company invited everyone who'd made it out to this sleek bar in The Rocks, where we ate copious amounts of food and drank whisky and wine paid for on the corporate credit card! It was unbelievable! They treated us like rock stars, like we were the kings of the world! And it makes all the blood, sweat and tears that went into this year so worth it! It's all been for the best, because now, I'm going to be rich as hell! I'm going to buy a great big house in Manly and drive a Ferrari and life is going to be so damn good! Fuck yes! Fuck yes, fuck yes, fuck yes, fuck yes, fuck yes!!!!!

27th October, 2011

Throughout most of the honours year, my marks had been so good that I had a shot at the university medal, which requires getting an average of at least 90% across your thesis and all of your subjects. But as much as I tried not to let this happen, I've been easing my foot off the gas pedal a little bit ever since I got my job, and now, I've probably squandered my chance. It's unfortunate, because the medal would've been really nice, but now that the need to ace honours has dissipated, I've found it impossible to motivate myself to study anywhere near as hard as I used to. Instead, I've been spending more time writing *Lovesick,* and as a result, I've been much, much happier – so much so that other people have been noticing it.

'You've seemed a lot less on edge the last few weeks, don't you reckon?' Corey said.

'Yeah, man,' Brent agreed. 'For a while there, you were reminding me of how you were a couple of years ago – drinking all out of control and being kind of quiet and moody the times you've been sober.'

'I'm really glad to see you doing better, Jimmy,' Olivia said one Saturday while we were lying on the beach together. 'And I'm so glad that honours is almost over and that you're about to start the job you want.'

Hell, I'm really glad too. I can't wait to get really rich!

2nd December, 2011

As expected, I missed out on getting the university medal. But, I still got first class honours, and to celebrate, Olivia took me out to lunch at Hugo's in Manly.

'I'm so proud of you, Jimmy,' she beamed. 'You got first class honours and the amazing job you've always wanted!'

'Thanks,' I smiled.

'Here's to you,' she said, raising her glass of champagne.

We chinked glasses, smiling at each other.

'You must feel on top of the world,' she said.

'Yeah, I really do. Honours is finished, I got the job I dreamed of, and I'm going to Cambodia in a couple of days to explore a new culture and just write and write and write. Life is great.'

'There you go again,' she frowned playfully. 'Abandoning me in the summer as usual.'

I laughed.

'Aw Liv, don't say that!'

'Such an abandoner,' she pouted.

'No, Liv don't pout,' I said, trying not to look at her. 'You know I can't resist you when you pout!'

She giggled.

'That's why I do it!'

I laughed.

'Will you forgive me if I bring you back a present?'

'Hhmmm ... depends what the present is.'

'What would you like?'

'I don't know – it's up to you to surprise me!'

'You do love your surprises, don't you?'

'As you often like to remind me ...'

'Remember that year when your mum and I organised that surprise birthday party for you?' I chuckled. 'We'd just gotten back to your house from uni, and when everyone yelled "surprise!" you were so shocked you dropped your notes all over the floor!'

'Yes! And little Snowy my dog was so excited that he peed all over Brent's shoe!'

'And then you got really, *really* drunk!'

'Hey! I wasn't *that* drunk!'

'Of course you were! You were so unsteady on your feet that you had your arms wrapped around me to stop yourself from falling.'

'I had my arms wrapped around you because I loved you, not because I was drunk!'

'I beg to differ. You were hammered.'

'I was in love.'

'You were hammered.'

'You take that back, Jimmy,'

'No.'

'Take it back!'

'No.'

'Take it back!' she smiled, jumping across from her chair to the bench I was sitting on.

'Uh-uh,'

She started tickling me.

'Liv stop it!' I laughed, trying to defend myself.

'Not until you take it back!' she teased.

'Liv, please! Cut it out!'

'Take it back then!'

I managed to grab one of her hands and start tickling her waist with my free one.

'Hey!' she cried, jerking away. 'Jimmy, stop!'

'Only if *you* stop!'

'Um, kangaroo medium rare?' a befuddled waiter holding two plates interrupted.

'Ah, yeah. Thanks,' I said.

'And the prawn linguini?' he added, placing a bowl of pasta in front of Olivia's seat.

'Thank-you.'

He walked away. Olivia gave my tummy one last quick tickle before jumping back into her seat and giggling at me across the table.

We ate our meals, had another glass of champagne each, and then because it was a beautiful day and we were having such a great time together, we decided to grab some towels from my place and lie on the beach together. As the sun warmed our nearly naked bodies and groups of friends and couples in love talked and laughed around us, conversation turned to Olivia's PTSD.

'I've been feeling OK, lately,' she said. 'But I'm still too scared to drive. I'm just so, so scared, you know?'

I rolled over onto my side, and propped myself up on my elbow to look at her.

'You know that time we tried together ... do you think ... do you think it set you back at all?'

Olivia shrugged.

'I don't know. It was so nerve-wracking ... so terrifying ... but I don't know if it set me back at all.'

'Hey Liv, I've been thinking … what if we took an easier route? I mean it's a bit hectic around here with the people and the cars and the hospital and all that, but what if we tried somewhere much quieter? Maybe like a parking lot at night? Or somewhere with hardly any other cars on the road?'

She shrugged again.

'I'd try it if I thought it would make a difference, but to tell you the truth, it would probably just be the same. I just don't think … I just don't think I'm ready yet.'

She sighed, scrunching up her face in a pained sort of expression.

'And lately, I've been thinking ... I've been thinking that maybe ... maybe I'll never be ready. I mean it's been more than a year-and-a-half now, and I'm still scared stiff, you know? So what evidence is there to suggest that given more time, I'll be able to do it? What evidence is there to suggest that I'll ever be able to drive again?'

Instinctively, I reached out my hand, and gently started caressing her forearm.

'Olivia, I ... I know you're going to get through this. You're going to get through this because you're strong, and because you're committed to getting through this, and because you're getting the right help to get through this. I don't know when, but I know there's going to come a time when you and I hop in a car together and go for a drive somewhere. The sky's going to be blue ... the sun's going to be shining ... you'll have the window wound down and your arm resting on the sill with a cool breeze blowing your hair to one side, and we'll talk and laugh as if we were never in that car accident last year. And after that, there'll be days when you drive to uni again, and after you've finished your master's degree and become a qualified psychologist, there'll be days when you drive to your office. When you get married, you'll drive with your husband on your wedding day in one of those limousines or those Ferrari's with the fancy white ribbons on the front, and when you have children, you'll get a big SUV and pick them up from school, and then drive them to soccer training or a ballet recital, and you'll take them to the zoo, and to their friends' houses, and to parties, and to lots of other places as well.'

I paused for a moment, gazing into her deep blue eyes.

'You're going to be OK, Liv. I'm not sure when, but I know you're going to be OK. I just ... I just know it.'

Lying on her side, she gazed right back at me, smiling her warm, vivacious, breathtaking smile before she took my hand in hers, brought it to her lips and kissed it ever so softly. In that moment, we would've looked like a couple to all those passing by, and as we held each other's eyes with our fingers intertwined, I wished with all my heart that I'd end up being that guy I spoke of – the forever blessed one who would end up marrying her, having a family with her, and sharing the rest of his life with her.

23rd December, 2011

I'm on my flight home to Sydney after spending the last two-and-a-half weeks in Cambodia. I had a really great time, seeing the iconic Angkor Wat at sunrise; meeting children who keep wild pythons for pets at the floating village on the Ton Le Sap Lake; eating fried cockroaches, crickets and tarantulas for dinner one night and snake, crocodile and ostrich another; visiting the heartbreaking "killing fields" where over a million people were murdered during the Khmer Rouge Regime; going on a two day party cruise around Sihanoukville; and volunteering at an underprivileged school in Battambang. But my most unforgettable experience occurred when I first arrived in Siem Reap and was wandering the dirty streets lined with beggars, trying to find a hostel. As I was doing so, I noticed a book stall on the side of the road, and of course I stopped to have a browse. As I scanned the titles, the owner emerged from the other side of the stall – a dark-skinned, 30-something year old Cambodian man, who tragically had his left arm amputated at the wrist, and even more tragically, had his right arm amputated at the elbow.

'Hello,' he smiled in a thick Khmer accent.

'H-hello,' I stammered, doing my best to smile and suppress the pang of anguish that had instantly swept over me.

'America?' he asked cheerfully.

I shook my head.

'Australia, mate.'

He nodded enthusiastically.

'Ah! Kangaroo!' he laughed.

I laughed along with him, just like I had when Fumio – the guy who I'd met at the internet café in Japan a year-and-a-half ago – had made the kangaroo reference himself. But unlike with Fumio, it was fake, forced laughter, even though the man continued chuckling genuinely. Due to the language barrier, I knew that that was unfortunately the end of the conversation, so I returned to looking at the books, all the while wishing that I could continue talking to him. I really wanted to know his story. I really wanted to find out what had happened to him. And above all else, I really wanted to know how he'd managed to keep such a sunny disposition despite everything he'd so obviously been through. But I knew I'd never get the chance.

After a few minutes, I decided to get a copy of *Life of Pi*, and a second book about Asia's sex slave industry to try and better understand it. I pointed to the books, indicating to the man that I wanted to buy them.

'Ten dollars, American,' he said.

I knew it was overpriced for Cambodia, but given the circumstances, there was no way in hell I was going to haggle with him. I gave him the ten dollars, smiled as warmly as I could, and walked away to continue my search for a hostel, filled with a gut-wrenching sadness for the guy.

Eventually, I found a place to stay. I checked into my room and started unpacking, thinking about the Cambodian man all the while.

That poor bloke, I lamented to myself. *It must be so hard for him to go through life that way ...*

Then, as I was taking the books I'd bought from him out of their bag, a piece of paper fell to the floor. I picked it up and started reading it.

Tok's Story

It happened in 1988. I was a government solider, in command of three or four men near Banon Village, in the western province of Battambang.

It was a mad time. There were three separate resistance groups – the Khmer Rouge, supporters of King Sihanouk, and those following (former premier) Son Sann.

I didn't actually want to be a soldier. In fact only about half of us wanted to do the job – many people were forced to fight against their will.

On the morning of the accident, I'd been training new recruits on jungle warfare techniques and survival skills.

I was taking a break from training when it happened. I went to get some food, but there was thick foliage all around us, and I had to clear a path to get through.

I bent over to pick up something on the way. How was I to know it would go off?

I don't remember much else after that. When I woke up, I looked down, and saw that both my hands were gone.

I wanted to kill myself. There was no future for me. What could I do? How could I get a job, get married and support a family? How could I even eat?

There was a grenade in a bag attached to my waist. It was there from the training exercise earlier.

140

I arched my body around and tried to reach it. I wanted to pull out the pin, but my friend saw me just in time and took the grenade away.

I was taken to a government hospital in Phnom Penh, where the authorities paid for my treatment because I was a soldier. I didn't have enough to eat, though, and my family had to send food parcels.

Gradually, after the pain subsided, I stopped wanting to kill myself, and dared to think about having a future.

I was in that hospital for nine months. When I eventually left, I was too embarrassed to go back to my family and let them feed and pay for me, so I stayed in Phnom Penh and became a beggar there for over a year. I was very unhappy during that time.

My mother eventually came to the city to find me, and she took me home and looked after me.

But I had to go back to Phnom Penh for more treatment on my arms, and I used up all my money on hospital bills and ended up back on the streets.

Then an aid worker found me and brought me to Siem Reap.

I was given a job working with Rehab Craft, selling local crafts and gifts to tourists visiting the temples at Angkor Wat.

Life was beginning to get better. Then I met a woman, got married and had two children.

I also really wanted my own business, so in the year 2000 I gave up my job with the charity to set up my own stall selling books on the streets of Siem Reap.

I'm very happy now that I have a family and have this job. Life is worth living again.

It was such a moving story that as soon as I'd finished reading it, I returned to his stall to firstly, give him a sizeable donation to help pay for his ongoing medical expenses and children's school fees – and secondly, to take down his contact details, since I found his plight so uplifting and inspiring that I had the thought of writing his memoir after I'd finished *Lovesick*. After all, it's a story that the world should hear, and I could use the proceeds to continue supporting him and his family. That's the exact kind of thing that invigorates me: meeting incredible people, writing incredible stories, and giving back to the world. That's the exact kind of thing that gets my juices going.

I wish I could start writing it right away – or at least as soon as I've finished *Lovesick*. But unfortunately, both of those dreams will have to be put on hold, because in a few weeks, I start full-time employment as a management consultant.

Part III

Be careful what you wish for

The week before I started work, I spent most of my $15,000 signing bonus decking myself out with a brand new wardrobe. In a single shopping bonanza, I bought seven suits, ten shirts and 12 ties from a variety of different designers; two pairs of cufflinks from Pierre Cardin; one Hugo Boss belt; one Luis Vuitton belt; one Versace wallet; one pair of Aquila shoes; one pair of Tom Ford shoes; and last but certainly not least, I bought a $5,000 Rolex – a gift to myself for getting into a Big Four Consulting Firm, and a symbol of the wealth I was sure I'd attain.

On my first day, I was titillating with excitement. I rose at 7am, had a hot shower, ate a bowl of cereal and fresh fruit for breakfast, and then slipped into my favourite outfit before giddily bouncing down to the wharf. On the way to the city, I sat up the front of the ferry overlooking the glittering sea, and felt the cool breeze ruffle my hair as I wrote the next couple of paragraphs of *Lovesick*. The company's plush offices in the Governor Philip Building were only a few blocks from Circular Quay, and when I arrived, I made small-talk with the other graduate consultants for ten minutes until one of the second year employees gave us a tour and introduced us to everyone. We were then placed on different projects to work on before breaking off to speak to our team leaders so we could get caught up to speed and be assigned our roles. My leader was called Gus – an overweight, balding, middle-aged man with a deep, tough voice who wore a beautifully tailored Armani suit and a pair of Tom Ford shoes that I knew from shopping at the store cost over $1,500.

'You're going to be working with myself, another partner called Steve, five associates and two second year consultants,' he said to me and Jane, a thin Chinese girl who'd just started working at the firm as well. 'A major computer company wants to expand into being an internet service provider, and we've been hired to advise them on how best to make the transition.'

He spent the next hour explaining more about the project before setting us to work at our desks. I'd been told to research the state of the Australian internet service provider industry and summarise my results into a PowerPoint presentation. Gathering data on how many people used the internet in Australia, for how long they used it for, for what reason they used it for and so on and so forth got pretty boring pretty quickly, but I was drunk on the euphoria of working for a top consulting company with views of Sydney Harbour, and that intoxication took the edge off the dreariness of the task. I was also buoyed by the thought of having lunch with Olivia – a rare, special meeting in the middle of the week to tell her all about my first day of work. But ten minutes before I was due to meet her, Steve – who was the other partner on the project – told Jane and me that we were going for sushi. The last thing in the world I wanted to do was cancel on Olivia, but shirking lunch with a partner on day one of the job would've been career suicide, so I apologetically called to cancel, promised that I'd make it up to her, and tried to hide my disappointment as best I could as I followed Steve out the door to a Japanese restaurant a couple of blocks away.

As we ate edamame, California rolls and plates of sashimi, Steve told us more about the project with Computer Company X (for confidentiality reasons, I can't divulge their real name). After that, we all returned to the office, where I continued busying myself with my research. Then at four in the afternoon, I attended a meeting with the rest of the team. My job was to take the minutes – Jane won the coin toss – and for the next hour-and-a-half, both of us sat their spectating. On a few different occasions, I had what I thought was a really good idea. But no one ever asked for my opinion, and being my first day and all, I was too scared of speaking to ever open my mouth.

After the meeting finished at half-past five, I returned to my desk, and did another three hours of research until Gus said I could leave. By then, I was knackered, having worked for almost 12 hours straight. As I trudged back to the wharf, I relished the idea of closing my eyes in the cabin on the ferry and having a little snooze on my way back home. But when I reached Circular Quay my Blackberry started vibrating, so instead of sleeping, I had to answer emails all the way to Manly, and then for another 15 minutes when I got home before I was finally able to curl up in bed and exhaustedly close my eyes.

Like I said, on my first day, I was drunk on the idea of working for a top management consulting firm, of being surrounded by people who drove Porsches and owned five million dollar houses, and of wearing an outfit that altogether cost more than my and Corey's eight week trip to Asia combined. But like all intoxications, it was a temporary one, and the hangover, when it hit me in the ensuing days, weeks and months, literally almost killed me.

Why was there a hangover to begin with? you may ask. Well firstly, contrary to what I'd read in the recruitment brochures and what I'd been told during the information sessions, the work of a management consultant – at least in my own personal opinion – was hardly "challenging", "stimulating", "diverse" or "cutting edge". Apart from when I'd sit in on meetings – usually doing nothing more than taking minutes – I'd spend all day, every day researching things like "the average price of internet services in Australia" or "the average amount of money households spend on internet usage per month" before summarising my research into anally-formatted PowerPoint slides. It was the complete opposite of stimulating, diverse and cutting edge, and the only thing challenging about it was trying to get it finished by its deadline without having a panic attack. It was so stressful that every day, I felt like I was in a never-ending race against the clock:

I have to have these PowerPoint slides ready by 6:30! I'd fret. *Will I get it done in time? Will I? Will I? I'd better work faster ... I'd better work faster ... shit, I really need to fucking hurry!*

In fact, there was so much time pressure that for lunch, I'd usually just get a takeaway sandwich from the cafeteria downstairs and eat it at my desk while I worked, otherwise I'd feel like I was losing time – which is how I felt even when I'd take just ten minutes' break to get a takeaway coffee for a much-needed pick-me-up, and if it was a particularly busy day, I'd also fret that I was "losing time" whenever I had to go to the bathroom. Working as diligently as I did, though, I always completed everything punctually – but even that accomplishment resulted in only a thimbleful of satisfaction, since within minutes, there'd always be more research to be done, more summarising to do, more Powerpoint slides to make, and another anxiety-provoking deadline just around the corner.

Not only did I find the work boring and stressful and seemingly endless, but it also encroached on every single aspect of my life. Instead of writing my beloved novel on the tranquil ferry ride every morning as I'd planned to, I was on my Blackberry answering emails so that I wouldn't be behind schedule when I arrived at the office at half-past eight. I'd then work until lunch, which like I said, would most days just be a takeaway sandwich at my desk – and even when I did go out it would usually be with one of my superiors to talk about work, which hardly qualifies as a "lunch break" anyway. After that, I'd work until about eight-thirty before taking the ferry home – once again emailing on my Blackberry instead of nourishing my soul and writing my book. Of course, if it was a particularly busy time, I wouldn't be able to leave until much later. Ten o'clock, for example, wasn't out of the norm. Midnight happened from time to time too, as would three- or four am. On one horrific day, I worked until a quarter-past-six in the morning, took a cab home to shower and sleep for two hours, and then returned to the office at 10am to pick up from where I'd left off.

Weekend work was common as well. At least one Saturday or Sunday out of every three, I'd find myself working from home. Other times, I'd have to come into the office – regardless of what I was doing or what I had planned. One time, I was having brunch with my parents who I'd barely seen all week, and was forced to leave for the city to enter a bunch of numbers into an Excel spreadsheet at my desk. Another time, I was fast asleep after working 70 hours that week from Monday to Friday, and was woken at nine o'clock on Saturday morning to come in and crunch data until five. The week before my team was due to finish up the internet project, I was having dinner with the boys on Saturday night when I was called at ten o'clock and made to work until four in the morning, before having to return to the office five hours later and work all Sunday. But the worst time I was interrupted was after I'd just had lunch with Olivia for the first Saturday in two weeks, courtesy of my insane work schedule. We'd just had a lovely seafood platter at Bluewater on the beach, and for the first time since I'd last seen her, I was relaxed and enjoying myself as we talked and laughed and even flirted a bit too. Olivia had been doing better – at the restaurant, she'd said that bit by bit, she was continuing to recover from her PTSD, and that she was feeling confident that one day, hopefully not too far away from now, she'd be able to drive again. I was really happy for her, and filled with excitement by the idea that if Olivia conquered her illness, then maybe, given a little more time, we might be able to rekindle our love. Thoughts of the future I hoped we could have together danced through my mind as we walked smiling along the beach, as we lay on the sand amongst all the other couples, and as we chatted and giggled beneath the soothing sun that gently warmed our nearly naked bodies. But then to my nauseous dread, my Blackberry started ringing.

'Hello?' I sighed.

'Jimmy – Gus. I need you to bring me the lawyer's report for the bank merger.'

'I'm sorry?'

'It's on my desk at the office. I need you to pick it up and bring it to my place.'

I gritted my teeth furiously. *How can this piece of shit,* I seethed in my head, *who lives not ten fucking minutes from the city himself, have so little respect for me and my time that he wants me to interrupt what I'm doing on my day off and trek all the way to the city from Manly, just to pick up a fucking document and deliver it to his house like a fucking courier?*

'Jimmy, did you hear me?' Gus asked.

'Yes.'

'Well, when can you get the file here?'

'Not today,' I said.

'What?'

'I said I can't do it today. I'm too busy.'

'What are you doing?'

'I'm ... seeing someone very important to me. We've planned this for a long time. I'm sorry, but I can't leave now.'

'What are you doing?' he repeated.

'We're at the beach. In Manly.'

'How about you both take a taxi into the city to pick up the lawyer's report, and then drop it off at my place on the way to Bondi Beach.'

'I'm sorry, but that's not going to work.'

'Why isn't it going to work?'

'Because ... my friend ... she doesn't like driving in taxis.'

'I'm sure she'll be OK just this once.'

'She won't be, actually.'

Gus sighed.

'Look, *Jimmy,*' he spat. 'I need that lawyer's report here by four o'clock. You're a smart guy – just figure out how to get it here. And let me tell you something else: you won't go very far in this industry if you can't be relied upon.'

Shaking my head vehemently, I buckled under pressure.

'OK,' I muttered. 'I'll work something out.'

'Good,' he replied. 'I'll see you before four.'

And then he hung up.

So that's how I'd describe the first three months of what I'd previously believed would be my "dream job": boring, stressful, and a burden that poisoned every facet of my life.

What about all those fancy dinners? you may ask.

In reality, they didn't happen very often, and even when they did, they were in my "free time" – which I would've much rather spent with my friends and family.

What about the ski trips, sailing regattas and weekend holidays to Fiji?

Same as with the dinners, except they happened even less frequently. In my first three months, we only did one such event – golf on a Saturday – and I would've much rather spent the day with Olivia than a pack of wankers like Gus.

What about all the interstate and international travel?

I never would've thought it, but the travel was even worse than staying in Sydney. Because I'd work just as hard away as I would at home, there'd be hardly any time to explore the city, and instead of coming back to my family at nine or ten or eleven o'clock at night, I'd retreat to my empty, lonely hotel room and either do even more work, or, too exhausted to write, watch Netflix by myself until I fell asleep.

But you're getting paid really well, right?

Yes, I was – better than almost any graduate I knew and close to six figures in my first year out of uni, with the capacity to earn well over a million each year by the time I was 35. But that's when I started realising the life-shattering reality that money, despite how much I thought it would, cannot buy happiness.

And, there was no greater teacher of this lesson than my $5,000 Rolex. When I bought it, I'd felt a primal thrill – a rush of bliss so intense I was on a high all day, and the next day, and even the next day after that. But as day three turned to day four turned to day five and then six and seven and so on and so forth, I felt a milder and milder buzz whenever I checked the time, and after a few weeks, I'd gotten so used to it that the high had completely worn off – by which point, my $5,000 Rolex brought me only marginally more pleasure than my previously-worn $50 watch did. And of course, wearing an expensive watch didn't make doing 70 hours of boring, mundane work a week worth it. It didn't make giving up my free time to be Gus's slave worth it. It didn't make having hardly any time to see my parents, my friends or Olivia worth it. And obviously, it didn't make nosediving into depression again worth it, either.

Diary Entry: 15th May, 2012

Every week is the same: more boring work, more stressful deadlines, more late nights, more weekend work, and more having to cancel plans with my parents, my friends, and dear sweet Olivia. And as the weeks pass and the emotional toll mounts, I feel more and more anxious, more and more on edge, more and more miserable, more and more depressed. I just want to escape – to run away from the office and never return. To go somewhere – anywhere – where I don't have to be a management consultant. But I can't, I can't do that, and because I can't, I want to drink. The cravings come and the cravings stay – on the way to work, while I'm at work, and of course on the weekend – because I feel so drained and exhausted and fed up and frustrated, and because I know that in less than 48 hours, I'll have to return to my desk again. I try to fight them but they just keep coming, and sometimes they become too strong to fight, so I spend $300 at a bar slamming drink after drink until I can't feel my Blackberry vibrating in my pocket anymore.

And I think I'd be able to handle it, I just might be able to handle it if I could see some light at the end of the tunnel. But when I look around me – at all the people who are older and more experienced and who've been slogging away in the trenches for years if not decades – all I see are the bags under their eyes, their prematurely greying hair and their receding hairlines. I realise that they're stressed out people who do work that, while more challenging than the entry-level bitch tasks I'm forced to do, still doesn't really interest me at all – and they have to do it all day long and all through the evening, only to arrive home when their kids are in bed and their wives aren't far behind them. I used to envy those men their sports cars and their mansions, but the more I look beyond the material wealth, the less I want to see, and the less I want to be them when I'm their age one day.

And it makes me wonder, has this all been just one big mistake?

Have I spent the last five years striving for a career that I don't even want?

Isn't there more to life than just working hour after hour after hour in an office 48 weeks a year?

Is the only time I'm ever going to get to enjoy myself again or make lasting memories – like doing it in a Hello Kitty themed sex room, watching a live cock-fighting tournament or getting a ballcuzzi on a boat in the middle of Ha Long Bay – going to be during my four measly weeks of annual leave?

So I'm self-destructing, I'm exploding at the seams. What the fuck am I supposed to do? What the fuck am I supposed to do? I can't quit, because it'd be a waste to abandon a career I've spent so long pursuing, and because I'm not sure what I'd do instead, and because I want all the money I know I'll have coming to me so that I can give my future family a really good life. But I also can't stand the thought of staying in this job either, because it's making me hate my life, because it's making me want to get my old steak knife and slash up my arms and watch the blood spurting out everywhere, just so I can feel something different, just so I can release some of my built-up tension and finally settle down a bit. So what the fuck am I supposed to do? What the fuck am I supposed to do? WHAT THE FUCK AM I SUPPOSED TO DO?

Denial

As my parents, my psychologist Dr Kendall and Olivia had all counselled, I should've quit right then. Working 70 hours a week as a management consultant was making me depressed, and since there wasn't much to suggest I'd ever start enjoying it, I should've packed up my things and walked out the door. But abandoning a job you've spent years pursuing – particularly one that everyone considers to be the "Holy Grail" of professional careers, and one that I knew would afford me and my future family the most comfortable life imaginable – takes a great deal of courage. And at that point in time, I didn't have it in me to turn my back on the path I'd always followed. As a result, I did what everyone else who's too scared to change their current circumstances does: try to make the best of their bad ones. And when you're in a high-paying job you don't like, that means spending lots of money outside the office to try and escape your misery, and put as much distance between yourself and your work as you can.

So that's what I started doing. On the weekends, when I wasn't at work, I'd try my damnedest to have as much fun as possible. If I had the day off, I'd spend my Saturdays with Olivia, and of course, it was by far and away the highlight of my week. Then at night, I'd go out with the guys and get ridiculously shitfaced on premium bottled beers, fancy cocktails and top shelf whiskey. The next day, $300 poorer and horrifically hungover, if I wasn't forced to work, I'd sleep in and then try to do something memorable – like go race car driving, parachuting out of a plane or jetboating on the harbour – activities that cost a lot of money but gave me an adrenalin rush, a temporary high, and just like drinking did, an escape from my despair.

But when I tried to do that – when I tried to use money to buy me happiness – I became the very epitome of a dog chasing his tail. Alcohol – even premium bottled beer, fancy cocktails and top shelf whiskey – is still a depressant after all, and so will ultimately cause everyone who's trying to use it to find happiness far more misery than joy. And, as much as I tried to distract myself with the thrill of new adventures, it was always in vein, because even while I was zooming around a race track or the water or while I was tumbling through the sky, I was conscious of the fact that my high was only temporary, and that when it was over, all I'd be left with would be my depression. But even still, I kept at my job, convincing myself that I couldn't quit because I'd spent years working for this career and it would be a waste to abandon it, because I needed to make lots of money to take care of my future family, and because I didn't know what else to do instead. Meanwhile, I hoped against hope that somehow, some way, things might magically improve, and that I might all of a sudden start enjoying my life again.

I'd hoped that the New York trip might be that turning point, because like so many people whose lives are riddled with problems that they're not ready to face, I clung to the belief that a change of scenery might make everything better. It began like all the domestic trips did – working on my laptop at the Qantas Club lounge, and then working for most of the plane trip too. When I arrived in Manhattan it was just after five o'clock in the afternoon, and since I'd finished everything I'd needed to on the plane, I had a free evening, and I took advantage of it by doing a night tour of the city. It started off in the loud, crowded, brightly-lit Times Square, where we weaved in between all the businessmen, couples and groups of friends and marvelled at its grandeur before frolicking on to Bryant Park, the Empire State Building, New York Public Library, the Original MetLife Building, Grand Central Terminal, Saks Fifth Avenue and St Patrick's Cathedral. Most of the other people on the tour were young adults like me – backpackers from places like London, Canada and even Australia, and despite the fact that I probably made more money than all of them, I found myself envying their carefree lifestyle, envying their freedom, envying their joy that I felt so far removed from. After the tour, they were going to go drinking at a bar before kicking on to a club and dancing the night away, and they asked me if I'd like to go with them. Of course I wanted to. I yearned to with every fibre of my being. But unfortunately, I had to be in the office at half-past eight, so as they all hoarded into cabs together laughing and giggling and giddy to start their night of revelry, I hailed one of my own, and went back to my hotel room all by myself.

During my first week in New York, I worked 14 hours a day, but thankfully, I was given Saturday and Sunday off, and after having a sublimely heavenly sleep in until a quarter-past eleven, I worked on a PowerPoint presentation for a couple of hours before taking a walk to Soho to have lunch with Fumio – the guy who I'd met at the internet café in Japan more than two years beforehand.

We hadn't kept in touch. In fact, I hadn't spoken to him once since the day we'd met. But we were Facebook friends, and the week before I'd left Sydney, I discovered through one of his status updates that he was in Manhattan, so I messaged him suggesting we catch up sometime during my stint there. He was a good guy, and in a foreign city, it's always nice to see a friendly face. Plus, I knew that if there was anyone who would understand my misery, anyone who would understand the truth about how devilish those "Holy Grail" jobs could truly be, it was Fumio – who around the time we'd crossed paths, had just turned his back on a lucrative law career to pursue his dream of travelling around the world.

I saw him at a café near his apartment. He looked the same as he had when I'd met him in Japan – his black hair swept to one side of his face, his skin clear brown and his shoulders slim – although he did dress a little more "westernised", rocking a white Ralph Lauren polo, faded blue jeans and black Nike high tops with the big white tick. And of course, his English had also improved significantly during his two years of travelling.

'Jimmy my friend!' he exclaimed with a big wide grin, shaking my hand warmly and clapping me on the back.

Like I did most of the time those days, I felt depressed, but there was something about Fumio – the excitement in his voice, his infectious smile, or maybe just how happy he seemed to be – that made me loosen up and smile genuinely back at him.

'Hey Fumio. It's been a while, mate.'

'It sure has been, my friend! I had a feeling I'd see you again – but in Sydney, not New York!'

I laughed.

'How long have you been here?'

'About six weeks now.'

'How're you finding it?'

'Amazing, man! In New York, there's so much to do. Doesn't matter what time it is – morning, noon, evening or even in the middle of the night – there's always something to do. Perfect for a young man who wants to enjoy himself!'

'I'll bet. It's an incredible city, isn't it?'

'Of course! Maybe my favourite one yet!'

'Where else have you been since I last saw you?'

'Ah, Jimmy! Since we met, I have been to plenty of places, my friend! I started in China – travelling for a bit and then working in Beijing. Then some friends and I went to Hong Kong and we worked there for a while, but they both fell in love with two girls – two sisters, believe it or not! – so they stayed and I went to Singapore for six months, and you'll never guess what I did there, my friend! I worked at Universal Studios – as a stunt man in a show to entertain the visitors! I must say I was very good, and they were very sad when I left to London, but that was even more fun, because for the first time in my life, I wasn't in Asia. I was in your world – the *Western* world – and I liked it very much! Your world is very funny, man! No one takes their shoes off when they visit each other's houses, and all the young people live together instead of with their parents. And so much drinking, Jimmy! You people drink so much that I couldn't pour the beers quickly enough! But you people know how to have fun! You know how to party! And we partied so much over there – almost every day, my friend! I stayed in London for about six months, and I made some very good friends too, and after we'd all saved some money, we travelled around Europe together – to really incredible places like Switzerland, and Spain, and France, and Germany, and Amsterdam! Oh, Amsterdam! Man was *that* fun! And then I started an online business and made some more money, and then I bought a plane ticket to New York City and here I am!'

There was so much passion, so much energy and excitement in his voice that I really enjoyed listening to him.

'Tell me more, Fumio,' I said as we ordered a couple of pastrami sandwiches and a round of margaritas. 'Tell me everything, mate.'

'Like I said, China was the first place I went, and I had a very good time there! For the first two months I just "backpacked", as you English speaking people say – meeting lots of different people along the way. One of those people was Chao – I met him in Beijing, and together, we climbed The Great Wall, paddled along the Yulong River on a bamboo raft, did some trekking in the mountain ranges, and hugged the giant pandas at Chengdu. Of course, we did some very strange things too, because we were in China, after all! We bought live crabs from a vending machine in Hangzhou; visited a dwarf theme park near Kunming where all the workers were under four foot three; ate rabbit head in Chenzhou; seahorse, lizards and starfish at some other markets; and, believe it or not, urine eggs!'

'*Urine* eggs?'

'Yes! They are regular eggs, but boiled for an entire day in the urine of ten year old boys!'

'No way!'

'Yes way! This is China, man! They do some very funny things! And I'll tell you something else crazy that happened with Chao – when we were visiting his hometown called Wuhan, we got stuck in a really bad traffic jam. We didn't move for over an hour, and I asked Chao how long the traffic jam was likely to last for, and he said anywhere from a few hours to a few days to over a week!'

'Over a *week?*'

'Yes Jimmy, over a week! I couldn't believe it either! I was panicking like I was a crazy man, but Chao – he just laughed! He was laughing his head off while I was panicking! And I said to him, 'Chao, how can you find this *funny,* man? We could be stuck here for *days!*' And he kept laughing and laughing as he called someone on his mobile phone, and then not long afterwards, three men arrived beside our car on motorcycles – two on one of them and one on the other. Chao then got out of the car and climbed on the back of one of the bikes, and indicated to me to hop on the other. Then, he gave his car keys to one of the men who got in the driver's seat, and paid him to wait in the traffic jam and drive the car back to his place when the traffic jam was over! Meanwhile, the other two men drove us to a bar on their motorcycles and we all got drunk!'

'What the hell?' I exclaimed.

'Yes, Jimmy! It is an actual service provided by an actual company! And a very necessary one too, when you have 1.3 billion people in a country and traffic jams that can last for over a week!'

I shook my head in amazement.

'Yeah, I guess it is.'

'Absolutely it is! If we'd been stuck in the traffic jam for a week, I would've been late for my bartending job in Beijing!'

'Yeah, what was that like?'

'Ah, very good, Jimmy! I had lots of fun meeting new people and pouring lots of drinks for them. The other workers were very nice too, and I became very good friends with them. There were many nights when we would all sit around a table drinking *baijiu* together, and we would get very drunk indeed! The funniest time was when me and my friend Hua had a competition to see who could drink the most without being sick. I was so sure I was going to win, but little Hua had a much stronger stomach than I expected, so it was me who vomited all over my shoes! The way we'd set up the bet, the winner got to choose a punishment or a dare or something for the loser to do, and guess what Hua decided for me!'

'What?'

'He made me be a "rent-a-boyfriend"!'

'A *what?*'

'A rent-a-boyfriend!'

'You mean like a ... like a *prostitute?*'

Fumio roared with laughter.

'No Jimmy you crazy Australian! In China, rent-a-boyfriends do not have sex with the girls – they just pretend to be their partner at family functions so that the girl's family stop pestering them to find a boyfriend and get married!'

'O ... K ...'

'Yes, Jimmy! It was so funny! I was pretending to be Chinese, you see, and I can speak Mandarin because I learned at school and because I had lots of private tuition, but I do not know very much about China compared to a Chinese person! So this girl – Ting I think her name was – she invited me over to her grandparent's house to meet her family, and they started asking me thousands of questions about where I lived and about my family and everything like that, and I tried my best to answer them, but I made too many mistakes! And Ting's family figured out that it was all pretend, and they yelled at me to leave the house and never come back!'

'Oh dear ...'

'Oh dear is right, my friend! Man oh man did Hua and everyone else at the bar enjoy *that* story!'

'I bet they did, mate,' I laughed. 'I bet they did.'

'Of course, I was learning English as well,' he continued, 'five afternoons a week at a language study school. The first class I went to had a very crazy teacher, who as coincidence would have it was Australian too! He was trying to teach us the names of the animals, so what he did was, he would write its name on the chalkboard, and then pretend to be that animal so we could guess what it was. It was so funny – he was barking and hissing and meowing and mooing and growling and making all sorts of other noises, and then when it was time for the kangaroo, he made little paws with his hands underneath his chin and started jumping around the room! And it made me think of you, Jimmy! It made me think of you!'

I laughed again.

'I'm glad, Fumio, I'm glad.'

'Yes, man! But this class with the crazy teacher was too easy for me, so I had to move to a more advanced one, and that's where I met Kuo and Liang – who I studied with for four months before we went to Hong Kong together!'

'What was that like?'

'Oh it was the best, Jimmy! I did the same things as I did in China – bartending and going to English classes – but also, I started playing basketball again. It used to be my favourite sport when I was younger, but then I had no time to play because I was studying so much or working really long hours as a lawyer – so in Hong Kong, I got back into it. There are a lot of courts at Victoria Park in Causeway Bay where I was staying, and every afternoon, I would join in playing with the other locals before work. In the beginning, Kuo and Liang would play with me too, but then like I told you, after a few months they met two sisters in the craziest way I have ever heard of, and they fell in love with them and stopped playing basketball with me.'

'How did they meet the two sisters?'

'It's quite a story, Jimmy my friend! They had hired a car to go for a drive around the island, and then as they were cruising around one day, they saw two very beautiful girls driving beside them in the exact same car – a blue 2007 Toyota Ractis. They thought it was some sort of sign, so they decided to follow the girls – which they did for the next 15 minutes until they accidently crashed into them.'

I laughed.

'That is a pretty crazy way for them to meet.'

'I'm not finished yet! Now, no one was hurt in the collision, but the two girls were a bit upset, so they decided to call the police. Everyone waited around for about 20 minutes until two sexy police officers arrived, and decided that no one would be charged. Anyway, the girls then drove home, but my friends Kuo and Liang needed to have their car towed since their engine was no longer working properly, and the sexy police officers offered to drive them home. And on the way, everyone hit it off, and they decided to double date later that night.'

'That's an even crazier way of meeting someone!' I laughed.

'I'm still not finished yet! Now, what happened was, they had all decided to meet at one of the girls' houses that night, and the girl had written down her address on the back of her business card and given it to Kuo. But somehow, he lost it! So he and Liang spent two hours looking for it – even picking through the dirty rubbish to see if they'd thrown it out by mistake! But they couldn't find it anywhere, so Kuo tried to remember the name of the street and the house number, and after looking at Google Maps, he thought he'd found the place. So they both turned up to where they thought the girls where, but instead of it being their house, it was another pretty girl's house! Her parents were away so she was having a party with her friends, and to cut a long story short as you English speaking people would say, Kuo and Liang hit it off with her and her sister, and they fell very much in love. In fact, they are both getting married to their girls later on this year!'

I shook my head in disbelief.

'That really is a crazy way of meeting someone!'

'Isn't it, Jimmy! So after that, they stayed in Hong Kong and I moved to Singapore.'

'Where you worked as a stunt man for Universal Studios?'

'Yes! There was a whole big group of us – Sally the gorgeous blonde girl, Robert her muscly protector and husband in the play, and me and a bunch of other guys who were all the evil pirates. We would all do a live show together – a few times each day in front of lots and lots of spectators. It would always start with Robert and Sally rowing a boat together in the water, on the way to a beautiful island for their honeymoon. But then me and the rest of the pirates would appear out of nowhere in our great big pirate ship and kidnap Sally by lifting her out of her little rowing boat! Robert would cling on to her to try and save her, but we'd shake him loose on the ship and make him walk the plank! He'd fall into the water and we'd all think he was dead, so we'd start singing a song about how we were the kings of the sea and then at the end of it, we'd all aim our guns at the audience and spray them with water! Then, we'd tie Sally to the mast of the boat and continue back to our homeland. As we'd be cruising away, Robert would climb out of the water dripping wet and start racing around the audience, weaving in between the aisles of the crowd with his finger to his lips, instructing them all to be quiet before he'd sneak up on to the boat and then *bam!* There he was! One by one the pirates would charge at him, but he'd fight each of us off with a barrage of acrobatic punches and kicks, and then while we'd all be lying sprawled out on the deck, he'd untie Sally. The pirates would be really mad then, so we'd get up and surround them both in a circle. There'd be nowhere for them to run, so they'd climb up the mast! And when they did, they'd slide down the edge of the sail, dive into the water, climb into Robert's boat and start rowing away! And the pirates would all be going crazy! We'd all be yelling and screaming and jumping up and down, and then we'd drop a rowboat into the water and start chasing after them! Both boats would stop at an island and we'd all set to square off in the sand, and the pirates would start laughing, because there were eight of us and only two of them, and we'd think we were going to beat them. We'd turn to the spectators and raise our arms in the air hoping they'd cheer, but then Robert and Sally would boo us, and at their encouragement, all of the spectators would join in booing us too! When Robert and Sally turned to the crowd everyone would start cheering for them, and the pirates would get even angrier, so we'd charge at them and all start fighting. There'd be a lot of punching and kicking and yelling and screaming and amazing sound effects going on, but somehow, Robert and Sally would always be winning! They'd be beating all the pirates! And in the end, they'd knock us all unconscious, row back to the pirate ship, tear down the scull and crossbow flag and then sail off into the sunset together!'

I laughed.

'Sounds like fun, mate.'

'Oh yes, lots of fun! And the cast – we were all living at the hostel near Universal Studios together, and at night, we'd all drink and tell stories – especially me and Sally! We became very good friends, and then we became more than friends, and then guess what happened, Jimmy.'

'What?'

'We had sex!'

'Oh yeah?' I laughed.

'Oh yeah indeed! We had sex together! So I'm not a virgin anymore!'

'Wait … time-out. You were a *virgin* before you met Sally?'

'Yes!'

'But ... but you were twenty-*seven!*'

'Yes! Quite young for a Japanese man to lose his virginity.'

'Quite *young?*'

'Well, maybe not *young,* exactly. But something like one in four Japanese men in their 30s who've never been married are virgins, so it's not uncommon either, my friend!'

'What?' I gaped. 'How? Why?'

'Many reasons. A lot of us Japanese men are very scared of failing, so we're really nervous about getting into a relationship. Of course, our economy has also not been very strong over the last 20 years or thereabouts too, so it's been harder to get a well-paying job, which has made a lot of men lose their self-esteem. And you know how it is – no self-esteem, no girlfriend.'

'Fascinating …' I marvelled.

'Yes, but I no longer have this problem, Jimmy, because Sally and I had sex! And not just once, but lots of times! And not just in Singapore, but in Europe as well!'

'You guys went to Europe together?'

'We sure did! Sally is from London, and when she wanted to go back, I went with her! We both got a job in a pub, and after we'd worked there for a few months and saved up some money, we went travelling together all over Europe, to really beautiful and amazing places like Paris and Barcelona and Munich and Berlin, and lots of places in Switzerland and The Netherlands and Belgium as well! And during that time, I started an online business as a life coach, because everyone always says I'm such a happy guy, and I figured I could make an online course where I could teach other people how to be happy as well, you know? Because being happy is a skill like anything else, Jimmy, being happy is a skill! And it worked! I am selling a lot of courses – enough to let me keep travelling comfortably and to save some money – and I want to keep travelling, I want to travel forever, because it's my dream – my *passion,* you know? But Sally, she wanted to settle down and get a stable job, buy a house and have a quieter sort of life. So when I asked her to come to New York with me, she said no. And then, we broke up.'

'Oh I'm sorry,' I said. 'I'm really sorry to hear that.'

'I am sorry too, but that is life, isn't it? We go through good times and we go through bad times, and we just hope that we go through many more good times than bad. And overall, Jimmy, I am definitely having more good times than bad. When I was a lawyer, I was very, very sad – very, very *depressed,* you could say. But now, I am very happy, because for the first time in my life, I am doing exactly what I want to be doing. It may not be the "right" life for everyone – like Sally, for instance – but it *is* the right life for me, and because I'm living the right life for me, I am very, very happy.'

'That's good, mate,' I said, nodding my head thoughtfully. 'That's really, really great.'

Fumio called over the waitress.

'I'm very sorry, Jimmy,' he said, finishing off his margarita. 'I've been dominating the conversation! Let me buy you another drink and then you can tell me all about everything *you* have been doing during the past two years!'

So we ordered two more drinks and then I filled him in on what had been happening in my life, focusing on the recent present – how I was a management consultant, but I hated it. When I did so, Fumio sighed.

'This is a big problem that a lot of people face,' he said solemnly. 'When we are young – when we are in school and university – we are taught to study hard so that one day we can get a "really good job" – and when people talk about getting a "really good job", what they mean is becoming a lawyer, a doctor, a management consultant, or any other job that pays really well. So instead of thinking about what type of job they might actually enjoy and then trying to do that, many people just work very hard to try and get a really high paying job, without much consideration for whether or not they'll even like it. Then of course, when they get that high paying job, they often realise that they don't in fact like it, and that they've spent years pursuing a career they don't actually want. That's exactly what happened to me, and most unfortunately, my friend Jimmy, it sounds like it's happened to you as well. We both fell victim to the biggest myth that plagues the working world: that getting what society considers to be a "good job" – which society defines as a *well-paying* job – will make us happy. But the truth is that a "good" job and a well-paying job are often not the same thing. For some people they are – if they have a well-paying job that also makes them happy. But if they have a well-paying job they hate which makes their lives miserable, then how can anyone say that they have a good job?'

He sighed.

'At the end of the day, Jimmy, I don't think there's such thing as a universally "good" job or a universally "bad" job. In my opinion, there are just jobs that contribute to making us – as individuals – happy, and jobs that contribute to making us unhappy. The way I see it, if our job leads us to be happy and live the life we want, then we have a good job. But if it doesn't, then no matter how well-paying it is, we have a bad job.'

I sighed a long, long sigh. Everything Fumio had said had been along the lines of what Jessica had told me the previous year, just after we'd visited the slum in India together. Back then, I'd thought she was full of it. But now, after management consulting had led me straight back into depression's waiting arms, I couldn't help but agree with her and Fumio's conclusion.

'Well then by that definition, I have a terrible job.'

'So why don't you quit? Why don't you leave and look for a job that you do want to do? One that actually *does* make you happy?'

I repeated all the same excuses I'd used to brainwash myself, but Fumio wasn't buying it.

'I understand how you feel,' he said, 'because I've been there too. In fact, a while before I quit my job at the law firm, I felt exactly the same as you do now. But it's like what they say about the frog in the kettle. If you put a frog in a kettle of cool water, his natural instinct is to stay, because he likes it. However, he will also stay if the water gradually heats up and he starts to feel uncomfortable, because he fears the unknown, and because despite it being uncomfortable, it's not yet uncomfortable enough to spur him on to face that fear. In fact, the only time he'll jump out of the water is when the water gets so hot that it becomes completely unbearable.'

Fumio paused for a second, looking at me seriously.

'It's exactly the same for somebody like you who doesn't like their job. The water you're in is very hot, but as long as you can tolerate it – even if only just – you'll stay, because you're terrified of change and the uncertainty that comes with it. But for your sake, I hope the water gets so hot that you jump out and quit. It will be harder in the short-term – and you may even feel jealous of those around you who are still able to tolerate it for the time being – but you'll be better off in the long run, because accepting a life of endless discomfort or misery is hardly a way to live.'

He paused again, avoiding my eyes this time.

'Then again, it's better than being burned alive – which is unfortunately what happens to the frog if the water gets to boiling point and he still stays put.'

Fumio was exactly right. While the water I floundered in was blisteringly hot, I could still grit my teeth and bear it. Yet as the days passed in New York and the toll on my psyche continued to mount, the water got hotter … and hotter … and hotter … until on one Friday morning – less than two weeks after my catch-up with Fumio – its heat became unbearable.

It was nearing the end of a torturously long week. The project we were working on was scheduled to be presented to the client on Monday, and as was usually the case leading up to the delivery date, we were under immense pressure to get it finished on time. From the previous Monday to Thursday I'd worked an average of 18 hours a day, and it had broken me. On Friday morning, as I tried to wash myself awake in the shower, I found myself shaking – literally trembling from head to toe at the prospect of having to spend another 18 exhausting, mind-numbingly boring, soul destroying hours doing something I could no longer stand – so much so that I slipped to the floor and broke down in tears, crying and crying with my head buried in my hands.

I don't know how long I stayed there. Maybe half an hour, maybe 45 minutes, maybe a whole hour – doing nothing but sobbing uncontrollably as water from the faucet slammed down on my back. When I finally emerged, eyes blurred red and my legs still quavering, I discovered I had six missed calls from people on my team, demanding to know where the hell I was. I phoned them all back telling them I'd been up most of the night with food poisoning, and that there was no way I could possibly make it in. They were furious, ordering me to call a doctor immediately and do whatever it took to come to the office as soon as possible. But instead, I collapsed on my bed in an exhausted heap, and rang the only person I felt like talking to.

'Hello?' she answered.

'Liv …'

'Jimmy? Is that you? Is everything alright?'

'No … no it's not.'

'Why?' she panicked. 'What happened?'

'I'm just … I don't know. I'm ruined. I *hate* my life. I hate it so much that I just want to die …'

We talked for the next three hours. I told her everything – not sugar-coating a thing – and she tried her best to console me, like she'd done so many times before.

'You're going to get through this,' she assured me, 'just like you've gotten through everything else. But you *need* to quit your job. You just have to. It's as simple as that.'

As usual, I said I couldn't, and regurgitated all the excuses that held me prisoner of my misery – the first one being that I couldn't quit because I'd invested so many years pursuing a career in management consulting, and abandoning it now would be a waste.

'Jimmy that makes no sense at all!' she cried. 'It doesn't make sense being depressed for the next 50 years of your life just so you don't waste the four years you studied to be a management consultant! By that logic, a battered woman would never leave her abuser, because it would be a waste of the time she'd previously invested in their relationship. People would never get divorced for the same reason. Dammit, no one would ever go about correcting any wrong decision they'd ever made! You can't

168

live that way, Jimmy. You can't be a prisoner of the past. Sometimes, you have to let it go and make a new life for yourself.'

The second excuse was that I needed to keep my high-paying job so that I'd be able to give my future family a really good life.

'Jimmy, giving your future family a "really good life" isn't all about being able to provide for them financially. It also involves spending time with them; and being there for them emotionally; and being an active, attentive, thoughtful and caring husband and father. And it's really hard – pretty much impossible, even – to be all of those things when you're working insanely long hours and you're really depressed every day. I'm telling you, your future wife and kids would much rather be less wealthy and have a happy husband and father who enjoys his life than be filthy rich but have a husband and father who's miserable and hardly ever home.'

And my final excuse: what the fuck would I do if I quit management consulting?

'What do you mean "what the fuck would you do if you quit management consulting"?' Olivia exclaimed. 'You still have a commerce degree with first class honours in economics, so you could still get whatever other corporate job you want. Or you could work for the Reserve Bank or go into economic policy. Or you could focus on writing and try to make a career out of that. Or you could go back to uni and study something completely different. After all, you're only 23! You can still be anything! Absolutely anything!'

And I must admit, even in my shattered state, everything she said made logical sense, and as a result, I should've logged on to my computer right then and there and emailed my boss to tell him I was through. But I still couldn't bring myself to do it. It was just too huge a move, and at that point, despite the urge to get a knife from out of the drawer and slit my wrists, the water, so to speak, still wasn't quite hot enough yet for me to face all my fears. And, I was still in denial. Instead of accepting that management consulting just wasn't for me, I desperately hoped that I might be OK after a day off, or that maybe the next project I was on would be more interesting, or that God would intervene and somehow make me enjoy my work. Olivia pleaded with me to change my mind, but I just couldn't do it. To her grave disappointment, I just couldn't do it.

'I'm so w-worried about you, Jimmy,' she cried. 'I'm worried th-that if you don't leave your job, you're going to get more and more depressed. I'm worried that if you keep going the way you're going, that one day you'll snap and end up killing yourself ...'

'I won't kill myself.'

'But I'm scared that you might!'

'I won't.'

'Pl-please don't,' she sobbed. 'Please d-don't kill yourself. I'm telling you, Jimmy ... if you do, it will hurt me more than anything else we've ever been through together. It will hurt more than the abortion ... more than our break-ups ... more than our car accident ... even more than my PTSD. It would ruin my life, Jimmy, because unlike everything else we've been through together, I will never get over it. Never, ever, ever, ever.'

And at that, she exploded into tears, bawling so hard I could barely understand her.

'Pr-promise me you won't do it, Jimmy ...' I only just made out. 'Promise me you'll never kill yourself.'

I wanted to kill myself. I really, really did. But if there was one thing I could never do, it was intentionally hurt the woman I loved.

'OK, Olivia. I promise you ... I will not kill myself.'

When we finally hung up I felt horrifically distraught, and I needed to do something – anything – to loosen the noose around my neck and escape the depression that was ruthlessly throttling me. They say that people turn to suicide when their pain exceeds their ability to cope with it, and while I'd promised Olivia that I wouldn't kill myself, I hadn't promised her that I wouldn't drink – which next to suicide, is one of the most numbing forms of escape there is. So I got a glass from the cabinet, some ice from the freezer and the bottle of duty-free bourbon from my bag and started drinking on my bed until I passed out.

I came to in the afternoon with a nauseous gut, dry mouth and a throbbing headache, and emotionally, I felt just as ghastly as I'd felt when I'd woken up that morning. Once again, my mind turned to suicide, as I fantasised about slashing my throat, slitting my wrists, jumping off a bridge, throwing myself in front of a speeding train, overdosing, hanging myself, or since I was in the USA – the land of loose gun laws – I envisioned buying an automatic and blowing my brains out. But I knew I couldn't do that to Olivia, and since I felt too queasy to start drinking again, I decided to try and escape my anguish by fucking it away.

After doing a Google search, I located the closest brothel and lethargically dragged myself there. When I arrived, I waited in a room while one by one, a handful of girls came in and out so that I could choose who to sleep with. Since I wanted to bang one of them to run away from my despair as opposed to for pleasure, I didn't care who I did, so I told the manager to just fix me up with whoever she wanted. That ended up being a tanned, black-haired, 20-something year old woman called Cassandra, and I fucked her hard and fast up against the wall. It gave me about 20 minutes of relief, but when I was finished, I could feel depression's hands around my throat again, squeezing, choking, strangling the life out of me. Unable to face it, I then told Cassandra to do whatever she wanted to me – something to make me forget about all the "bullshit I was going through now", as I'd phrased it. She said it would cost extra, and I said I didn't care. She said she'd tie me up and whip the shit out of me and I told her to go for it.

One of the reasons some people with depression cut themselves is so that they can feel something – feel anything – that's not mental pain, because when you're tearing a blade through your skin, gritting your teeth and watching blood seep out and dribble all over the place, you're in so much physical affliction that you temporarily escape your mental anguish. And that's what it felt like to be tied to a cross against the wall and flogged. I screamed every time she whipped my back, but on the whole, I felt better, because it was less painful than my depression – even when I started bleeding, even when she'd whipped me so many times that there were tears in my eyes, even when she strapped on a dildo and started fucking me in the ass – no lube or anything.

'Ah! Ah! Ah! Ah!' I gasped in agony.

'Tell me to stop,' she snarled aggressively in my ear.

'Stop …'

'Louder!'

'Stop … stop!'

'Now scream, "stop raping me!" '

'Stop raping me …'

'Louder!'

'Stop raping me …'

She slammed my face into the wall.

'Louder!' she bellowed.

'Stop raping me!'

My eyes were watering. My nose was full of blood – as was my ass. I knew I wouldn't be able to walk properly the next day, but my session with Cassandra had given me some reprieve from my depression and possibly prevented a suicide, so I considered the $300 it had cost me money well spent.

Rock bottom

I returned to Sydney the following week, and after being given a day to shake my jetlag, I was right back in the office. Being the start of a new project, the hours had eased up a bit, but I was still miserable, still exhausted, still depressed, and still in desperate need of escape. And on the weekend, that escape came in the form of Stereosonic – a raucous, rowdy, daytime music festival.

I went with the boys – Corey, Brent, Sean, Chris and Steve. We arrived at about midday, and joined the crowd of people lining up to get in. After a few minutes, we found ourselves talking to a couple of blokes, and before long, they offered us some pills. Given that I was on two types of medication for my bipolar disorder – and two very strong types of medication at that – there was no way – under *any* circumstances – that I should've been taking any drugs. But, dying for some relief and emboldened by the dangerous "it won't ever happen to me" mentality, I bought one with Brent. It was wrapped up in a little bit of glad wrap, and I lodged it in my cheek to hide it. But as we were approaching the front of the line, a sniffer dog came and sat beside me. In an anxious panic I quickly swallowed the pill – but not before a copper saw me and yanked me out of the line.

'Alright, you're coming with me,' he said, grabbing me by the arm.

My heart was beating furiously as he led me to the police headquarters. As soon as we got there he started interrogating me, asking whether I was carrying any other drugs, whether or not I had a criminal record, and a bunch of other questions like that. After checking his database and frisking me thoroughly, he was satisfied that I wasn't a previously-offending drug dealer, but just another young guy keen for a weekend thrill.

'You know, I could charge you if I wanted to,' he said. 'But to be honest, I have more important things to worry about, so I'm going to let you off. However, I *am* going to confiscate your ticket, so you can forget about going to the festival with your friends.'

I handed over my ticket and he let me go. But, what he didn't know was that I'd printed off a spare one in case I'd lost it, so instead of going home, I waited for him to disappear before doubling back in and catching up with the boys.

'Dude! What the fuck happened!' they all exclaimed.

I told them the story and they all laughed their heads off, particularly Brent who was already munted off his pull.

'Pity about the dinger though, bro,' he said in my ear. 'This shit's fucking unreal! I am *flying* right now!'

And flying he was – jumping up and down, punching the air and dancing his ass off, all with a big fat smile spread across his face. And I wanted that bliss. I wanted that ecstasy. And since I'd already envisioned myself experiencing it when I'd bought the pill, not experiencing it now seemed an impossible option.

'Be right back,' I said to Brent.

I ran to the bar, bought four beers, took them into a cubicle in the bathroom, and then sculled them one after the other to try and make myself puke. I gagged repeatedly but couldn't manage to vomit, so I filled one of the cups up with liquid soap and then started chugging that. It made me gag as well and cough up bile into the toilet, but still not enough to throw up the pill. I hadn't wanted to shove two fingers down my throat, but I was so desperate for the drug, so desperate for a release that I jammed them down there, holding them up against my tonsils as I coughed and spluttered before finally hurling all over the ground. Someone outside the cubicle called out to me asking if I was OK. I muttered "yes" as I searched for the pill in the puke before I found it, unwrapped it, popped it, and then got the hell out of there.

For the next hour, I was OK as I danced with the boys and drank some more beers, waiting for the high to kick in. It came on gradually and then it came on fully, and for a while, I was just like Brent – jumping up and down and screaming and having a great time. But then my vision started to get fuzzy, and then I wasn't really sure where I was anymore, and I have this vague recollection of pulling out my dick in the middle of a mosh pit and pissing in my empty beer cup, and hearing all this yelling and shouting, and then I kind of remember falling to the floor, and hearing a lot of commotion around me, and then for the first time since I'd started working as a management consultant, I remember feeling relieved, and unburdened, and calm, and above all else free ... so free ... so unbelievably, wonderfully free.

Part IV

Wake-up call

She was holding my hand when, after much longer than usual, my eyes finally scratched open.

'Oh Jimmy! Oh Jimmy!' Olivia cried, bursting into tears and smothering my face with kisses. 'I'm so glad you're awake! I'm so glad you're alive!'

She threw her arms around me and sobbed into my neck. I was so confused ... so disorientated ... having no idea where we were or how Olivia or I had come to be there. Squinting over her shoulder, I groggily tried to survey my surroundings. The walls were pale green and lifeless, but for a small TV protruding from a stand in front of me. Directly below it were two cheap yellow armchairs, with Olivia's handbag lying face-down on one and what I recognised as my mother's coat tossed over the other. Beside me there were all sorts of medical machines and instruments doing something or other – but which I was shocked to realise were connected by needles and plugs to my arms and chest. I couldn't make sense of it. The last thing I remembered was being at Stereosonic, dancing with the boys to Avicii.

'What ... what happened?' I murmured groggily, gently pulling Olivia off me. 'Why am I in ... why am I in hospital?'

It was a while before she managed to stop crying, and compose herself enough to be able to speak. And then, with her face erased of everything but sadness, she whispered:

'You broke your promise to me, Jimmy.'

I squinted at her uncertainly.

'Huh? Liv, what are you talking about?'

'You promised me you'd never kill yourself, and yesterday, you tried to.'

'What? No, I just – '

'The doctors said they found drugs in your system. They said that you'd overdosed.'

I shook my head.

'Overdosed?'

'Yes. You had a drug overdose. You could've died.'

I couldn't believe it. Me, Jimmy Wharton, had almost died? Because of some sort of *drug overdose?* I cast my mind back to Stereosonic, trying to figure out what the hell had happened, what the hell had gone so horribly wrong when gradually, it started coming back to me: buying the pill as we were lining up to get in, swallowing it and the plastic it was wrapped in because of the sniffer dog, puking it back up again in the toilets, dropping it properly, dancing like mad in a mosh pit and then everything slowly, steadily, melting away from me.

'I didn't try to kill myself,' I said.

'But the doctors said they found drugs in your system.'

'I took a pill at Stereosonic with Brent, but only one – just to have some fun.'

'But you're on medication for bipolar disorder!' Olivia exclaimed. 'What did you think was going to happen?'

'I don't know. I guess I wasn't thinking.'

'You're fucking right you weren't thinking! How could you be so stupid?'

'You're right – it was dumb. But I didn't break my promise to you,' I stressed, squeezing her hand. 'How could you … how could you possibly think I would ever do that?'

As we stared at each other, tears lacquering both our eyes and slowly rolling down our cheeks, my parents appeared in the doorway and rushed towards me.

'Thank God you're alright! Thank God you're alright!' they cried, hugging me tightly.

For the rest of the afternoon, there was the emotional talk you'd expect, the 'I'm so glad you're OK' and the 'we were really worried' kind of stuff, while the doctors and the nurses intermittently came in and out, doing what they needed to. Olivia was there the entire time, reiterating what my parents were saying about how glad she was that I was OK and about how worried I'd made her, and while I knew that she meant every word, I also knew that underneath it all, she was furious with me. For as long as I'd known her, I'd always thought of her as one of the most caring people I'd ever met. Over the years, she'd dabbed Betadine on my bruises when I'd been in a fight, rubbed antiseptic cream into my wounds when

I'd cut myself, and stayed up all night with me when I'd been suicidal, holding my hand and telling me over and over again that everything would be alright. But she was also one of those people who believed that everybody has a responsibility not only to themselves, but also to the people who love them, and that for that reason, it's selfish of that person to do something stupid that puts their life at risk – and taking ecstasy at a festival when you're on two heavy medications for bipolar disorder certainly qualified. Consequently, I knew that sitting beside her overwhelming relief that I was OK was irate anger – at the fact that it was my very own idiocy that had nearly killed me. And in my books, that was fair enough, too. Like Olivia had said over the phone in New York, if I killed myself, it would ruin her life, and she would never, ever, ever get over it. When I thought about it like that, she had every right to be mad with me, and as the afternoon wore on, I became consumed with guilt for what I'd done not only to her, but also to my parents, and the boys, and everyone else who cared about me.

When visiting hours were almost over, Mum and Dad hugged me close to them, whispered again how glad they were that I was alright, and reiterated that they'd be back as soon as the hospital opened the next day.

'We'll give you two a minute,' they then said, looking at Olivia and me before stepping outside.

As soon as they'd done so, I started apologising.

I'm sorry, Liv,' I said. 'I'm really, really sorry.'

She shook her head.

'This is because of your job, you know that? It's because you hate your job that you took that pill.'

I nodded softly.

'Yeah. I know.'

'Are you going to quit now?' she demanded.

I looked away.

'Well, it's not that simple.'

'Yes it is.'

'But I've worked so hard for this career and – '

'Who gives a fuck?' she exploded.

Her outburst shocked me into silence. All I could do was look at her face that was glowering with fury.

'What's happened to you?' she eventually asked. 'You're not the Jimmy I fell in love with.'

'Huh? Olivia, what – '

'What happened to the Jimmy who was the best 15 year old surfer in the world?' she challenged. 'What happened to the Jimmy who after everyone said he'd amount to nothing more than a washed up jock when he got injured said "Really? Watch *this!*" and then ended up coming first in Year 12? What happened to the Jimmy who let me abort his unborn baby, even when he loved it and believed it was murder? What happened to the Jimmy who used to face his alcoholism head on, and his depression, and all the other problems in his life, and fight like hell to try and beat them?'

She sighed, shaking her head exasperatedly.

'You used to be so courageous, Jimmy. You used to be so brave. When did you become so scared? When did you become so pitifully afraid?'

And at that, she turned on her heel and walked out the door.

I was exhausted, but I hardly slept a wink that night. How could I, after what Olivia had said to me?

What the fuck is she talking about? I'd seethed as soon as she'd left the room. *I'm still the same brave, courageous guy I've always been.* But as the night wore on and her parting words echoed in my mind, I realised that, as hard as it was to admit, she was right. After all, the only reason I hadn't turned my back on management consulting yet was because I was scared – of the unknown inherent in starting from scratch. And, if I no longer had the strength to face my fears, then I was no longer the fighter that I'd always believed myself to be.

And with that realisation, I finally did what I'd needed to do, and then called up Olivia as soon as I knew she'd be awake.

'I just did it,' I said. 'I just quit my job.'

I obviously couldn't see her, but at that moment, I knew she was smiling.

'Yeah?' she asked. 'For real?'

'For real.'

'That's great, Jimmy,' she said. 'I'm really glad to hear that.'

'Yeah.'

'How do you … how do you feel?'

I sighed.

'To be honest, I don't … I don't really know. I guess on the one hand, I feel relieved, because I'll never have to work another day as a management consultant. But on the other hand … on the other hand I feel … *terrified*. I mean ever since I left high school – six whole years ago – I've been striving for a goal … and I achieved it. But all achieving it did was make me wake up every morning wanting to kill myself. It's like, I got exactly what I wanted, and it turns out that I didn't actually want it, and now I've thrown it all away, and I'm left with nothing. So what the fuck am I supposed to do now? What the fuck am I supposed to do?'

I sighed again, frantically shaking my head.

'I just want to be happy, Olivia. Honestly – all I want is to live a happy, healthy life. But evidently, I don't know how to do that. I try so hard, but at the end of the day, I really have no idea what I'm doing.'

For a while, Olivia was silent, carefully pondering her response before she finally spoke.

'I think that's it in a nutshell, Jimmy – at the end of the day, all you want is to be happy, but for years now, being happy has never been your *direct* focus. Your goals have always centred around being "successful" and being "rich", and while accomplishment and wealth can contribute to a person's happiness, in many instances, they also don't – which is how a person can find themselves having achieved everything they'd wanted to, but still be unhappy.'

She paused for a moment.

'So instead of focusing on being "rich" and "successful" and blindly hoping that being rich and successful will lead you to happiness, try and focus first and foremost on building a career – and a life – that makes you happy. If doing so leads you to be rich and successful as well, then that's fine. But if it doesn't, then that's fine too, because you'll still be happy, and like you've said, that's all you want.'

My mind was spinning.

To be happy, try and focus first and foremost on building a career – and a life – that makes you happy.

It was such a simple concept, but like Olivia had said, it's not something I'd ever done before. Like she'd said, I'd always obsessed over achieving a different goal like being rich or successful, and assumed that achieving that goal would make me happy. But in reality, that way of thinking had only led me to be depressed, and I knew that if I wanted my life to head in a different direction from the way it had been heading, then I needed to start approaching it in a different way.

'So if I did that,' I began. 'If I set being happy as my highest goal and threw myself into achieving it, then do you think I'd be able to do it? Do you think I'd actually be able to be happy?'

'Of course I do, Jimmy,' she said. 'After all, you've always been able to do anything you've set your mind to, and if you set being happy as your highest goal and then throw yourself into achieving it, I have no doubt that you'll be able to do it. I have no doubt that you'll be able to be happy.'

Goodbye, Australia

For the first couple of weeks after I'd quit my job as a management consultant and been discharged from hospital, I felt OK – maybe even pretty good. I relished the joy of not having to work in an office, and with my newfound freedom, I spent my days resting, recuperating, reading and writing *Lovesick*. That's what the doctors and my psychologist Dr Kendall had encouraged me to do – just relax for a little while, do the things I enjoyed, and put off making any major decisions about my future until I was ready.

But then, I crashed again – at the reunion my honours cohort had organised to celebrate the one year anniversary of our graduation. I'd arrived in a good mood, excited to see some old friends and catch up on their lives. But when I got there, everyone mostly talked about their jobs in the corporate world – about their lives as investment bankers, management consultants, stockbrokers, economists and internet start-up founders – while I was forced to say that I, on the other hand, was currently unemployed. Admittedly, the majority of my ex-classmates said that they envied me my freedom, and my "bravery", as they called it, to turn my back on a traditional career and follow my own path. But as they talked about their work and their plans for the future with such clarity and direction, it reinforced the horrifying reality that I, on the other hand, at the age of almost 24 and after five years of university, had absolutely no idea what to do with my life. And as the night wore on, I started to hear the scared Jimmy Wharton, the one who was too afraid to quit management consulting shouting in my head.

What the fuck were you thinking? Quitting a job as safe and secure as management consulting?

How the fuck can you possibly start over from scratch again?

You're not going to amount to anything anymore! You've completely and utterly screwed up your life!

And that voice was so loud, so convincing, that by the time I'd arrived home, I believed it – I believed every single word it was telling me. And then, back came my depression with a vengeance.

It would be so easy, I thought, *getting a knife from the kitchen and slitting my wrists. Or cutting my throat. Or jumping off a bridge. It would all be way easier than trying to work my way out of this fucking nightmare of being unemployed, having no idea what to do for a career, having no idea how to be happy, and having no idea about anything anymore. Damn Olivia, damn my parents, damn my friends and everyone else who cares about me. If it wasn't for them, I'd be able to do it. I'd be able to kill myself and end my misery. I'd be able to kill myself and finally be free.*

As I sat alone in my room, listening to the cicadas chirping in the midnight air, so depressed that in those moments, I literally loathed the people who loved me for burdening me with my own existence, I decided to get drunk to at least give myself some temporary reprieve. After stealing a bottle of bourbon from my parents' liquor cabinet – both of whom were sound asleep – I sat down at my desk with a glass of ice and three cans of Coke and started drinking away. After the first glass, I decided to amplify my attempt to escape by taking a wank, so I fired up my laptop to watch some porn. But at that moment, I noticed that Fumio was online, and instead of me watching videos of two girls licking each other's clit, the two of us ended up talking for the rest of the night.

When I'd turned on my computer, the last thing I thought I'd do was book a one way ticket to Brazil. But after speaking to Fumio for almost three-and-a-half hours, that's exactly what I did.

'I know exactly how you feel, man,' he said, 'because I've been there before. I know how scary it can be starting all over again. I know how confusing everything can seem. I know how hard it can be to envision a future where you're happy again. But if there's one thing I know even better than all that, it's how to overcome all of those worries and fears and rebuild your life so that you're happy again. As soon as I quit my job, that's what I threw myself into doing – seeing different therapists, reading countless self-help books and travelling all over the world to meet all sorts of people from all walks of life – all to try and learn how to be my happiest self. As a result, I made myself really happy again – so much so that now, I actually make my living through my online course that teaches other people how to be happy as well, and through my life coaching business where in private consultations, I teach people the same thing. You should let me teach you, Jimmy, because you're where I was two years ago, and if you let me teach you the things that I learned that helped me to be happy again, then I really believe that you will end up being happy, too.'

He then explained that at the start of the new year in a couple of weeks he'd be heading to Rio de Janeiro to hang out for a month before *Carnivale* started, and that if I went and joined him, he'd teach me everything he'd learned about how to be happy – and for free as well. On the one hand, it seemed absurd to just pack my bags and go with so little time to plan. But on the other hand, I genuinely had no sense of direction, no clarity on the future, and no idea what steps I needed to take from there in order to be happy – so travelling to Brazil to be taught by someone who'd walked in my shoes and had already figured all of those things out seemed about as good an idea as any. So with a bit of persuasion, he was able to convince me, and the next thing I knew, in a whirlwind two weeks I was saying goodbye to all my friends and packing my bags to move halfway across the world, with no idea when I'd be back and no idea how my life would look when I did return – assuming, of course, that I actually would.

On the day I was due to depart, Mum and Dad drove me to the airport, and because she'd really wanted to come and see me off, Olivia took public transport. My parents hugged me and said they'd miss me – Mum crying as she did so, and Dad with tears in his eyes too. Then, it was Olivia's turn.

'I c-can't … I can't b-believe you're actually going,' she sobbed.

'I know,' I said. 'I can't really believe it either.'

'I mean it's just so … so *sudden*, you know? So out of the blue.'

'Yeah. Yeah, it is.'

She wiped her eyes.

'What if we … what if we never see each other again?'

'We will, Liv,' I said. 'Of course we will.'

'But what if we don't?' she wept. 'You don't know what's going to happen overseas. You don't know who you might meet or how your life might change. What if you get a job over there? What if you fall in love with someone? What if you build a brand new life and never come back?'

Tears were now running down my cheeks too.

'We'll see each other again, Liv,' I repeated. 'We'll see each other again.'

She wrapped her arms around my neck, and buried her head in the nape of my neck.

'I c-can't imagine us being so far apart,' she cried. 'I can't imagine not being able to pick up the phone and call you … I can't imagine us not spending our Saturdays together anymore … I can't even imagine what it would be like wandering down to The Corso, and knowing for a fact that there's no chance I'll see you there …'

'I c-can't imagine it either, Liv,' I wept, gently rubbing her back. 'I'm going to miss you so much.'

For a while, we just stood there, holding each other, neither of us wanting to ever let go until finally, Olivia lifted her head from my shoulder, so that our faces were only inches apart. For the last time, I gazed into her sea-blue eyes, and then, as if it was the most natural thing in the world, we leaned forwards, and for a few magical, enchanting, celestial seconds, our lips met, just like those of countless other lovers who'd parted right there before us. But then, it was over, and I was at the departures entrance, waving back at her through the dozens of bustling people before turning the corner and disappearing out of sight.

Learning how to be happy

In time, it would become one of my favourite cities in the world – this sun-drenched, South American wonderland pulsing between majestic mountains and breathtaking beaches; thronged with bronze, beautiful people speaking mellifluous Portuguese; and so laid back that time often doesn't seem to exist. But unlike most wanderers, my first memories of Brazil's Rio de Janeiro aren't taking the train up to Christ the Redeemer to snap the obligatory selfie and marvel at the jaw-dropping, bird's eye view of the city, nor are they of strolling along the boardwalk of Copacabana- or Ipanema Beach; watching a soccer match at Maracanã stadium with 100,000 other screaming fans; listening to samba music at the bopping live music halls at Lapa; surfing the waves off Prainha; hiking through the lush, dense rainforests of Tijuca; sipping on an *açaí* at a local bakery, restaurant or juice bar; going to a *churrascaria rodizio* and chowing down on unlimited servings of sirloin steak, pork ribs, chorizo, chicken hearts, fillet mignon and grilled banana and pineapple; or drinking and dancing the night away to more samba music, bass-heavy hip hop, favela funk, sultry bossa nova or electronica. On the contrary, my first memory of the city was taking a cab from the airport through the hustling, bustling, horn-beeping streets and being dropped off on the steps of an apartment complex in Ipanema where Fumio was living, anxiously about to embark on a pilgrimage of self-discovery.

'How are you, my friend?' he beamed, giving me a hug when he opened the door.

I shrugged.

'I don't know. Not good. But I'm trying to hang in there.'

'Don't you worry, Jimmy my friend. We'll have you fixed up soon.'

I sighed.

'I really hope you can help me. I've been so scattered lately. So confused. And even though I know it's theoretically possible, I can't see myself ever finding a way out of this mess, or ever being happy ever again.'

'Wow, OK, we have a lot of work to do. Should we wait a few days before we get to it so that you can shake your jetlag and do a bit of sightseeing? Or do you want to jump into things right away?'

I was so tense, so on edge about the state of my life, and I was desperate to be free of that distress as soon as possible.

'If it's OK with you, then I'd like to start now.'

So we went around the corner to a *buffet a quilo* restaurant, where customers would serve themselves food like they would at a buffet in Australia, but instead of paying a fixed price, they'd weigh their plates at the counter and then pay by the pound or portion thereof. We loaded our plates up with three different cuts of beef, salmon, codfish pasta bake, mashed potato and *feijão* (Brazilian black beans), and after weighing and paying, sat down to talk.

'OK,' Fumio began. 'I guess it's fair to say that so far, your life has followed a very similar trajectory to my own, in the sense that you worked your ass off to get a high-paying corporate job, hated it once you got it, started suffering from depression as a result, and then after much deliberation, did the sensible things and quit – only to find yourself feeling lost, scattered, thoroughly unsure of yourself and afraid of the future.'

I nodded through a mouthful of pork. He had it down to a T.

'When I felt this way,' Fumio continued, 'I took a really hard look at my life, and I realised that the reason I wasn't happy was because up until that point, I hadn't made decisions that led me to be happy. Now, that may sound really obvious to you, but it was a very important observation to make, because it made me realise that making decisions that lead a person to be happy is a skill just like anything else – and just like any other skill, it's possible for people to learn it, to practice it, and to eventually even master it. So with that in mind, I became a student of "happiness" – as unusual as that may sound. I saw multiple therapists, read dozens and dozens of books on the subject, talked to hundreds and hundreds of people from all walks of life, and as you know, I've travelled all over the world – not just to tend bar, but to observe different cultures and meet different types of people – all to be able to better understand "happiness". And in time, I learned so much that I was able to transform myself from a miserable, depressed law firm drop-out into a happy, self-actualised life coach who through an online course I made, now teaches other people all over the world how to be as happy as I am.'

He paused to take a bite of his fillet mignon steak, and because it was so good, he held up his index finger, asking me to give him a moment so he could quickly finish the rest of it before he continued.

'To tell you a little more about the course, it covers a range of important topics that are essential to master if you want to be your happiest self – like how to build a career that makes you happy, how to stop worrying about things that are out of your control, why you shouldn't take people's actions towards you as personally as you probably do, and a lot of other things as well. Now, obviously you could've watched the course online like everybody else, but I wanted to talk to you about everything face-to-face so that you can ask questions, and so that I can try and help you implement everything into your life – starting with the first module we're about to discuss, because it's the lessons in that module more so than anything else that helped me get my life back on track and find happiness again. And, given where you're at in your life, I'm confident that once you learn them, you'll be able to do the exact same thing.'

I nodded.

'OK. I'm ready for it.'

So we polished off our meal, ordered a popular domestic beer each (Antartica Cerveja), and then dove into it.

'Alright Jimmy, to cut a very long story short, after quitting my job at the law firm and delving into all the research I did about how to be happy, I eventually learned that I had to build a career – and a life – that satisfied my "core values".'

'What do you mean by "core values"?'

'The things that mean the most to you in the world – like what gets you excited, what inspires you, what gives you a buzz, and what you're thinking about during those times when you're lying in bed and you feel so alive that you can't fall asleep. Whatever those things are – whether it's making money, travelling, being creative, spending time with your friends and family, playing sport or whatever else – *those* are your core values. And, what I learned was that in order to build a career and a life that makes you happy, you need to first identify your core values, and then set about building a career and a life that spends as much time satisfying them as possible – because it's when you're satisfying your core values that you'll be your happiest self.'

'How so?'

'For example, two of my primary core values are travelling and helping people. But, I became a lawyer, which is a career that is much more aligned with satisfying a core value of "making a lot of money", as opposed to satisfying the core values of travelling and helping people. So when I was a lawyer, I was really depressed. Now, I'm certainly not knocking being a lawyer – after all, it's a great job for someone if it satisfies *their* core values. But, it didn't satisfy *my* core values, so being a lawyer didn't make me happy. So I quit and started focusing on satisfying my core values of travelling and helping people – and as a result, I'm now much happier.'

He paused, looking at me carefully.

'Now Jimmy, I'm not entirely sure what your core values are, and if you're like a lot of other unhappy people, then you may not know yourself. But I can almost guarantee that whatever they are, those core values were *not* satisfied by management consulting – which is why you didn't enjoy it at all. And if you want to build a career and a life that makes you happy, you first need to identify all of your core values, and then construct a life that satisfies them as much as possible.'

I didn't sleep much at all that night, so consumed was I with what Fumio had said. As I sat up in bed in the spare room of his apartment, I asked myself the same questions he'd raised at the *buffet a quilo*:

What gets me excited?

What gives me a buzz?

What am I thinking about during those times when I'm lying in bed and I feel so alive that I can't fall asleep?

I pondered and pondered, and eventually, I had a list written. And, from that list, there emerged a very clear lifestyle that I undoubtedly knew would make me happy – but it was one that was so unconventional, so idealistic, so utterly difficult to achieve that I'd never seriously considered it before, and considering it now made me feel just as excited as it did scared.

The next morning, Fumio and I went to a bakery and each ordered an *açaí* – a purple Amazonian berry blended into a tropical smoothie – which we ate with freshly cut banana, strawberry and granola as we picked up from where we'd left off the previous day.

'So Jimmy,' he began, 'let's see this list of core values that you came up with last night.'

I handed him a piece of paper from my wallet, and he started reading it straight away:

- I value writing fiction, and above all else, writing fiction that I believe will have a positive impact on the world – like helping people understand depression.
- I value travelling. I love exploring new cultures and meeting lots of different people.
- I value spending time with my friends and family.
- I thought I valued making a lot of money, but while I was a management consultant, none of the expensive things I bought ever gave me any lasting joy, and I was miserable doing what I was doing even though I was getting paid really well for it. So, I don't think I value money as much as I thought I did.

Fumio read through the list a couple of times, nodding his head slowly as he did so.

'So Jimmy, are you saying that writing your book, travelling, and spending time with your friends and family are the things that give you a buzz, and that excite you more than anything else in the world?'

'Yes.'

He nodded.

'Well then it's no surprise you were miserable being a management consultant, because that's a job that ignores every single one of your core values – after all, nowhere have you written that solving business problems or making companies more efficient gives you a buzz; you worked such long hours that you had hardly any time to do the things that actually do excite you like write and spend time with your friends and family; you got to travel a bit, but you'd work so hard while you were doing so that you never got to experience that place's culture or meet any of the local people anyway; and the lucrative salary you were paid and the material wealth it afforded you were things that you turned out not to even value that much.'

'Yes,' I nodded. 'Looking at it like that, it's easy to see why I hated management consulting.'

'Ahuh. Now, like I said yesterday, to actually have the happy career and life you want, you first need to envision a career and a life that satisfies these core values you've identified, and then work your ass off to try and build it.'

That was the part that really scared me.

'I think … I think I've already envisioned that life,' I said shakily. 'But when it comes to actually building it … I'm not sure if that's something I can really do.'

'What is that life?' Fumio asked.

It seemed so outlandish, so pie-in-the-sky that I felt embarrassed even saying it.

'I'd love to make my living as an author … and travel around the world while I write my books.'

'That's awesome!' Fumio said with a perfectly straight face. 'That would definitely satisfy your core values, and I can really see you being happy doing that.'

'Of course I'd be happy doing that!' I blurted out. 'But writing is always just something I've done for fun. How can I possibly make a career out of it?'

'What do you mean "how can you possibly make a career out of it"?'

'Living a life like that … it's just too …'

'Too what?' Fumio pressed.

'I mean it's just … like there's a reason people talk about "starving artists", you know? Authors don't get paid very well, so it's almost impossible to make a living out of it.'

'Isn't J.K. Rowling a billionaire?'

'Yeah. So?'

'So there's clearly a lot of money in writing.'

'Well, yes,' I admitted. 'But you've got to be really good to get any of it.'

194

'Don't you believe that if you worked really hard then you could be really good too? And haven't you said that the book you've started writing is really topical, and that it has the power to help the 350 million people in the world who suffer from depression to not feel so alone, and to help everybody else in the world understand the illness better?'

'Yes, but – '

'So your book is really marketable, and could probably sell really well. So why can't you make a living as an author, and travel around the world while you write?'

'I just don't think … I just don't think I can.'

'But why not?'

At a loss for words, I shook my head, before eventually shrugging my shoulders.

'I don't know. It just doesn't seem possible.'

Fumio sighed.

'You know what it sounds like?'

'What?'

'That you're scared.'

'Scared?'

'Yeah. It sounds like you're scared of following a path that's much less secure than most other paths – and one that doesn't guarantee you a pot of gold at the end of it.'

'OK, you're right – I admit it. But don't I have a right to be scared? Like you said, there's no guarantee I'd be able to "make it" as an author. There's no guarantee that following that path is going to work. So what if I don't make it? What the hell's going to happen to me then?'

'I don't know, mate. But what I do know is that if you ignore your core values, you will never find happiness. The only way for you to be happy is to accept what your heart wants, and fight like hell to try and get it. And for whatever reason, Jimmy, your heart wants you to be an author, and it wants you to travel and experience things, and have a positive impact on the world. I understand that writing is a scary, insecure, highly competitive path with no guarantee of success, but if you pursue it, and you can make it work, then you know you'll be happy. But if you don't pursue it, then you know – from your previous experience as a management consultant – that you have no chance of being happy. So while you're allowed to be scared of going all out and trying to make it as an author, you should be even more scared of not doing so.'

I stared down at my nearly-empty glass of *açaí*, nodding my head ever so slightly.

'I think you might also be getting held back by society,' he said,

'By society?' I frowned, looking back up at him 'How?'

'Think about it, mate – when you were growing up, how often were you ever told by anyone – at any point in time – that you could write books for a living?'

'I don't know. I don't think anybody ever told me that.'

'Exactly. The only careers you were told about and were encouraged to pursue were traditional jobs like being a lawyer, a doctor, an engineer, a teacher, or a management consultant, and as a result, you've subconsciously been brainwashed into believing that careers that are outside of the box – like being an author – are not really feasible, or are too idealistic to pursue wholeheartedly. It's the same with so many of the people I've met travelling over the last two-and-a-half years. When I was living and backpacking around China, Hong Kong, Singapore, Europe and America, so many people would say to me, "you're so lucky to be able to travel full-time", or "I wish I was able to do what you're doing" – and I'd be like, "dude, *anyone* can do what I do! Anyone can get a job at a bar and travel around the world if they want to! You've just got to stop dreaming about it and have the determination to go out and do it!" And while *your* dream, Jimmy – travelling around the world supporting yourself as an author – is much more difficult to achieve than travelling around the world supporting yourself as a bartender, it certainly is possible. Don't abandon it just because all the people and institutions who gave you career advice when you were younger weren't imaginative enough to envision it, or weren't daring enough to pursue it, or weren't skilled enough to achieve it. If you can dream it, Jimmy, and you work your ass off, then you can live it. And don't let anyone tell you otherwise.'

For the next few days, I was still on the fence – being pushed forward by my burning desire to do it, but held back by my fear of failure, and, like Fumio had said, the deeply-ingrained notion that being an author wasn't a valid career path to pursue. But the more I thought about it, the more my excitement got the better of my fear, and like Fumio had said, I'd never be happy if I didn't follow my heart, so one morning, I just woke up and said, *fuck it, I'm going to give it my all to try and make it as an author, and I'm going to start by spending today writing* Lovesick *down by Ipanema Beach*. I stayed there from nine in the morning until seven at sunset, and as I wrote, I felt so liberated, so inspired, so utterly at peace with the world. Not only that, but as I was walking back to Fumio's apartment at twilight with the cool summer breeze in my hair, I felt on such a natural, blissful high from having spent the whole day doing the thing I love; I felt so excited about all the different scenes I was going to write the next day; and I felt so invigorated by the idea that maybe, just maybe, I could do this forever. It was the complete opposite of how I'd feel after spending the whole day slaving away as a management consultant when I'd leave the office feeling miserable, drained and exhausted, and I think it was that contrast, more so than anything else, that made me realise that I was, finally, on the right path. For the first time in months, instead of dreading my future, I looked forward to it with passionate, unbridled excitement, and I couldn't wait, I couldn't wait, I just couldn't wait to start my new life.

Olivia's diary entries: 15th January, 2013

Nothing is the same without him. The beach. The Corso. Sydney. My life. It was strange going to work for my first paid, full-time job as a psychologist at the hospital yesterday, and not being able to share it with him in some way. I know that if he was here, he would've met up with me for lunch, or taken me out for dinner, or at the very least called me afterwards so that I could tell him all about it – and even though he sent me a really sweet Facebook message wishing me luck and saying how proud he was of me, it's just not the same. It's just not the same as having him here. In the past when he'd go on holidays, I was only half-joking when I'd tease him saying that he was abandoning me, because I really would miss him. But now, knowing that he's travelling indefinitely, knowing that he may never come back makes my heart ache, and fills me with an emptiness so strong that I can't even put it into words.

It's not like I don't feel happy for Jimmy – after all, I'm so glad that he's feeling better, I'm so glad that he's got direction in his life again, and I'm so glad that he's going to dedicate himself to trying to make it as an author, because I think it will make him happy, and because I know he can do it. I just wish he didn't have to do it travelling around the world. I just wish he was doing it in Manly, like he always has, so that I can be with him throughout his journey, and he can be with me throughout mine. I want to be there to encourage him whenever he gets writer's block, to hold his hand and remind him that everything is going to be OK whenever he gets scared and doubts himself, and to celebrate with him when he finishes Lovesick, *when he gets it published, and when it becomes a bestseller. And I want him to be here with me so that I can share my life with him too, particularly the moment when I drive a car for the first time. I don't think that day's far off now, but where will he be for me to throw my arms around him? He'll be somewhere in Brazil, with people I've never met before, maybe with another girl's arms wrapped around him, building a whole new life of his own – while meanwhile, I'll be here, wondering, will he ever come back to Manly?*

We talk about gratitude

As January entered its twilight moments and *Carnivale* quickly approached, I continued living off my savings and keeping my expenses down, spending my days writing at the beach and my night's progressing with Fumio's course. In the previous week, we talked about the importance of having healthy, deliberate habits that contribute to building the kind of life you want, and the importance of letting go of anger and forgiving those who've wronged you so that you can find internal peace. After all of that, next on the agenda was the module about gratitude.

'Gratitude is an extremely important concept,' Fumio began, 'because not only does having gratitude make you appreciate everything so much more than you otherwise would, but it also gives you the positive attitude you need to be able to navigate your way through your trials and tribulations, and find the light at the end of the tunnel.'

'Absolutely. In fact, I've actually experienced that myself.'

'Yeah? How so?'

'A couple of years ago I went to Singapore, and just before I left, Olivia broke up with me. I was really depressed for about a week when I got there, but then my best mate Corey did something really nice for me, and I was reminded that even though Olivia and I had split up, I still had a lot of amazing things going for me – like the fact that I was much healthier than I was at the start of that year, that I was about to spend the next two months travelling all over Asia, and that I was surrounded by great friends like Corey. I then realised that if I can instead make a conscious effort to focus on all that's good in my life – if I can make a conscious point of being mindful of and grateful for all the blessings that I have – then I'll be able to find light even on my darkest of days, and be able to prevent myself from tumbling into depression every time adversity strikes. And after I'd made that realisation, I felt a whole lot better.'

'That's basically the crux of the entire module,' Fumio said. 'A lot of people mistakenly believe that having gratitude involves making light of your suffering, or guilt-tripping yourself into feeling better because there are other people in the world who are far worse off than you – but that's not what it's about at all. Instead, it's about being grateful for all the blessings in your life *as well as* feeling sadness, anger or worry for whatever difficulty you're going through – and thereby maintaining a healthy, accurate perspective of your situation, instead of dwelling so much on all the negative aspects of your life that you forget about all the positive aspects.'

'That's it, mate.'

'So how come you haven't been doing that lately, Jimmy?'

'Huh?' I frowned.

'Here you are, telling me that in the past, you've used gratitude to pull yourself out of a depressive episode. But when you were talking to me on Facebook the night I convinced you to come to Brazil, you were feeling suicidal, because you were terrified of the future, and you had no idea what to do with your life.'

'Yeah,' I said, not really getting it. 'So?'

'So,' Fumio continued,' 'if you were in touch with everything you had to be grateful for, your thinking would've been something more along the lines of, *OK, I don't know what to do with the rest of my life, and that uncertainty and lack of direction really scares the shit out of me. But, I'm really lucky to be surrounded by supportive friends and family who will be there to help me figure it out. I'm also really lucky that I've been blessed with a very smart mind, which means that when I do work out what to do going forwards, chances are that I'll succeed at it.* And if you'd thought more along those lines, Jimmy, then there's no way you would've catastrophized your difficulties like you did, and as a result, there's no way you would've been feeling suicidal.'

I sighed.

'Yeah, that's fair enough. As usual, you're right, man.'

Fumio beamed.

'Of course I'm right! And because I'm right, you need to work harder at practising gratitude – so that you're more mindful and conscious of all the blessings in your life.'

'But how does someone actually *practice* gratitude?' I asked. 'I would've thought that being conscious of how lucky you are just involves reminding yourself of all your blessings every day.'

'I guess at its core it kind of does, but having gratitude is so central to being happy that it's become a field of study in and of itself – leading to books and articles being written about it, studies being undertaken, and in this day and age, apps being developed to help us become more aware and grateful of all the beauty, joy and pleasure that exists all around us.'

'Do you know what some of those techniques are?'

'Of course, my friend! I teach some of them in my course, and I practice a lot of them myself as well.'

'Which ones?'

'Well, one of the biggest things for me personally is, instead of turning a blind eye to all the poverty, suffering and injustice in the world, actually making myself aware of it, and then doing something to help – which is why I donate 5% of the proceeds of my online course to Japan's biggest mental health charity, and why I'm going to Paraguay in July to spend three months volunteering at an underprivileged school. Not only does this sort of thing give you perspective and cause you to feel more grateful for all of the positive things in your life, but there's also nothing more rewarding than to offer your time or money to help other people. After all, just watching a little kid's face light up when you give them a yoyo, or having someone say, "thank-you, you've helped me, you've had a positive impact on my life", is truly one of the most beautiful feelings you can experience.'

I nodded.

'Yeah, I've really got to do more of those things.'

'Ahuh. Another thing you can do is to keep a "gratitude journal".'

'What's that?'

'So every night before you go to bed, write down five things that you're either thankful you were able to do that day, or five things that you're grateful for in general.'

'You do this every night?'

'Yep. Want to know what I wrote last night?'

'Sure.'

He unzipped his backpack and retrieved a diary that he opened to yesterday's date.

'OK, here are the five things I said I was grateful for yesterday:

1. *I'm grateful to wake up every morning in Brazil and go for a run along Ipanema Beach, which must be the most beautiful beach I've ever seen in the world.*
2. *I'm grateful to have been able to go to a* Churrascaria *for lunch, and eat as much meat as I could fit in my stomach.*
3. *I'm grateful to have access to the internet, so that I could talk to my ex-girlfriend Sally on Skype this afternoon.*
4. *I'm grateful to be able to afford an apartment with air conditioner, which I know will keep me cool throughout the night.*
5. *I'm grateful to have the freedom and the money to be able to travel around the world doing something I love for a living.*

'This list only took me five or so minutes to write, but doing this exercise every night really helps me focus on all the positive things in my life. In fact, studies have shown that gratitude exercises such as this – simple as they may be – actually result in increased alertness, enthusiasm, determination, optimism and energy.'

He paused, smiling at me.

'And of course, decreased levels of depression.'

Olivia's diary entries: 29th January, 2013

Jimmy's such an inspiration – the way he's left behind everything he's ever known and moved to the other side of the world, the way he works hard every day to try and make it as an author, and of course, the way he's thrown himself into Fumio's course to try and fulfil his overarching goal of being happy. In the few weeks he's been in Brazil, he's already made so many positive life changes – from deciding he wants to be a writer, to saying Grace before every meal and keeping a gratitude diary to remind himself of all the good in his life – and I am so, so proud of him. He's back to being the brave, courageous, determined Jimmy I've always known. He's back to being the Jimmy I fell in love with.

Seeing how much Fumio's course is helping him has also inspired me to take it myself, because even though I don't suffer from depression, I could always be happier. That's something I've noticed studying psychology over the years and particularly now that I'm working in the field – that the majority of people only seem to become interested in learning about how to be happier once they're particularly unhappy. *But I think it's something we should always be studying, because even if we're already happy, why not try to be even happier? And then once we're even happier, why not try to be even happier still? Why not endlessly continue studying, learning about and pursuing happiness, so that we can try and live the happiest life possible?*

Then again, while I do believe that even happy people should continue learning about happiness, can I really still call myself happy? I've always felt I could – even during the last two years while I've been recovering from my PTSD – but ever since Jimmy left, I don't really know. And if I'm being completely honest with myself, as I'm about to start Fumio's course, I actually find myself hoping there'll be a module about emptiness – because that, above all else, is the strongest emotion I feel these days.

We talk about worrying

'What's your biggest worry in the world, Jimmy?'

'My biggest worry in the world?'

'Yeah. You've been doing well lately, mate – pursuing a career you really enjoy; tapping into your core value of travelling by exploring a new part of the world; making sure you spend time talking to your friends and family back home on Facebook; building healthy habits into your life like going for a one hour swim every morning; and practising gratitude by keeping a gratitude diary and saying Grace before every meal – and, as a result of all this, you're feeling much, much happier than when you arrived in Brazil a month ago. But, because this life is still new to you, I have a hunch that you still stress and worry far more than it's helpful to, and that if you could minimise that, you'd be even happier. So, I'm asking you – what's your biggest worry in the world?'

Fumio was right – I *did* have one big worry that regardless of how much I was currently enjoying my life, shadowed me throughout every day – which is why when he asked, I was able to respond without hesitation.

'My biggest worry in the world right now is that I'll never make it as an author … and that as a result, I'll always be broke … and that because I'll always be broke, I'll never be able to get married and support a family … and that consequently, I'll end up dying alone and depressed.'

'Just as I thought, man – which is why today, I want to show you how you can stop worrying so much, OK?'

'Sounds good.'

So we ordered an *açaí*, and then jumped straight into it.

'Now Jimmy, when we find ourselves worrying, the first thing we need to do is to take a few minutes to *dissect* our worry. Specifically, we want to ask ourselves if there's anything we can do to fix the problem that's troubling us. Now if the answer's yes, then we need to turn our attention to doing everything we can to fix it. But, if we find that we're worrying about something that is out of our control, or too far-removed from the present for us to need to worry about right now, then it means that our worrying is unproductive, and isn't doing anything more than stressing us out and compromising our happiness.'

He paused to have a spoonful of his *açaí*.

'Let's now dissect your biggest worry, and let's start by you answering whether there's anything you can do right now to stop that worry from becoming a reality.'

'Yeah, there is – right now, I can work really hard to write the best book I can, so that I minimise the chance that I'll never make it as an author.'

'Which you're already doing, right?'

'Right.'

'So let me rephrase my original question, then: is there anything *more* you could be doing right now to stop your worry from becoming a reality?'

I thought about it.

'No,' I eventually said. 'I don't think there is.'

'Which then means that you worrying about not making it as an author is really unproductive, and isn't doing anything more than stressing you out.'

'Yeah, OK,' I admitted. 'I guess I can see that. But I can't help it, you know? I'm so scared of the possibility of it happening that I can't stop myself from fretting about it.'

'You can't help it now, but I want to show you how you can stop worrying about it so much – or hopefully at all. Here's what you do: the next time you find yourself worrying that you're never going to make it as an author, and that as a result, you'll always be broke, never have a family and end up depressed, I want you to *challenge* that worry.'

'*Challenge* it?'

'Yes. When we're jumping to conclusions, fretting over "what-ifs" and going crazy thinking about all the worst possible scenarios that could ever take place, what we're usually doing is viewing our circumstances in a much darker light than they really are. That sort of pessimistic thinking often comes really naturally to us, but in order to prevent our worry from destroying our lives, we need to retrain our brains to think about our circumstances more realistically – or in other words, in a brighter light.

'Now to do this, we need to start by zeroing in on our worrying thought. Then, instead of accepting it as a fact, we need to challenge its validity by asking the following questions. Firstly, *what evidence is there to suggest that what I'm worrying about is likely to take place?* And secondly, *is there a more positive, accurate way that I could be viewing this situation or circumstance?*

'Do you want me to answer those questions now?'

'Yep. Start with the first one: what evidence is there to suggest that what you're worried about is likely to occur?'

I thought about it.

'Well, there's no guarantee that I'll be able to make it as an author, so of course there's a chance that I may not.'

'OK. And what about the evidence supporting the fact that you may in fact be able to make it as an author?'

'Ah … well, I guess if I work really hard, then there's also a chance that I *will* be able to make it.'

'Sure, but I'd take it a step further. I'd say that if you work really hard, then chances are that you *will* make it as an author, because you've proven yourself to be really, really smart, and capable of achieving anything you set your mind to.'

I smiled reminiscently.

'That's what Olivia always tells me.'

'She's right. Now, how about the second question: is there a more positive, accurate way you could be viewing this situation or circumstance?'

'Yeah, how you said, I guess – by believing in myself, and knowing that with my work ethic and intelligence, I'm capable of achieving my dream.'

'That's true, but once again, I'd take it a step further by adding that the assumption you made that not making it as an author means you'll always be broke, which means that you'll never be able to get married and support a family, which means that you'll wind up alone and depressed, is a very, *very* negative way of viewing things. After all, if you're struggling to make ends meet as an author, then there are still lots of other things you can do in the field to help you get by.'

'Like what?'

'You're the writer – you'd know better than me.'

'But I don't know.'

'Come on, Jimmy!' Fumio pushed. 'Think! If you were struggling to make ends meet as an author, what could you do to keep yourself afloat?'

It was at least a minute before I was able to speak.

'I guess … I guess I could keep doing high school tutoring. It pays a good hourly rate, and it would still give me lots of time to write.'

'There you go. What else?'

'Um … I guess I could also write articles and stuff for newspapers and magazines.'

'You sure could. Hell, you could probably even start your own online publication, right? About an issue you really care about, perhaps?'

'Yeah …'

'Or you could go back to university and do your masters in creative writing – maybe even your PHD, too – and become a professor.'

'Hey, that would be kind of cool – nurturing young talent and all of that.'

'Sure! If you'd be interested in developing talent you could also be a literary agent, which would be pretty interesting too.'

'Yeah … yeah it would be.'

Fumio smiled.

'You see Jimmy, I really believe you'll make it as an author – you're too gifted and hard-working not to – but if you do end up struggling to make ends meet, then you're hardly destined to end up broke, alone and depressed. In fact, you're much better equipped to be able to deal with such an outcome than you think you are – which is apropos, because studies indicate that even if what we're worried about *does* occur, then 80% of us handle it better than we originally thought we would. So you need to give yourself credit for being more resilient than you think, and be mindful of the fact that even if your biggest fear of not making it as an author *does* come true, then there still exist a multitude of opportunities that will allow you to support yourself and your future family.'

'Yeah,' I nodded. 'Yeah I guess I can see that.'

'That's good mate, so every time you find yourself worrying, you need to challenge that worry by using the techniques we've just talked about, OK?'

'OK.'

'Sweet. Aside from that, just try to enjoy yourself. After all, you're living in Brazil and writing full-time – right now, you're *already* living your dream! So experience it to the full. Milk it for all it's worth. Live wholly in the present, and try to enjoy every moment as much as you possibly can.'

I nodded.

'Yeah. I think I tend to live a bit more in the future than the present, so that's something I need to work on.'

'Worrying about tomorrow's rain only stops you from enjoying today's sunshine,' Fumio said.

I laughed.

'That's kind of corny, mate.'

'Yes it is my friend, but it's also very true!'

'I guess you're right.'

'Of course I'm right! Now, let's go get a big steak with a huge side of beans and mash. All this talk about worrying has made me hungry.'

Carnivale

'Alright Jimmy, do you remember yesterday when we touched briefly on the importance of living in the present?'

'Ahuh.'

'One of the keys to being your happiest self is understanding that the present is all we have. Right now, this moment is everything, but if we fret about all of the what-ifs that could've happened in the past or that could happen in the future, we'll rob it of its joy. That's why the happiest people in the world live in the moment, because they realise that if they focus on enjoying and making the most out of all the individual moments of their lives, then all of those individual enjoyable, enriching moments will add up to an enjoyable and enriching life.'

'Yeah,' I nodded. 'When I look back, I can see that the times when I'm the happiest are the times when I'm living in the present just like you say – like when I'm writing, or swimming at the beach on a hot summer's day, or hanging out with Olivia on a Saturday afternoon. But it's hard to remember to just live in the moment, you know? So many times I just find myself stressing about the future or something without remembering to stop and enjoy what's right here in front of me.'

'Of course, mate – nothing comes more naturally to the human mind than worrying. But it's all a matter of practice. And to that end, it's now officially *Carnivale,* so for the next week, we're going to stop doing the course and just enjoy the moment. All we're going to concern ourselves with is having a great time, and appreciating how lucky we are to be in Rio de Janiero during the summertime at one of the best festivals in the world. Can you do that?'

I smiled at him.

'Yeah. I think I can.'

'Good. Then let's go to a bloc party.'

'A party? *Now?*'

'Yeah.'

'But … but it's eight o'clock in the *morning!*'

'It's *Carnivale*,' Fumio said by way of explanation. 'So get dressed quickly and then we'll wolf down some breakfast – we don't have long until the *bloco* starts.'

Because I'd been so absorbed in writing *Lovesick* and implementing everything I'd been learning with Fumio, I hadn't been focusing on *Carnivale* and all the chaos it encompassed. But at nine am, I found myself in the thick of my very first bloc party, which reminded me of the opening scene of the James Bond movie *Spectre* as we joined tens- if not hundreds of thousands of locals and tourists dancing down the street by Copacabana Beach, all following a giant float blasting music from its speakers that was so far ahead of us that we couldn't even see it through the throngs of people. Like everyone else we drank cans of beer and Skol Beats bought from locals selling them out of eskies along the way; intermittently tipped bottles of water over our heads because the sun was so strong and we were in the middle of a sweating, dancing, endless caterpillar of people; and since so many others were dressed up wearing flamboyant feathered wigs, superhero costumes, fluoro-coloured skirts and pants, brightly-patterned budgie-smugglers, painted-on masks, non-painted-on masks or hardly anything at all, Fumio and I both bought policeman's helmets and those floral Hawaiian things you wear around your neck, and continued bopping and weaving our way through the crowd until after two hours, we'd finally made our way close enough to the front so that we could see the singers, dancers and DJs doing their thing on the huge pink float with *"Bloco Favorita"* written across it. When it was nearing midday, the float finally stopped moving, and as everyone threw their hands in the air and jumped up and down to the music, I remember getting up on Fumio's shoulders and looking behind me as I fist-pumped to the beat, and seeing dancing, crazily-dressed people as far behind me as my eyes could see.

'This is unbelievable!' Fumio screamed in my ear once I'd gotten back down.

'It sure is, brother!'

'Are you living in the moment!'

'Yes!'

'Are you enjoying yourself?'

'Fuck yeah!' I screamed, putting my arm around him as we continued jumping up and down.

Then the next thing we knew, two brown, beautiful Brazilian women wearing bright pink tutus, white polos and glittery pink eye masks with feathers sticking out of them approached us out of nowhere.

'Where are you from?' the shorter one with a taut, tanned body asked me.

'Australia.'

'Ah, Australia! Welcome to my country!' she exclaimed with a smile, placing her hands on my chest and kissing my cheek.

'Thanks! So you're from Rio?'

'No, Sao Paulo. Roberta's from Rio,' she said, pointing to her taller blonde friend who was talking to Fumio. 'How are you enjoying *Carnivale* so far?'

'It's incredible! Are all the *blocos* this big?'

'Not all of them, but some of them are even bigger.'

'Even *bigger?*'

'Yes, the biggest ones draw crowds of over two million people.'

'Two million people?'

'Yes!' she laughed at my astonishment. 'Us Brazilians like to party!'

'I can see that!'

'I like your costume.'

'I like yours too.'

'Can we swap hats?'

'You want to wear my policeman's helmet?'

'Yes, and you can wear my mask.'

'With the bright pink feathers?'

'Yes!'

'I don't think so,' I laughed.

'Why not?'

'I think your mask will look better on you than it will on me.'

'You don't know that until you try it!' she giggled, making a play to take my hat which I fended off with a smile.

'I don't need to try it to know that I'd look stupid wearing it.'

'No one cares if you look stupid, Australian man. After all, you're at *Carnivale!* You can do anything you want here and no one will say a word.

It's all about letting go. It's all about doing what feels good. It's all about enjoying yourself and living in the moment.'

It was that phrase that did it, and the next thing I knew, I'd given her my helmet and put on her ridiculous pink-feathered mask.

'You look beautiful, Australian man,' she giggled.

'I can't believe I let you talk me into this,' I said, shaking my head with a smile.

'I can't believe it took so long for me to convince you!'

At that moment, Fumio burst out laughing.

'Hey, she forced me into it,' I said, assuming he was cackling at the sight of me in the mask.

'No, it's not that,' he replied, with his hand cupped over my ear. 'Her friend just asked me why you haven't kissed her friend yet.'

'What? We've only been talking for five minutes.'

'Well, apparently that's long enough, and since you haven't made a move, her friend thinks that you might be gay!'

I shook my head with a smirk, and then looked at the girl I'd been talking to who, as soon as our eyes met, grabbed my hand and started dancing with me. We smiled at each other as we did so, and with her mask off, I realised she was even more beautiful than I'd originally thought, with her soft twinkling eyes; long feminine lashes; shimmering brown hair; smooth olive skin; and her full-lipped, white-toothed, beguiling smile. Knowing I'd be crazy not to go for it, I danced up closer to her, and when our faces were only inches apart, I kissed her. She tasted delicious, and with all due respect to Olivia, her lips were the softest thing to ever touch my own. She kissed a little quicker than I was used to, used more tongue, but it was passionate and sexy in a primal kind of way as we pressed up close against one another and ran our hands all over each other's body. Then she turned back around to the float and started waving one of my hands in the air and grinding her ass on my crotch as everyone chanted *'Blo-co Favor-ita! Blo-co Favor-ita!'* at the top of their voices, and I remember thinking that I never wanted the moment to end.

Unfortunately though, the chanting at midday signalled the *bloc* party's finale, but to keep the good times going, my gorgeous Brazilian girl Bianca and her friend Roberta invited us to a barbeque at their other friend Isabella's place.

'You should let me show you around Rio,' Bianca said as we walked hand-in-hand towards Isabella's apartment on Ipanema Beach. 'I can be your tour guide!'

'That sounds amazing,' I smiled.

After weaving through the crowds of costumed people and the car-jammed streets, the four of us arrived at Isabella's building. We took an elevator up to the top floor, and then the next thing we knew, Fumio and I were drinking chilled Coronas as we gazed out at the breathtaking view of the beach, surrounded by at least a dozen Brazilian women.

'I'm a little bit nervous, my friend,' Fumio whispered with a giggle in my ear. 'I've never been surrounded by so many pretty ladies before.'

'Neither have I,' I admitted. 'But try not to worry about it, mate – they won't bite!'

'So what's it like to live in Australia?' Bianca asked, returning from the bathroom to sidle up to us, and affectionately slip her hand in my own.

'It's good,' I found myself saying, even though I wasn't sure if I actually lived there anymore.

'But isn't it quite dangerous?'

'What do you mean?'

'Aren't there lots of deadly animals there? Like sharks and crocodiles and snakes and stuff?'

I couldn't help but laugh.

'Is that what everyone outside Australia thinks?'

'That's what I thought,' said Isabella, who was tall and tanned and blonde and who I just automatically assumed was a model.

'Me too,' agreed her pretty, caramel-haired younger sister called Sophia.

'I've heard this too, Jimmy,' said Fumio, whose cheeks I couldn't help notice were slightly flushed with self-consciousness. 'In New York I went out for drinks a few times with an Australian girl I met, and more than once she was asked if she'd ever been bitten by something.'

I laughed again.

'Well, you'd have to be really unlucky to get bitten by anything, If you swim between the flags at the beach you'll be safe from the sharks, and all the dangerous land animals never come near the cities.'

'What about kangaroos?' Bianca asked. 'Do you ever see them in the streets?'

I thought about making a typical Australian traveller's joke and saying that we all had kangaroos as pets, that we'd sometimes ride them like horses to work, and that little kids could often be seen bouncing around in their pouches. But I decided not to perpetuate misinformed cultural stereotypes and just tell the truth.

'Nah,' I smiled. 'You never see them in the cities either.'

They all nodded thoughtfully.

'And where are you from?' Sophia asked Fumio.

'Japan,' he replied, with a slight tremble in his voice.

'I don't know anything about Japan. What does it have that's interesting?'

'Well … um … our toilets are pretty crazy.'

'Your *toilets?*'

'Ahuh,' he swallowed.

'How?'

As Fumio – perhaps unwisely – started talking about anus perfumes, vulva cleaners and automatically-warming toilet seats, Bianca led me to the other side of the balcony so that we could start cooking some food.

'This is called a barbeque,' she said, placing some chicken onto a grill. 'Do you have these in Australia?'

I burst out laughing.

'Yes, Bianca. We have them in Australia.'

'Oh, that's good!' she said with a completely straight face. 'And what do you do back home? Like for work?'

'I'm an author,' I said, for the first time ever.

'Oh, wow! Really?'

'Ahuh.'

'What kind of books do you write?'

'Well, the book I'm writing now is a love story.'

'A *love* story?'

'Yeah.'

'Wow … you're like every girl's dream!'

'I don't know about that,' I laughed.

'No seriously, you are!'

I laughed again.

'So do you write lots of sex scenes?' she asked excitedly.

'Yeah, quite a lot.'

'Can you read me one?'

'Sure.'

'Now?'

'Yeah, if you want me to.'

So I pulled out my phone, logged on to the internet, and retrieved my book that was stored on my email. Because she wanted to completely focus on what I was saying, she decided to stop preparing the barbeque, and because we were both quick to agree that it was a little bit loud on the balcony with everybody talking, she suggested that I read it to her in a bedroom.

Being a flashy apartment on Ipanema Beach, the room was high-ceilinged and spacious, with palatial, white marble walls; black marble furniture lined with books; and a crystal chandelier that hung above the queen-size bed in the centre of the room – which, after slipping off her shoes, Bianca lay down on.

'OK, Australian man,' she smiled, rubbing the mattress beside her in a slow, circular motion. 'Come here next to me and read your best scene.'

So I kicked off my shoes and lay down facing her, feeling a stirring of horniness as I began:

I popped the champagne cork, breathed in the subtle aroma permeating through the air before I slowly poured the golden liquid over her taut, bare, sun-kissed skin. I watched it roll down the contours of her body, my eyes drawn in particular to the stream between her breasts and the small, overflowing lagoon that had formed in her belly-button. When the bottle was dry, I placed it on the floor beside the bed, and as I knelt over her, I began to lick the champagne from the dimple in her chin. Then, I moved to her ears, circling them with my tongue, unable to resist nibbling on her lobe as her breathing began to deepen, and as she started to moan ever so softly.

'Wow …' Bianca murmured, quavering slightly beside me as her eyes fluttered open and closed. 'Keep going …'

Next, I moved to her neck, feeling her shiver as I grazed my teeth against her skin … backwards and forwards, backwards and forwards, backwards and forwards ... my lips tingling as I tasted the acidulous champagne and then softly kissed my way down to her chest, nuzzling my face between her breasts as I tongued her cleavage. Her moaning grew louder as I worked my way to her nipples, circling them slowly, then faster ... faster ... and as I felt them harden, I began squeezing them tightly between my thumb and forefinger. Her back arched up off the bed in response and she released a high-pitched cry, before my tongue swirled down to her navel and then her waiting vagina. It traced around her lips and then I dove for her clit, flicking it with quick fast licks as she clenched her legs around my head.

'Oh fuck ... oh fuck ... oh fuck!' *she screamed. 'If you keep doing that you're going to make me come ... ! You're going to make me come ... ! Oh, fuck! If you keep doing that you're going to make me come!'*

With my mouth dripping with her juices I kept on going, faster and faster, before with a loud, convulsing, uncontrolled shriek, she climaxed all over me. Trying to catch her breath, she lay there quivering, but stretched to, quite possibly, the horniest I'd ever been, I lubricated my throbbing cock with her come, pulled her down towards the edge of the bed by her ankles, lifted her up by the buttocks and then began thrusting myself inside her. She wrapped her legs around my waist, and then when she'd regained her strength, she used her stomach muscles to pull herself upwards, so that our torsos were writhing against one another's, and then with her arms around my neck and her head resting on my shoulder, we just kept going, and going, and going until gasping and shaking, I could feel myself coming, and in that moment, my knees were so weak that I fell forwards on top of her, screaming with my eyes clamped shut and my mouth wide open before we just lay there in a heap on the bed — exhausted, panting, and holding each other.

'Wow ...' Bianca murmured again once I'd finished. 'You're good, you know that? You're really, really good.'

'Thanks,' I whispered, feeling really glad that she'd appreciated my writing, and even more horny after reading the scene. And then, as we lay there on the bed looking into each other's eyes, one thing kind of led to another, and we started making out before inevitably re-enacting the scene in my book — right down to me pouring and licking champagne off her trembling body, fucking her standing up as she lay down on the bed, and then continuing to do so as she straddled me with her head resting on my shoulder – before, within a minute of each other, we both had our orgasms.

'Wow … you have sex even better than you write, Australian man,' Bianca smiled as we lay there naked together, staring up at the crystal chandelier.

'Thanks,' I laughed, turning over to face her. 'You're really good for my ego, you know that?'

She giggled, and leaned in to kiss me.

'You know, we should be each other's *amores de Carnivale.*'

'What does that mean?'

'It's a saying used to describe our lover during *Carnivale* – a time when we're not worried about the future, when we're not worried about commitment, when we're not worried about anything but living in the moment, and having the best, most passionate sex we can possibly have.'

'Sure,' I said breathlessly, feeling my erection return at the thought of making love to this exotic goddess for the next week. 'We can definitely do that.'

And so we spent the whole of *Carnivale* together. Some days, we'd sunbake arm-in-arm at Ipanema- or Copacabana Beach while making out, watching locals play *futevolei* (foot volleyball), or just sipping on *açaís* and coconuts while eating snacks sold by street vendors such as *esfihas* (flat bread with various Middle Eastern spices), *coxinhas* (deep-fried chicken pockets), *queijo coalho* (grilled cheese dipped in herbs on a wooden stick), and a variety of different meats and fish. Other days, we'd paint each other's face, dress up like idiots and head to a *bloco,* where we'd dance along to the music with Fumio, all of Bianca's friends and the thousands of other people there before kicking on to the next *bloco,* and then the next one after that, and then eventually on to a nightclub. On one special night, we all went to the *Sambodromo* to see the *Carnivale* parade, and drank beers in the packed-out stadium while watching the best samba schools in the world put on incredible performances on top of huge, stunningly decorated, brilliantly coloured floats that slowly moved from one side of the arena to the other. Of course, it goes without saying that every single night, Bianca and I also fucked like animals.

Then on the last night of *Carnivale,* she took me to a place called Lapa. Arguably having the best night life in Rio, the bars and clubs were so packed that people were spilling out onto the sidewalk; the sidewalks were so packed that people were spilling out into the streets; and the streets were so packed with people drinking and talking and dancing to the cacophony of reggae-, samba-, brega-, hip-hop-, funk- and salsa music that with almost every step you took, you had to push your way through a slim gap in the crowd to try and get to where you wanted to go – which for us, was a popular Brazilian samba club.

'Alright, Australian man,' Bianca smiled, 'tonight, I'm going to teach you how to samba, because you can't say you've been to Brazil if you haven't tried it at least once!'

'Um … alright,' I murmured nervously, feeling intimidated at the sight of everybody around us quickly shaking their hips and expertly shuffling their feet on the dancefloor. 'But it looks really hard.'

'It's not *that* hard. Here, I'll show you,' she said, placing my right hand on her back, her left hand on my shoulder, and taking my opposite hand in hers. 'Now, starting with your right foot, you want to go forward, and then backwards; then with your left foot, forward and then backwards; and then again with your right foot, forward and then backwards; then your left foot again … no! Not like that! You have to bend your knees more! And relax! You're too tense at the moment! OK, try again … right foot forward, right foot back; left foot forward, left foot back … no, bend your knees more. And lean your torso over more. No, not that much!'

'I don't think I can do this,' I said. 'It's too hard.'

'Of course you can! If you can write such good sex scenes, then you can definitely learn samba!'

We continued trying, and while I did kind of get the hang of the most basic steps, I never seemed to be able to do it in time with the music, plus I kept staring down at my shoes to make sure I was getting my footwork right instead of looking at Bianca, which she said totally took the romance out of it – so after a little over an hour, we gave up on the samba club and went to a funk bar down the street where a nine person band on stage played to a small but jam-packed, bopping room of people. We danced along with the rest of the crowd, me behind her with my hands on her hips, and her hands on top of mine tapping to the rhythm. Then at various intervals, her left one would slide up my arm, and cup me behind the head as she'd grind her ass on my crotch before swivelling around to kiss me hard and fast and frantically until the band would hit the chorus, and we'd re-join the rest of the crowd screaming with joy, bouncing to the beat and having the time of our lives.

'Now *that* was more my kind of dancing!' I exclaimed after we'd finally left the club at four in the morning when the band had stopped playing.

'I've got to admit,' Bianca smiled, 'that was a hell of a lot of fun!'

Hand-in-hand, we weaved our way through the main street that was still teeming with drinkers and dancers, before reaching a congregation of street stalls with long lines of people queuing up to order burgers, pizzas, cakes and meat platters.

'It's such a shame that *Carnivale's* over,' she lamented as we joined the shortest line.

'Yeah, it is. What time is your flight back to Sao Paulo tomorrow?'

'In the morning – at eleven o'clock.'

At that moment, our eyes met, and we looked at each other sadly.

'I'm going to miss you,' I said.

'Me too, Australian man. But you're going to come and visit me in Sao Paulo, right?'

'Yeah, I'd love to.'

'I can show you all the best places and the funnest spots to go out, and if you're still there in April, then we can go to the Lollapalooza music festival together!'

'That'd be great,' I smiled, leaning in to kiss her. 'That'd be really, really great.'

We talk about not taking everything personally

But like so many plans made between travellers, they never eventuated. When I messaged Bianca to ask how her flight was and to say that I'd enjoyed spending *Carnivale* with her, she never replied. When I followed up a few days later telling her that I'd found a cheap flight from Rio to Sao Paulo and asking whether it would be a good time to visit, she said that she was 'really busy with work', and that if I came, she 'may not have time to see me'. When I asked her if sometime in the next two weeks would be better, she didn't reply.

'Is that why you've been a bit grumpy the last couple of days?' Fumio asked.

I nodded.

'Yeah.'

'Why do you think that is?'

'What do you mean?'

'I mean why do you think Bianca not replying to your messages has made you feel that way?'

'Because I liked hanging out with her, and it sucks that I'm never going to see her again.'

'Are you sure that's the only reason?'

I met his eyes. He raised his brows to encourage me to dig deeper, and when I did, I realised that there was indeed a bit more to it.

'Well I guess … I guess I also feel … *rejected* by her. And, combined with the fact that Olivia rejected me too, I guess I feel that maybe there's just something about me that girls don't like, you know? That maybe there's something wrong with me. And I guess that's shaken my confidence in myself.'

Fumio nodded softly.

'I understand, mate,' he said. 'It's natural for us to blame ourselves whenever we get a negative reaction from someone, and automatically conclude that it's a consequence of our own personal failings or shortcomings or what not. But like I say in my course, when we do this, we're completely ignoring the fact that the way someone reacts to

220

us is not only a reflection on us, but also a reflection on *that person* and *their* circumstances.'

'How so?'

'Well for example, let's say that a person gives their boss what they feel is a really good piece of work, but their boss isn't particularly enthusiastic about it, and as a result, that person then concludes that their boss doesn't value their input and that they're the weak link in their team. But, isn't it also possible that their boss was just in a bad mood because of something else that's entirely unrelated to them, and that their boss's less-than-enthusiastic response to their work was just a projection of that bad mood?'

'I suppose,' I shrugged.

'What about when a person's partner says they're not in the mood to have sex, so they then conclude that their partner could be losing interest in them. Now, anything's possible – maybe their partner *is* losing interest in them. But isn't it also possible that their partner's just tired and not in the mood? Isn't it also possible that their partner's stressed out about something else, and for that reason, doesn't want to have sex? Isn't it also possible that their partner has something on early the next morning and just wants to sleep?'

'Yeah, it's possible.'

'And what about your current situation, Jimmy: Bianca not responding to your messages, and you as a result concluding that it's because there's something fundamentally wrong with you. But isn't it also possible that the reason she hasn't been speaking to you is because she's crazy busy with work? Or because she's scared of really falling for you and then getting hurt if you leave her to go back to Australia? Or because she met someone else? Or because she's coming off a recent break-up and on second thoughts, doesn't want to get involved with another person yet? Aren't any of these reasons possible – in addition to a bunch of other reasons that I haven't even mentioned?'

'Yeah,' I said. 'I guess they are.'

'And if you're honest with yourself, haven't you done the same thing before? Haven't you at some point decided not to pursue things with a girl for a reason that's actually completely unrelated to that person?'

'Hey, yeah,' I said, thinking back to Jessica.

Fumio nodded.

'Here's the point I'm trying to make: just because somebody has a bad response to something we do, we can't jump to negative conclusions about ourselves. When we do this, we are completely ignoring the fact that we are only a part – and often only a very small part – of that person's world. They – like us – have got a million things going on in their head that influence their decisions and their responses towards us, and for this reason, it's entirely possible that when they have a negative reaction to something we say or do, that it has absolutely nothing to do with us. And knowing this, and being conscious of it, can be a very powerful, soothing concept that can eliminate a lot of our stress.'

Olivia's diary entries: 20th February, 2013

As is usually the case these days, I've come home from work, kicked off my heels, made a hot chocolate, and curled up on the couch to continue watching Fumio's course on my laptop. I'm actually finding it really worthwhile, and since Jimmy's also doing it, it helps me to feel closer to him, and eases the pain of missing him ever so slightly.

Tonight's topic is regret. It seems that a few psychological studies lately have been centred around asking hundreds of people nearing the end of their life what their biggest regrets are, and then sharing their answers with younger generations so that they don't repeat the same mistakes. Having analysed all of the studies inside-out, Fumio talks about the responses in his course, which I'm now going to continue watching and taking notes on in my diary:

Many elderly people regret living the life that other people wanted for them, instead of the life that they wanted for themselves.

According to Fumio's course, this is one of the most common regrets – and also one of the most painful. The majority of respondents agreed that if you're not true to yourself and don't pursue your own dreams, then you'll always wonder what might have been – and that feeling will haunt you until the day you die.

They regret working so much

Everybody needs to make a living, but many elderly people regret working as hard as they did. As one man put it, 'looking back, I would've rather lived in a smaller house and driven a cheaper car in exchange for working less and spending more time with my friends and family'.

They regret not staying in better contact with their friends

Many elderly people found that over the years, they got so caught up in their lives that they gradually fell more and more out of touch with their buddies – only to regret it later on when they realised that love and companionship are the most important things in life.

They regret not listening to people older and wiser than themselves

Looking back at their lives, many respondents acknowledged that they could've made far fewer mistakes and saved themselves a whole lot of hassle, stress and pain if they'd made a point of listening to people with more life experience than themselves.

They regret spending so much money on material possessions as opposed to experiences

Looking back, many elderly people admitted that after initially feeling excited when buying a material possession, they gradually adapted to each of them, and consequently, that material possession eventually lost most of its ability to charm them. On the other hand, they said that the experiences they'd spent their money on became a part of who they were, helped them connect with other people, and gave them lasting memories that they still cherish to this day.

They regret not travelling more

Many elderly people lamented not travelling more when they were younger with minimal commitments, because they found that the more responsibilities they had and the older they got, the harder it became to see the world.

They regret not volunteering more

A lot of elderly people felt sad that they hadn't done more to make the world a better place.

They regret caring so much about what other people think

Many people reached the end of their life realising that what other people think of them really doesn't matter, and that if they'd known that earlier, they could've saved themselves a lot of worry and stress.

They regret not taking better care of themselves

Sickness and premature aging made many people wish that they'd eaten better, exercised more, and actually followed through with quitting smoking.

They regret holding on to grudges

As the saying goes, holding on to anger is like drinking poison and expecting someone else to die. At the end of their lives, many people realised it would've been better to have forgiven those who'd wronged them and lived in peace, rather than holding on to their anger and letting it eat away at them.

They regret being too scared of taking chances

Almost every elderly person interviewed regretted not taking the chances they could've taken. They all agreed that it would've been better to roll the dice and live with the outcome, rather than spending the rest of their life a prisoner of their fear and forever wondering what might have been.

The last lesson

'OK, Jimmy,' Fumio said, as for the umpteenth time in the last several weeks, we sat down at a *buffet a quilo* restaurant with our plates stacked high with different cuts of meat and a generous serving of *feijão*. 'We've finally reached the end of the course, and today, I'd like to share with you what I believe is the single most important lesson about happiness.'

He paused momentously, fixing his eyes on me.

'Are you ready for it?' he asked.

'Always.'

'OK, here it is: the single most important lesson about happiness is that in order to be happy, you need to set being happy as your highest goal. So many people set goals like getting a particular job, making a certain amount of money in a year, or getting married by a certain age – and then hoping that the achievement of those goals will then lead them to be happy. But a far more direct – and likely – way to find happiness is to set being happy itself as your number one goal, and then fight like hell to try and achieve it. Now, that doesn't mean that you don't set sub-goals like getting a certain job or making a certain amount of money – but it *does* ensure that the making of those sub-goals is in line with achieving your over-arching goal of being happy – as opposed to another overarching goal like being "rich", for example, which often doesn't lead people to be happy.'

'I know,' I smiled.

'Yeah, I guess you know as well as anyone that being rich doesn't mean you'll be happy.'

'No, I mean that I already know that the biggest key to being happy is setting happiness as your highest goal, and then fighting like hell to try and achieve it.'

'What?' Fumio exclaimed. 'Where on earth did you learn that?'

'From Olivia. That's exactly what we talked about after I quit management consulting, and since adopting being happy as my highest goal, I've been much, much happier.'

Fumio laughed.

'Well there you go, then,' he said. 'You know that it works. Just remember to always keep happiness as your number one goal, and to always, always, *always* keep on fighting for it – no matter how happy you are. Even if you already feel happy, keep on fighting for it so that you don't lose it, and so that you can be even happier still. Keep on trying to learn about happiness by doing courses like mine, and also by reading self-help books – which are the most underrated, underutilised resource in the world. Keep obsessing about happiness, keep striving for it, keep relentlessly pursuing it – and if you do that for the rest of your life, you give yourself the best possible chance of being lastingly happy.'

Goodbye Fumio, hello Olivia

Even after completing Fumio's course, I decided to stick around in Rio for another few weeks just to hang out with him, and to finish off the first draft of *Lovesick*. But as March rolled on and I'd sent the manuscript to my long-time mentor Pierce, I felt the itch to move on and see what the rest of South America had to offer. So, after going to one last *buffet a quilo* for lunch together and chowing down on all our favourite meats, it was sadly time for me to say goodbye to Fumio, who was planning to stay in Rio until June before beginning his volunteer stint in the capital of Paraguay.

'Thank-you so much,' I said, hugging him tightly and clapping him on the back. 'I was so lost ... so scattered ... so troubled when I came here ... but thanks to you, I now feel OK again. In fact, I feel the best I've felt in a very long time.'

'No problem, my friend,' he said. 'Just remember that you still have a lot of work to do, and to never stop fighting for happiness no matter what.'

'I know,' I said. 'This is only the beginning.'

I could feel him nodding into my shoulder before we eventually pulled away. When we did so, we smiled at one another, and I thanked him again before getting into my taxi, telling the driver to please take me to the airport, and then waving goodbye to Fumio before we turned the corner and were out of sight.

I spent the short flight to Montevideo, Uruguay reading over the Lonely Planet guide, learning about the city's eclectic, downtown architecture that's a combination of art deco, neoclassical buildings and worn-out skyscrapers; and looking at beautiful pictures of the avenue – AKA *"la rambla"* – that stretches along Montevideo's entire coastline and is lined with locals walking, jogging, biking, fishing, kite-flying, sunbathing or sipping the popular South-America tea known as *mate*. Of course, I also read about the local cuisine, and discovered that it included *asado* (barbequed beef), *milanesa* (schnitzel steaks), *chorizos* (sausages), *morcillas* (blood sausages that can either be sweet or savoury flavoured), *riñón* (grilled kidney), *chinchulin* (intestines), *chivito* (a sandwich full of steak, ham, cheese, tomato, lettuce and mayonnaise), *empanadas* (small pies typically filled with either beef or ham and cheese), and *flan con dulce de leche* (a sweet, custard-type dessert with caramel-esque sauce). As I departed the plane and walked towards baggage claim, I was salivating at the thought of getting a giant meat platter at Montevideo's largest meat market called *Mercado del Puerto*. But I was snapped out of my culinary imaginings and stopped dead in my tracks as soon as I noticed, standing right by the conveyor belt … Olivia.

Part V

Did you keep your promise to me?

I was so surprised, so shocked to see her that I couldn't move, couldn't speak, couldn't do anything but gape at her in astonished amazement. As soon as our eyes met, she froze too, and for several seconds, we just stared at each other breathlessly until the next thing I knew, she'd walked shakily up to me, and was nervously, anxiously looking into my eyes.

'L-Liv what are you … h-how … when did you …' I trailed off, still unable to believe it.

'J-Jimmy,' her voice quavered. 'I c-came … I came to ask you … if you kept your promise to me.'

I was so caught off guard, so thunderstruck, that in the moment, I didn't know what she was talking about.

'What … what promise?'

'You know …' she murmured. 'The one you made to me in Tweed Valley … when you promised that you'd move on from me. When you promised me that you'd let me go.'

My mouth went dry. I licked my lips, opened them to speak … but nothing.

'Just tell me,' she whispered as her eyes grew moist. 'Have you moved on … or do you still love me?'

As I stood there paralysed with shock once again, my heart started pounding in my chest, and my whole body trembled. I'd kept my feelings secret for the last two years, and for all the times I'd fantasised about us reuniting, making love, getting married, having children, and growing old in each other's arms, I'd never once imagined her asking me point blank if I still loved her, and what exactly I'd say in response. For I don't know how long, I just looked back into her watering eyes … speechless … inundated with disbelief, anxiety, fear, and maybe even a flicker of hope until, after what felt like forever, the words finally tumbled out of me.

'L-Liv,' I stammered. 'I tried … I tr-tried really hard to keep my promise. But as you know, I am a fighter, and what I eventually came to realise is that for better or for worse, there are certain things that I just can't give up on. And one of them … one of them is you.'

I clenched my face, all of a sudden on the brink of crying myself.

'Even after all these years,' I choked. 'Even after everything that's happened … I still feel as if you're the one for me. I still love you as much as ever, and no matter what you say, I think I always will.'

As tears began to leak from my eyes and my heart lay splayed open at Olivia's mercy for the thousandth time, I waited desperately for her response – knowing that she might be angry that I'd broken my promise; knowing that she might be disappointed, since as she'd put it in Tweed Valley, if I held out the hope that we'd get back together and I didn't move on from her, then I'd end up old and alone. Hell, for all I knew, she could've thought I was pathetic – for holding on to the fantasy like a love-sick puppy even though she'd literally gotten down on her hands and knees and begged me not to. But as I continued gazing at her, wondering what on earth was going through her head, her face gradually melted into a smile.

'I knew it,' she beamed. 'As I was flying here, that's what I was counting on – the fact that you're a fighter. The fact that you're so strong that you can't help but follow your heart no matter what.'

My whole body started shaking even more so.

'L-Liv what are you … what are you trying to say?'

She wiped her eyes, and reached her arms up around my neck.

'I'm tr-trying to say …' she smiled through tears. 'I'm trying to say that I'm glad you broke your promise … because the reason why I'm here is to tell you that I love you too, and that I want more than anything for us to get back together again.'

I stared at her … astounded … unable to believe my ears, before her hands slid up to my cheeks, and she pulled me in to the most ethereal, enraptured, enchanting kiss.

Oh my God! my mind hysterically raced. *I'm kissing Olivia! I'm kissing Olivia! I'm in Uruguay and I'm kissing Olivia! She came here for me! She came all the way here for me! To tell me she loves me! To tell me she wants to be my girlfriend again! Oh my God, Olivia is my girlfriend again! Olivia is my girlfriend again! After everything that's happened, Olivia is my girlfriend again!!!!!!!*

I was so suffused with joy, so flooded with ecstasy, so wondrously, ardently, deliriously euphoric that I started kissing her faster, harder, hungrier, and she kissed me back just as eagerly as we held each other tightly, gripped fistfuls of each other's hair, ran our hands all over each other's back and pressed our bodies so close together that my hard on was right up against her crotch, before unable to help ourselves, we started grinding against one another – which prompted a 50-something year old English woman to tap me forcefully on the shoulder and disgustedly tell us to "save it for the hotel room". So we grabbed our stuff, raced elatedly up to the first taxi in the rank, and jumped in the back seat with our hands all over each other.

'San Jose Hostel,' I said to the driver, thrusting a piece of paper towards him with the address written on it before Olivia and I frantically started kissing again with my fingers in her hair, her hands underneath my shirt and her bare, sun-kissed legs lying over my lap as we forgot about the taxi driver, forgot we were even in a taxi and just kept kissing, and kissing, and kissing until we heard a pounding on the clear screen that divided the front and the back seats. It was the driver – we had arrived! Snatching up our luggage, we tipped him big and then rang the doorbell of the hostel before wrapping our arms around each other and starting to make out again, unable to keep our hands off one another even for the few seconds it took for us to get buzzed in. As soon as we were we bolted hand-in-hand up the stairs, immediately asked if I could change my reservation from a dorm to a private room, paid the money, giddily said we'd take the tour later and then there we found ourselves, alone in a bedroom, like we'd been so many times before, but never with so much lust, never with so much unbridled desire as I fumbled with the buttons of her blouse, as she pulled down my shorts and underwear, and when they were around my ankles, she pushed me onto the bed, tore them from my feet and took my balls in her mouth, tonguing them rapidly as I grunted through gritted teeth, clenched a fistful of her hair before she started licking my shaft, and when I was dripping wet from her saliva, she took my aching cock in her mouth. I let out a small cry as soon as she did so, and moaned as she moved her head up and down, up and down, really taking me up to the back of her throat, jerking off the bottom of my dick that couldn't fit inside her, just the way she knew I liked it as my whole body quivered beneath her, as I reached for her hand, clutched it in my palm before knowing I was getting close to coming, she rolled off me onto her back, and took my hand to start rubbing her crotch over her short denim shorts.

235

I got to my knees and quickly undressed her before I buried my face in between her legs, felt her juices moisten my forehead, eyelids, nose and cheeks as I started licking her clit, massaging her hot, sweaty, writhing thighs as she shrieked and panted, and as I started tonguing her faster, I slid my fingers insider her, furiously stroking the very back of her pussy as she arched her bottom off the bed so that I could get deeper inside her, as she gyrated her hips in sync with my fingers, as she cried out even louder and wrapped her legs around my head.

'Oh fuck!' she screamed. 'You're going to make me come! You're going to make me come!'

And I wanted her to, I wanted her to come so fucking badly, I wanted her to squirt all over my face and I wanted to lick it all up, because when you're with the woman you love, it really does taste great, and then I wanted to wipe whatever was left all over my prick and then use it as lube to start fucking her, because I had to be inside her, I had to be side her, after so long apart I had to be inside her, so as soon as she came with a loud, high-pitched scream that's exactly what I did – licking my lips, lathering my cock and then pulling her down on top of me before, for the first time in over two long, lonely years, I entered her.

We both gasped as soon as it happened, and then started fucking hard and fast, too horny for gentility, too eager to take it slow as I held her firmly by the hips and rocked her on top of me, back and forth and back and forth as I moaned with passion, as Olivia screamed with her eyes tensed shut and her mouth wide open before I started squeezing her breasts, pinching her hard, erect nipples as the bed creaked and squeaked and banged against the wall, and even though her being on top had never been my favourite position, it was just how I wanted it since after so long apart, I was desperate to see her body, desperate to look at her tits, desperate to get myself off to her orgasmic face, her mouth making a perfect "O" when she climaxed all over again. Knowing I wasn't far off myself, I flipped her over and started thrusting even harder, pinning her arms down to the bed as she continued screaming, as her head tossed theatrically from side to side before she pulled my face towards her and started nibbling my neck, tonguing my ear, penetrating all the way inside it which made me go fucking wild and I could feel myself coming, I could feel myself coming …

'Oh fuck, Olivia!' I cried. 'Oh fuck, oh fuck, oh fuck!'

And then it was over, and in a panting, trembling, rapturous heap, I collapsed on top of her.

I don't know how long we lay there, doing nothing but holding each other. After all, when you're with the one you adore, the hands of time tend to turn unnoticed, and you can effortlessly while away hours just cocooned in the warmth of their arms. Eventually though, I rolled off her torso, and lay propped up on my elbow as we gazed into one another's eyes. I ran my fingers through her thin brown hair, and she brought my free hand to her lips, kissing each of my fingertips, one by one, before tracing her nails over the stubble of my jawline.

'What are you thinking about, baby?' she eventually smiled.

Baby ... it was a name that was so familiar, yet one that I hadn't heard her call me for such a long time that I savoured the sound of it in her mellifluous voice, before finally opening my mouth to answer.

'I was thinking about how when I woke up this morning, the last thing I expected was to see you, and for the two of us to spend the afternoon in bed together. And then, I was thinking about how happy I am that you're actually here and that we're back together again, and how I think this is honestly the best day of my life. And then ... and then I was wondering about what had changed your mind ... wondering what had caused you to go from begging on your knees for me to move on from you to flying half-way around the world to tell me you love me.'

She smiled again, inching her fingers up into my hair.

'It wasn't really one thing in particular that changed my mind ... more like a combination of things, I guess. As I continued to recover from my PTSD, I gradually started to think that maybe you'd been right in Tweed Valley when you'd said it was messing with my mind, and that my illness was the real reason why I was afraid of being with you – because the more time that passed, the less scary it seemed. Then when you left for Brazil, I just found myself missing you so, so unbelievably much. But what really tipped me over the edge ... what really tipped me over the edge was doing the module about regret in Fumio's course – when he said that what so many elderly people lamented was not taking the chances they could've taken, and therefore spending the rest of their life wondering what might have been. And Jimmy even though ... even though I was scared of coming all the way here, because I had to give up my job to do so, and because for all I knew, you may've already moved on from me and then I would've been heartbroken, I knew that if I didn't do it, and that if you fell in love with someone else and I never saw you again, that it would haunt me every day for the rest of my life. So I had to come. I had to come and take the chance.'

'Wow ...' I murmured breathlessly, still not quite able to believe that she was actually here and that we were one again. 'But Liv, you ... you could've just sent me a Facebook message, you know? Or just called. So why did you ... why did you come all the way to Uruguay to tell me?'

She gently pulled me in to kiss her.

'After everything we've been through together, don't you think me asking you if you still loved me was something that I should've done face-to-face? And, if you were still in love with me – if you'd actually waited for me to change my mind for the last two years even though I'd literally gotten down on my knees and begged you not to – then flying here to see you was the least I could do.'

'But what about your job?' I asked. 'You've worked so hard to get a position at Manly Hospital, and now you've ... now you've *quit?*'

Once again, she smiled her warm, beautiful, vivacious smile.

'A certain soon-to-be published author inspired me to follow my heart, and for the indefinite future, my heart yearns to travel with the guy I love. After all,' she winked, 'we have a *lot* of lost time to make up for.'

I stared at her blissfully, reflecting her jubilant, radiant grin before I kissed her, and then one thing led to another and we made love again, and then for a third time, and then one hour later, for a fourth – where, with our heads resting on the pillow, I lay behind her, and slowly and tenderly moved inside her to the rhythm of our breathing. If we could've, I think we would've stayed in there all night, but hunger eventually led us out to the sunset-lit streets, where we walked hand-in-hand along *la rambla*, marvelling at the beauty of the beach against the backdrop of the orange-yellow sky. I was so happy, so ebullient, so flushed with love that I beamed at all the walkers, joggers, couples and groups of friends passing by, and of course also at Olivia – the holder of my heart, the kindred spirit of my soul, my everything in that moment and I hoped forever. When we saw a *chivito* stand, we stopped and ordered two, and as we waited for them to be cooked, we kissed each other softly.

'Let me get these,' I said when they were ready. 'After you flew all the way here, the least I can do is buy you dinner.'

She giggled.

'Always the gentleman.'

Since my board shorts didn't have any pockets, she'd been minding my wallet in her handbag, and when the store owner told her the price, she took it out and handed him the money. As I picked up the food, I expected her to close my wallet and put it away. But instead, she just stood there staring at it, while her glistening lips widened into an awestruck smile.

'What is it, baby?' I asked.

With her face still glowing, she turned my wallet around to show me, and there it was: the picture of her smiling, with her hair brushed to one side and blowing slightly in the wind, and her warm blue eyes staring straight into mine. The picture that I'd carried with me in my pocket, every single day, during all the months I hoped and prayed that she'd come back to me.

'You never removed it?' she asked incredulously. 'You've actually kept it with you all this time?'

'Of course!'

She was smiling so giddily that she was almost laughing, before to my surprise, she eagerly rummaged through her handbag, retrieved her own purse and then excitedly handed it to me.

'What?' I said.

'Just open it!'

So I did so, and then the next thing I knew, I was staring at my very own face – a shirtless, grinning picture of myself that Olivia had taken at Manly Beach while we were still together. I was astonished.

'You've … you've carried this with you the whole time as well?'

'No,' she admitted. 'I only put it in there a couple of days ago – on the morning I took the flight to come here and see you. But while I was in the air, I'd take it out and gaze into your eyes, and talk to you, and sometimes, I'd even bring you to my lips and kiss you. I guess that in a way, doing so just made us feel closer.'

'I know what you mean,' I beamed, thinking back to all the times I'd done the same thing with her picture. 'I know what you mean exactly.'

'The woman sitting next to me though must've thought I was crazy,' she laughed, as we continued strolling along *la rambla*. 'And it didn't help that when she woke up in the middle of the night to go to the toilet, I was crying.'

'Why were you crying?'

'I had a nightmare,' she said softly, 'that when I arrived at the airport, I found you kissing another girl. And then while she was glaring at me, you said that it'd been over for years, and you told me to go back to Australia.'

I put my arm around her and gently caressed her shoulder.

'I'm surprised you were so nervous that I wouldn't want to be with you. Surely over the last two years, you must've at least suspected that I was still in love with you?'

'Suspected, yes – but I didn't know for sure. And then after being in Brazil for three months, who knew what you were thinking?'

'I was thinking about you, baby,' I said, slowing to a halt and gazing into her eyes. 'No matter where I've been, I've been thinking of you. And, no matter what happens for the rest of my life, I'll always look back on this day as the very best one, because you've given me the most incredible surprise I could've ever imagined.'

She leaned in to kiss me.

'I'm so glad you liked it,' she smiled. 'But if I was you, I wouldn't assume that today will be the best day of your life, or that I've given you the best surprise possible. After all, you don't know what else I have planned for you!'

I gawked at her.

'Liv, how could you have *possibly* planned anything more amazing than today?'

Once again, she leaned in to kiss me.

'You just wait and see,' she winked.

Uruguay, Argentina and Chile

For the next two weeks, we barely left the bedroom. All we wanted to do was rediscover each other's body, make love as if we'd never made love before, and hold one another in our arms and never let go. Seriously, that's pretty much all we did apart from swim and sunbake at the beach, eat meat platters and *chivito*, and go for runs along *la rambla* to work the fat off before taking a bus to Colonia and then a boat over to the Argentinian capital of Buenos Aires.

When you're in love, any city is wonderful to be in, but of course, some are more beguiling than others, and few South American cities more so than BA, where we walked hand-in-hand through the sunny streets admiring all of the lovely European architecture; sipped on freshly-roasted coffee at cute little cafés every morning while our legs rubbed beneath the table; drank the most delicious wine we'd ever tasted at one of Buenos Aires's luscious vineyards while staring into each other's eyes; watched hours of steamy, passionate Argentinian tango dancing at various *milongas* before making hot, sweaty love back at our hostel; fed each other different types of *dulce de leche* sweets; had a picnic lunch and went bird-watching at the luscious *Reserva Ecológica Constanera Sur*; sun-baked in each other's arms amongst the locals in the oasis-like *Jardín Botánico;* took a gondola ride through the Puerto Madero waterways; and danced up close together into the early hours of the morning at a few of the city's pulsing nightclubs.

And on the less romantic side, since we were in Argentina, we also of course went to a soccer match.

It was something our hostel organised – the manager Alejandro taking Olivia, myself, two Canadian guys, two Englishmen and two other Australian blokes, to ensure that we were safely transported to and from the arena and supervised during the game. I use the phrases "safely transported" and "supervised during the game" because as it turned out, Argentinian soccer matches could be very dangerous if you didn't follow the unofficial rules – as Alejandro so carefully explained to us on the bus ride over.

'OK guys, so today, you are lucky enough to be watching the Boca Juniors versus River Plate, which is one of the fiercest rivalries in sporting history, and a match that is known as the *Superclásico*. It's a rivalry that dates all the way back to the start of the 20th century, with Boca being seen as the club of Argentina's working class, and River representing the upper. They call Boca supporters *bosteros,* or "shit handlers", since before Boca built their stadium, a factory that used horse manure stood in its place; while Boca fans refer to River supporters as *gallinas,* meaning "chickens", because their team's been said to choke in big matches. Not only that, but Boca fans always, *always* ridicule them for the fact that River was forced to drop down to the second division in 2011 – which, as a side-story to show you just how seriously Argentinians take their football, was an event so devastating for the River fans that when it happened, crisis support lines reported a huge increase in calls, and demand for anti-depressant medication soared.'

'You *can't* be serious!' exclaimed one of the Canadians.

'I am, and it's because football's taken so seriously that Boca and River fans absolutely hate each other – to such an extent that garbage and cups of urine are almost always thrown at visiting fans during home games; opposition players have been pepper-sprayed and had rocks and bottles hurled at them; and countless fights and riots have broken out over the years – the most serious occurring at River's stadium *El Monumental* in 1968, which led to 78 people dying and another 150 being injured. For this reason, there will be hundreds of police officers on duty at the match today, and River and Boca supporters each have their own section of the stands to watch the game – Boca's obviously taking up the majority of the stadium since it's their home ground. Because we'll be sitting with them in the main section, unless you want to get punched in the face or leave the arena soaked in piss, it's absolutely essential that you cheer for Boca. This of course applies to me as well as you, even though if truth be told, I'm actually a River fan!'

'*Really?*'

'Yes! But if River score, you'll see me completely silent like everybody else, even though I'll be going absolutely crazy inside; and if Boca score, you'll see me jumping up and down and screaming – even though I'll be secretly devastated.'

Alejandro continued talking about the rivalry for the next quarter of an hour, answering our questions and telling us about some of the most renowned and dramatic moments in its 100 year history before the bus dropped us off a few blocks away from the stadium, and we found ourselves surrounded by thousands of Boca supporters wearing blue and yellow jerseys, waving blue and yellow flags and flying blue and yellow balloons – all of them either speaking excitedly about the upcoming match, banging raucously on the drums hanging from their necks, or throwing their right arm back and forth in the air while belting out anti-River songs – which, being half-Spanish and knowing the language, Olivia translated for me as:

> *"River, tell me how it feels,*
> *To have played in the second division,*
> *I swear that even as the years pass,*
> *We're never going to forget it.*
> *You were in the B,*
> *You burned the Monumental,*
> *The stain will never be lifted.*
> *What filthy chickens you are,*
> *You hit a player,*
> *You're all drunken cowards!"*

We arrived at the stadium 40 minutes before kick-off, and even then, most of its 49,000 seats were already full of screaming, cheering, chanting, singing, drum-banging, blue-and-yellow wearing, flag-and-balloon flying Boca Junior fans – except for the small section of red-and-white wearing River fans, who through a pair of binoculars that one of the Canadian blokes had brought, I could see were already being antagonised by the closest Boca supporters.

'This place is as crazy as the cockpit Corey and I went to in the Philippines,' I murmured in amazement to Olivia.

'It really is something,' she said. 'Imagine how wild it will get if Boca score a goal.'

'The whole stadium must go apeshit. I really hope we get to see it.'

But to the crowd's horror, River midfielder Manuel Lanzini scored a header within the first 45 seconds – which we later found out was the fastest goal in *Superclásico* history. All the Boca fans were dead silent, looking as if they were at their best friend's funeral – including Alejandro (although if you looked really closely, you could see the sides of his lips twitching to try and fight back a grin).

From that moment on, the atmosphere was vehemently tense – everyone agitated and on edge, and together surely combining to break the record for how many times the word *puta* was uttered in such a short time span. But six minutes before half-time everything changed, when Boca striker Santiago Silva kicked a right-footed goal from inside the far post.

The stadium fucking erupted! Everyone screamed their lungs out, jumped up and down, hugged the people next to them, punched the air and banged on their drums so furiously that Olivia and I could see our seats shaking! We could literally see our seats shaking! And then of course came the anti-River song, with nearly 50,000 people thrusting their right arm in the air and shouting it out in unison:

> *"River, tell me how it feels,*
> *To have played in the second division … !"*

The crowd remained on their feet for the rest of the half, passionately cheering and yelling and singing, as they did to start the second half as well – which ended up needing to be temporarily stopped when River's coach was sent off the field for insulting a ref, causing some of the closest Boca fans to bombard him with trash as he ran for the exit; others to launch fireworks into the air; others still to throw flares onto the field which sent blue and yellow smoke all through the stadium; and dozens of fans to scale the fence separating the pitch from the stands and shake it like mad while continuing to bellow out the anti-River song.

After 10 minutes, order was finally restored and the game resumed. Although there was a heap more singing, yelling, cheering, *puta*-calling, flag-waving, drum-banging and jumping up and down, the rest of the game was relatively uneventful in the sense that no more goals were scored, meaning that it ended in a 1-all draw.

'That was one of the craziest experiences of my life!' Olivia exclaimed once we were back on the bus.

'Mine too, baby.'

'Honestly, I never thought I could have so much fun at a sporting event!'

'Does that mean we can go to more sporting events now?' I smiled.

She giggled.

'Maybe! Particularly if you agree to come to some … dare I say "girly" events with me.'

'Oh dear. Like what?'

'Well … how about a tango lesson?'

'A *tango* lesson?'

'Why not? It's been so great to watch – you've even said so yourself! And I think it would be really fun to try.'

'Yeah it's been great to watch, but that doesn't mean I want to try it! I can tell you from experience that I am *not* good at Latin American dancing.'

'When have you tried Latin American dancing, Jimmy?'

'In Rio.'

'What, with a girl?'

'No with Fumio – we held each other in our arms, stared into each other's eyes and then pirouetted around the room together.'

'Very funny. So how come you can go dancing with another girl but not with me?'

'Think of it as I subjected another girl to my awful dancing, but I love you too much to subject you to it.'

'Nice try. But you know sweetie, you really should just say yes to me now – that way we can spare the formality of me pouting and you inevitably giving in to me, because we both know you can't resist me when I do that.'

'I don't know baby, you haven't tried to wield that superpower over me for so long that I just might be able to withstand it these days.'

'Oh you think so, do you?'

'Hhmmm … how about we play it safe and you agree not to pout?'

'Sure, if you agree to go tango dancing with me.'

'I told you, I love you too much to inflict my awful Latin American dancing on you.'

'Aawww, please?' she asked, turning her bottom lip inside out.

'Oh shit,' I laughed, already feeling myself begin to weaken. 'No, OK, I can do this!' I said, taking a deep breath and trying to compose myself. 'I can resist … I can resist …' But the more I looked at her the more I began to crumble, so I turned to stare out the window – only to crack a few seconds later when I glanced back at her mock-sad face.

'OK, fine! You win!'

'Yay!' she exclaimed, clapping her hands excitedly.

I shook my head with a grin.

'I can't believe I've let you talk me into this.'

'I told you you wouldn't be able to withstand my superpower,' she winked.

'You're meant to use your superpowers for good, not for evil.'

'Oh don't be like that,' she giggled, cuddling up closer and leaning in to kiss me. 'How about this – we'll just try it for an hour, and if you don't like it, we can leave. But,' she smiled, 'because you'll be with me, I have a hunch that you'll actually have fun this time.'

'Want a bet?'

'Loser buys drinks for the rest of the night?'

'You're on, baby.'

So the following evening, we went to a tango lesson at a *milonga*, where to my surprise and Olivia's delight, I actually found myself enjoying it – so much so that we even stayed back after the lesson to continue dancing, in what by then had turned into a sultry, dimly-lit nightclub.

'So I wonder what drink I'll let you buy me first,' Olivia teased as we did the basic step around the room with an impromptu turn thrown in here and there.

'Alright,' I laughed. 'I'll admit you were right.'

She giggled.

'I genuinely did think you'd like it – after all, tango is the lover's dance! Where we just get to stare into each other's eyes, and press up against one another as we twirl around the room.'

'I know. This is actually making me kind of horny.'

Olivia raised her eyebrows up and down at me with a cheeky grin, and leaned in to nibble my ear.

'Me too, baby. We're going to have the best sex tonight.'

'We have the best sex *every* night.'

'True, but tonight's going to be extra good.'

'And why is that?'

She smiled seductively.

'Ever heard of a love hotel before?'

'You mean the places where you rent the room by the hour purely to have sex?'

'Yes! How do you know?'

'They're everywhere in Japan.'

'What! Don't tell me you've already been to one?'

'Can I help it if women find me completely irresistible?'

'I can't believe this!' she laughed.

'What can I say, baby – I'm a playboy. You're lucky you snapped me up before somebody else did.'

'You're not a playboy,' she smiled, leaning in to kiss me. 'But you're right – I'm really, *really* lucky to be with you, and I'm going to show you just how glad I am that we're back together tonight, when I give you the best time you've ever had in a bedroom.'

'I can't wait for it,' I murmured, feeling my cock evolve beneath my pants. 'But seriously … how much better can our sex possibly get?'

'You'll find out,' she winked. 'I got talking to an Argentinian girl at the coffee shop this morning when you were writing at the hostel, and aside from her telling me about the best love hotels in the city, she also enlightened me about a new trick that you're apparently going to go wild for as well.'

Eager to see what she had in store for me, we soon walked to a *telo*, which is what Argentinians call their love hotels. Just like in Japan, they came about because it's culturally the norm to live with your parents into your late 20s or until you get married; and, just like in Japan, they also offer some sex-friendly features including branded condoms, porn on the television, surrounding mirrors, steaming Jacuzzis and HD video cameras, while boasting a variety of themed rooms where patrons can, for example, have sex in a spaceship, an Egyptian pyramid, or a Star

Wars themed room complete with blue mood lighting, fake control panels and robot decorations.

Upon entering the establishment, we found ourselves in a dim, narrow corridor lined with smoked glass windows. One of them then opened a crack, before a stray hand emerged waving a card key. Olivia proceeded to have a rapid conversation in Spanish with the hand that went mostly over my head before she nodded, and then started leading me through a labyrinth of doorways lit overhead by fluoro-coloured lights. We walked to the very end of the corridor, turned left, and then quickly slipped into the first room on our right.

To my surprise, it was immaculately clean, boasting a beautifully made bed opposite a plasma screen TV and a perfectly positioned video camera; a private bathroom with fresh towels, a gleaming mirror, liquid soaps, toothbrushes and a stack of condoms; more shining mirrors for walls and a ceiling; and a big, bubbling Jacuzzi just by the bed.

After we took our clothes off, I helped Olivia into the Jacuzzi and poured us each a glass of the champagne we'd ordered before being unable to control ourselves, we started fucking up against the jets – me moaning, Olivia screaming, her hands clutching my salty wet hair, my face buried in between her tits as she rode me up and down, while the water got rough and wavy and splashed all over the floor. Both of us were so absorbed in the moment, so immersed in our passion, so focused on how good we felt in each other's body that I didn't even notice accidently knocking over my champagne glass and it smashing on the floor as we cried out in ecstasy, and when I felt close to coming, I arched my head back from Olivia's breasts to the rim of the tub behind me, and for a split second, I caught sight of my open-mouthed, gasping face in the mirror on the ceiling before my eyes rolled into the back of my head and I came long and slow and hard. But there was barely time to catch my breath since as soon as I was finished, Olivia climbed over me onto the bed, and after towelling herself off with theatrical, moaning wipes, she asked me to join her so that she could show me her new trick.

Positioning me sitting propped up against the pillows, she encouraged me to spread my bent legs, and slide myself downwards at such an angle so that my dick, balls and ass were all exposed. Then, she started squeezing the shaft of my still erect cock, and with her other hand, gently circling her fingers around the rim of my anus. The latter took me by surprise, but it felt good, so I let her keep going as my skin turned to gooseflesh and I started panting all over again.

'You like that?' she murmured.

'Oh yeah ... is this the new thing you wanted to try?'

'Not quite.'

'What ...' I puffed. 'What is it, then?'

'Just close your eyes ... lean back ... and trust me.'

'Whatever you say ...'

'If at any point you want me to stop then of course just tell me, but I really hope you're going to like it.'

'Whatever you say ...' I repeated breathlessly.

So she kept on going, squeezing my dick and lightly tracing her fingers around my bum hole, tickling me in a sensual kind of way before she briefly stopped to lather her index finger with lube. Then, after she resumed massaging my cock, she gently slid her finger inside my ass, and in a "come here to me" motion, started rubbing it against my prostate gland.

'Oh my God!' I cried. 'Oh fuck! Oh *fuck!*'

'Do you like it?'

'That's so fucking good! That's so fucking good! That's so fucking strange but it's so fucking good!'

'It feels so good because according to my new Argentinian friend – and the internet confirms it – a man's prostate is actually where his G-spot is. So all I'm doing is the equivalent of you fingering up the back of my pussy.'

I wanted to ask her why no one else seemed to know about this, but I was so fucking aroused that I couldn't speak, couldn't do anything but moan and scream and gasp for air for the next 20 minutes, at which point, despite how good it felt, I wanted to be inside her, because that's where I always wanted to come, so after she slipped her finger out of me, I flipped her over on the bed and started fucking her doggy-style in front of one of the mirrors, relishing for once being able to see the orgasmic, open-mouthed look on her face in that position before I ejaculated inside her. Then, keeping her bent forwards, I fingered her clit furiously to get her off, until with a high-pitched, uninhibited shriek she came, and we collapsed back down on the bed together.

As I waited for Olivia to catch her breath, I held her in my arms, and looked up at our reflection on the ceiling.

'So, baby,' she finally sighed with a smile. 'Was that as good as the other time you went to a love hotel?'

'Not quite to be honest,' I grinned. 'But that's only because last time the girl and I did karaoke together afterwards. Then again, I suppose that's more this love hotel's fault for not having those facilities, as opposed to any knock against your sexual performance.'

Olivia laughed, and we cuddled together silently for a while before eventually drifting off to sleep – only to wake up in the morning and watch the night's performance on the plasma screen TV, and then repeat it all over again as we watched it for a second time.

After another week of eating meat platters, tango dancing, writing for me, and some sensual prostate-play that had become my new favourite thing to do in the bedroom, we flew down south to Bariloche, where over the course of the next week, we kayaked in the Nahuel Huapi Lake situated at the foothills of the Andes Mountains; admired the alpine-style, rock-and-wood architecture of the civic centre; put on a kilo or two each eating too much *Fra Nui* (fresh raspberries double-coated with white and black chocolate); and rode horses through the lush Patagonian woods before kicking on to Pucón across the Chilean border, where we went white-water rafting; relaxed in the soothing, spa-like outdoor hot springs while gazing up at the trees around us; and spent an entire morning hiking up one of the country's most active volcanoes, and an evening cuddled together outside as we marvelled at the red smoke that puffed from its apex. After that, we moved on to the Chilean capital Santiago, where we ate countless *empanadas;* lazed arm-in-arm around the lovely Parque Forestal; tried our hand at salsa dancing at a popular night spot called Bellavista; and took pictures together in front of all the amazing street art at nearby Valparaiso. After a 25 hour bus ride which included us having sex four times in the toilet, we arrived at the San Pedro de Atacama desert at the top of the country, where we saw the "Valley of the Moon" and its awe-inspiring sand formations that've been carved by wind and water, and also went star-gazing – which, because of Atacama's high altitude, barely-existent cloud cover, dry air and lack of light pollution, make it one of the best places in the world for it.

When we arrived at the observation point beneath a breathtaking blanket of glittering stars, our tour guide told us about the zodiac, about what makes a constellation, and about how to read a map of the sky. We then got behind the telescopes, and all *oohed* and *aahed* at the remarkable, close-up view of Mars, the moon, the vividly-coloured nebulae, different galaxies altogether, and Saturn with its surrounding rings. As if that wasn't incredible enough, as Olivia and I held each other close and sipped on a hot chocolate, we actually came upon a shooting star.

'Baby look! Look!' Olivia cried, jumping up and down and pointing at it excitedly. 'You have to make a wish! You have to make a wish!'

As I watched it streak across the sky, I felt the warmth of the woman in my arms. The woman who, like that star, had flown thousands of miles – all just to see me. The woman who, like that star, was so bright, so beautiful, so full of life – and who my love had burned for since the day I'd met her. And so, just before the star's spectacular soar inevitably tailed off, I silently offered up the following:

My wish is for Olivia and I to always stay together, and one day, for me to marry her, have a family with her, and go on to live a long, happy life with her.

The best surprise of my life

After the desert, we took the bus to Uyuni in Bolivia to see the world's largest salt flats, which consist of 10,582 square kilometres of uninterrupted, glistening whiteness that sit at the crest of the Andes Mountains. Since the best time to visit them is at sunrise, I assumed we'd get up early the following morning to check them out. But, Olivia asked if we could wait a couple of days.

'Sure, baby. How come?'

'Because the way the tours operate, you get driven to the salt flats in four wheel drives.'

'Oh,' I said. 'Right.'

'It's fine. Let's just relax here for a day or two while I figure out what to do about the car situation.'

'OK, no problem. Would you like me to help you take care of it at all?'

'No don't worry, I'll do it.'

'Are you sure?'

'Yep. You just concentrate on your novel, and keep working on trying to get that next draft to Pierce by the end of the month. And who knows? Given how impressed he was with the first one, it may be ready to submit to agents and publishers after that!'

So for the next two days, I continued editing my book at our hostel or in a café, while Olivia would be in town trying to sort out how exactly we'd get to the salt flats. Both nights, we met up in the evening for a popular Bolivian dinner involving some combination of quinoa, soup, potatoes, llama steak, alpaca steak or guinea pig, and each time, I asked again if she needed any help. But she would just smile, say that everything was under control, that believe it or not she was actually really enjoying herself, and for me to just focus on my writing to try and make my dreams come true.

On the morning Olivia had arranged for us to do the tour, our alarms went off at a quarter past five, and after dragging myself out of bed, having a long hot shower to wake up and then getting dressed into my warmest jeans, jumper and pea coat since it was freezing cold outside, I walked into the dining area of our hostel to find Olivia fixing us some ham and cheese rolls.

'Everything's ready to go, baby,' she said brightly. 'So get some breakfast into you and then we'll head off.'

I gave her a kiss, and then ate a sandwich before we both excitedly stepped outside – only to be greeted by two white four wheel drives.

'What the hell?' I frowned. 'Oh shit Liv, there's obviously been some sort of mistake.'

But instead of getting upset, she just stood there smiling at me.

'No,' she said. 'There's been no mistake.'

'Huh? What do you ... what do you mean there's been no mistake?'

'I mean that this is exactly what I asked for, baby – one car for our tour guide to lead the way to the salt flats, and the other one for you to drive so that we can follow him.'

My jaw dropped.

'You want ... you want to drive in a car ... with *me?*'

'Yes,' she smiled.

'Seriously?'

'Yes.'

'Are you sure?'

'Yes!'

And then, as I stood there stunned and gaping at her, she took me by the hand, and with that smile still spread across her face, she walked me to the driver's side door and opened it up for me.

'In you get,' she chirped. 'We'll miss the sunrise if you don't get a move on.'

Still overcome with shock, I tentatively did as she said, and then watched her skip around the other side of the car, signal to the guide in front of us that we were ready to go, and then hop in the passenger seat beside me.

'Are you *sure* you're up to this?' I asked uncertainly.

'One hundred per cent,' she beamed. 'Now hurry up and follow him – we can't miss the sunrise!'

So I turned on the engine, and looked at her to see how she'd respond. As you know, the first and only occasion we'd tried to drive together since the accident, she'd been shaking from head to toe before she was even inside the vehicle. But this time, she was calm, and relaxed, and wearing that smile telling me that everything was fine. So I gently pressed my foot down on the accelerator, and we began moving.

I started off slowly at first, glancing over at Olivia every few seconds to make sure she was OK. But all she did was smile at me, so I started going a bit faster, and since she kept on smiling, with mounting excitement I started going a little faster still, and then a little faster after that, and when we'd kicked it up to 90 K's an hour and she was still grinning at me, I was finally convinced that after almost three years, she'd conquered her demons.

'Woo-hoo!' I howled with glee, beeping the horn ecstatically and zooming after our tour guide. 'Didn't I tell you, baby?' I exclaimed. 'Didn't I tell you you'd beat this? Didn't I tell you that everything would be OK and that one day we'd be able to drive again just like we used to?'

'Yes you did!' she laughed. 'Yes you did indeed!'

I wound down the windows and felt the wind whooshing through my hair as I screamed elatedly again, and just like she used to, Olivia rested her forearm on the windowsill, and held my free hand in the palm of her own.

'I'm so happy for you, Liv,' I beamed. 'I'm really, really happy for you.'

'Thank-you so much, sweetie,' she smiled. 'For everything.'

'I didn't do much, baby. It was all you.'

'Aw, don't be modest, now. You were there for me every time I needed you, and you encouraged me every time I didn't believe in myself – and that meant so, so much to me. Plus, by always fighting so hard to overcome your own problems, you really inspired me, and set an example for me to follow to overcome mine.'

I gave her hand a little squeeze, and began stroking it gently with the tip of my thumb.

'You know Liv, if truth be told, it's really because of you that I'm even here today. It's really because of you that I'm actually healthy and enjoying my life again. I know a lot of other people helped, but you were the one who was always there for me – in every single way I could've ever hoped for.'

She squeezed my hand too, and brought it to her lips to kiss.

254

'We make a pretty good team, don't we?'

'The best,' I smiled.

For the next several minutes, we continued driving blissfully until the guide in front of us beeped his horn – at which point, Olivia told me to stop.

'But we'll lose him,' I said.

'Just trust me, baby,' she winked. 'That's the rule for the morning, OK? For you to just sit back, relax, and trust that I have a very, *very* special surprise for you.'

'What, *on top of* us driving together for the first time in years?'

'On top of it, and even better than it!'

I shook my head in astonishment, unable to conceive of such a thing.

'Liv what on … what on *earth* could you have organised that's a bigger surprise than this? Aside from you flying halfway across the world to say you love me, of course – which I still contend is the best surprise you could ever give me.'

She grinned at me.

'Well … we'll see about that.'

Utterly amazed by her, I leaned over to kiss her lips, and then eager to see what she had planned, I opened the door to step out of the car. As soon as I did so, I unexpectedly felt my shoes crunch on the ground beneath me. Since the previous night still hadn't given birth to the new day yet, I shone the light of my phone around my feet to be able to see clearly – at which point, I realised that the pure white salt I was standing on had crystallised into hexagonal rings that were about a foot in diameter, and coated with a thin film of water. Having read that the salt flats are perfectly horizontal and knowing that we were near the centre of them, I assumed that dawn would reveal countless of those white watery polygons, surrounding us as far as our eyes could see. But with the sun's slow rise, to our wonderment, each liquid hexagon became a small reflecting pool, and combined, they'd created the world's largest mirror, vividly reflecting the mountain range to our left, the blue sky spotted with fluffy white clouds above us, and Olivia and I with our arms around each other – the two of us gaping in awe at the horizon, where the salt flats were such a perfect reflection of the sky above that we could no longer tell where it began and where the land ended.

'Wow …' I murmured breathlessly. 'I think this is the most incredible thing I've ever seen …'

'Yes,' Olivia agreed.

I turned my head to look at her, and realised that her eyes were glazed with tears.

'Hey,' I said. 'Are you OK?'

Rotating out of my arms to face me, she stared into my eyes, and nodded her head ever so slightly.

'Jimmy, there's … there's something I'd really love to tell you …'

'What is it, baby?'

Never breaking our gaze, she took my hands in both of hers. For a while, she didn't say anything, didn't do anything but look at me with a damp-eyed smile that radiated joy, and amazement, and happiness … all at the same time. In that moment, she was, quite possibly, the most beautiful I'd ever seen her, and as soft, gentle tears began rolling down her cheeks and she opened her mouth to speak, she looked even more mesmerising, and I could feel my heart start to race in my chest.

'Jimmy over … over the years … we've been through so much together. We've been through so many highs, so many lows, and faced more challenges than I ever imagined … and there were times … there were times when I doubted whether our love was strong enough to overcome them … and other times when I was convinced it wasn't. But no matter what happened, you always believed in us. You always believed we could get through everything and live happily ever after. And today … today I want you to know that I finally agree with you. I want you to know that no matter what the future holds in store for us, that I know we can handle it, and that no matter what difficulties we encounter, that I'm committed to you forever. I want you to know that I love you with all my heart, Jimmy Wharton, and that nothing would make me happier than to marry you, to start a family with you, and to spend the rest of my life with you … which is why today, I want to ask you …'

And then to my disbelief, she knelt down on one knee.

'Jimmy will you … will you marry me?'

I stared at her … astounded … more surprised than I'd ever been in my life, before my eyes welled with tears and the words burst out of me.

'Yes!' I exclaimed. 'Yes of course!'

And then, she pulled me down on top of her, and we held each other tightly and wept with delirious, unbridled euphoria into one another's shoulders.

'Oh my God!' I cried. 'Oh my God, oh my God, oh my God! I love you, Olivia … I love you more than anything in the world …'

'I really love you too, Jimmy. And I'm unbelievably, unbelievably, unbelievably happy.'

And as we continued sobbing and clutching each other fervently on the angel-white salt, I found myself thinking back to each of the heart-wrenching times that we'd broken up, the car accident that had nearly destroyed us, and the morning in Tweed Valley when Olivia had gotten down on her hands and knees and begged me to let her go – and as I did so, I felt so, so glad that I'd never given up on her. And then, I found myself reflecting on all the days and nights that I'd been so depressed that I'd wanted to kill myself, and been so devoid of hope that I'd wholeheartedly believed I would never recover – and I felt so, so glad that I hadn't given up on myself, or on this thing called life – which truly is filled with beauty, joy and wonder if you only know where to look. But above all else, as I lifted my head from Olivia's shoulder, ran my fingers through her hair, and gazed at her ardently as tears continued to stream down my cheeks, I felt overwhelmingly, unimaginably grateful that after all I'd been through, I could now finally say:

'I'm really happy too, dear Olivia.'

And if you can say that you're happy, then what more can you possibly ask for?

The next book in this series is now available!

Let Me Tell You My Stories From South America, Jimmy

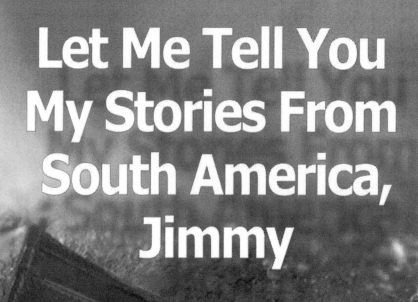

My dream is to be depression-free and happy

Danny Baker

Let Me Tell You My Stories From South America, Jimmy

The last time Jimmy saw his life coach and good friend Fumio Yakatori was in Rio de Janeiro, where Fumio taught him how to be much happier, before Jimmy moved on to Uruguay, received the biggest surprise of his life, and then ecstatically continued his travels around South America. But since parting ways, they've kept in touch, and in this book, Fumio tells Jimmy about his own epic adventure through the continent: beginning in Brazil's outrageous party capital of Florianópolis and taking him to the electricity-free, hippie town of Cabo Polonio in Uruguay; bringing him face-to-face with some of the world's most breathtaking lakes, icebergs and glaciers in the southernmost tip of Argentina; and seeing him go volcano-hiking, stargazing in search of aliens, and to the raunchiest coffee shop he's ever been to in Chile – at which point, he follows the backtracker trail to the Bolivian Salt Flats just like Jimmy and Olivia did, and after his own life-altering experience there, an unforeseen sequence of events leads him all the way to Colombia's portside city of Cartagena – where he embarks on a thrilling 7,500 kilometre journey that's his most unpredictable yet.

However, being Jimmy's life coach, Fumio tells him his weird, wonderful stories in such a way that he's continuously teaching Jimmy how to be the content, happy person he wants to be. After all, that's Jimmy's number one goal – to be depression-free and happy for the rest of his life – and after how helpful Fumio proved to be in Rio, then who better to help him achieve it?

An interview with the author, Danny Baker, about this book:

Q: Unlike in the series' first two books, this story is being told from Fumio's perspective as opposed to Jimmy's. Why is that?

I'll return to Jimmy and Olivia's love life soon, but right now, I want to focus a little more on the travel/"how to be happy" themes of *I Just Want To Be Happy, Olivia* – and this is best done with a backpacking life coach narrating the story.

Q: Yes, I noticed that many reviewers of *IJWTBH,O* said how "helpful" they themselves found Fumio's life coaching. Is that why you wanted to make more of it in this book?

Absolutely. I think fiction is at its most powerful when it's not only unputdownably gripping, but also when the reader can learn something important. So, the aim of this book – just like with *I Just Want To Be Happy, Olivia* and all future books in this series – is not only to thoroughly entertain my readers, but also to show them what changes they can make in their own lives to be the happiest versions of themselves they can be.

Q: That's great! And since you brought up future books, can you tell us a bit about those?

Sure. Fumio will be the narrator for the next four as well, and they'll see him travel to Europe, Central America, North Korea and Africa. After that – in book #8 – the story will continue from Olivia's perspective; in book #9 it will be from Jimmy's best friend Corey's; and in #10, it will return to Jimmy's point of view.

Q: Wow, you have ten books planned?

Yes, and I'd love to write many more. As long as I have something original, entertaining and helpful to say, then I'll keep extending this series for as long as I can.

Q: Interesting. Now, you've talked a lot about travel and happiness, but what about love? Will there be less of a "romance element" in future stories than there was in the first two books?

No, not at all. When you're writing a series, you have to keep true to the themes you started with, because they're what readers have come to expect. The way I see it, the *I Will Not Kill Myself, Olivia* series is centred around love, mental health, travel and "learning how to be happy" – and I will stick with these ingredients because I believe that if I do, then readers will love all future books in the series as much as the previous ones.

Also by Danny Baker

Depression is a Liar

A #1 international mental health bestseller

Depression is living in a body that fights to survive . . . with a mind that tries to die.

Depression is fear, despair, emptiness, numbness, shame, embarrassment and the inability to recognise the fun, happy person you used to be.

Depression is the incapacity to construct or envision a future.

Depression is losing the desire to partake in life.

Depression can cause you to feel completely alone – even when you're surrounded by people.

Worst of all, depression can convince you that there's no way out. It can convince you that your pain is eternal, and destined to oppress you for the rest of your days. And it's when you're in that horrifically black place, staring down the barrel of what you truly believe can only be a lifetime of wretched agony, that your thoughts turn to suicide – because depression has convinced you that it's the only way out.

But depression is a liar.

Recovery IS possible – and I can prove it to you.

My name's Danny Baker, and for four years, I suffered from life-threatening bouts of depression that led to alcoholism, drug abuse, medicine-induced psychosis and multiple hospitalisations. But over time, I managed to recover, and these days, I'm happy, healthy, and absolutely love my life.

Depression is a Liar is a memoir that recounts my struggle and eventual triumph over depression. It is highly recommended for the following people:

- People who don't believe that it's possible to recover from depression and find happiness again (I will show you that it is);

- People who keep relapsing over and over again, and accordingly believe that they'll never truly be free of depression (I'll explain why you keep relapsing, and tell you what I did to ensure that, over time, my relapses occurred less and less frequently before eventually petering out for good);

- People with depression who want to feel understood (you'll in all likelihood be able to relate to the majority of my story, and after reading it, I promise you that you'll feel far less alone);

- People whose perfectionistic tendencies contribute to their depression (being a perfectionist contributed to my depression in a major way, but I'll show you what I did to control those tendencies so that they stopped triggering my depression);

- People who drink and take drugs to cope with their depression (no judgement here – I did it too – but after seeing how much it exacerbated my depression, you'll hopefully choose to stop);

- People who are close to a loved one who suffers from depression and want to better understand the illness (I promise I'll give it to you straight and not sugar-coat a thing).

ABOUT THE AUTHOR

Danny Baker was born and raised in Sydney, Australia. In 2007 he took a scholarship to study commerce/law at Sydney University before trading in his textbooks in 2012 to pursue his dream of becoming an author. At the time of writing, he's published three books: *I Will Not Kill Myself, Olivia*, the sequel *I Just Want To Be Happy, Olivia* and a memoir, *Depression is a Liar*, which recounts his struggle and eventual triumph over depression.

To find out more about Danny's books or to get in touch, visit his website at www.dannybakerwrites.com.

33194615R00151

Printed in Great Britain
by Amazon